# PICK UP THE PIECES

Andrew White, the proprietor of a country garage, sees four of his mechanics run over a woman while they are on an unauthorized ride in a customer's car. Thinking there had been no witnesses, they fail to report the accident. White then blackmails the men. Soon desperate, they plan to steal White's savings, drawing lots to decide who shall break in, and agreeing that the thief shall remain anonymous. The next morning, White is found murdered, his savings stolen. But someone knows their secret and plans to profit by it . . .

J. F. STRAKER

# PICK UP
# THE PIECES

*Complete and Unabridged*

**LINFORD**
*Leicester*

First published in Great Britain

First Linford Edition
published 2005

British Library CIP Data

Straker, J. F. (John Foster)
Pick up the pieces.—Large print ed.—
Linford mystery library
1. Detective and mystery stories
2. Large type books
I. Title
823.9'12 [F]

ISBN 1–84395–856–2

Published by
F. A. Thorpe (Publishing)
Anstey, Leicestershire

Set by Words & Graphics Ltd.
Anstey, Leicestershire
Printed and bound in Great Britain by
T. J. International Ltd., Padstow, Cornwall

This book is printed on acid-free paper

# 1

## Hit and Run

Bert Wickery heaved his long, thin body from under the chassis of the ancient Humber and scrambled to his feet.

'That should fix it,' he said, wiping his hands on a greasy rag. 'Let's take her out now and see how she goes. We can paint the wing when we get back.'

'Pop' Wells (he had been christened Daniel, but few in Chaim were aware of that) swung his foot in disgust against a rear tyre.

'Only a damn' fool woman like Mrs Riley would waste money on her,' he said. 'Fit for the scrap-heap, that's all she is.'

'Mrs Riley?'

'No, that wreck there. Not but what Mrs Riley isn't as big a wreck herself, come to that.'

Harry Forthright gazed impatiently at the garage clock. He was a burly, coarse-looking man, shorter than Wickery but with greater breadth of shoulder. As he peeled off his overalls a tattooed snake writhed on a hairy right arm.

'Let's get a move on, then. It'll be after nine before we're through, and I need a drink.'

He wriggled into his jacket and began to tug at the heavy sliding doors.

'White's got a nerve, expecting us to work as late as this,' Wells grumbled, as he went to help him. 'Serve him right if we'd knocked off at six and left him to finish the job on his own. Suckers, that's what we are.'

'I'm not grousing,' said Wickery. 'I can do with the extra cash. Hullo — here's Dave.'

A young man, hands in pockets, a heavy muffler round his neck, sauntered into the widening beam of light that shone out on to the road. 'Haven't you chaps got any homes to go to?' he asked amiably. 'Talk about the slave-trade!'

'Got the job?' asked Wells.

Dave Chitty nodded, grinning. He would have been good-looking but for the too sloping forehead and the small, beady eyes that shifted restlessly behind his spectacles. 'Twenty-five bob a week more than I'm getting here. *And* prospects.'

'Lucky devil.'

'It's a break,' Chitty agreed. 'And am I pleased to be leaving this ruddy dump! Is the old man in?'

'No.'

'Oh. I came up to give him the good news, but it'll keep till the morning.' He stood aside as Wickery began to back the Humber out of the garage. 'Where are you chaps off to?'

'Nowhere in particular,' said Forthright. 'Just taking her out on test. Want a lift home?'

'I don't mind. Or, better still, let's go into Tanbury and have a drink at the George. I feel like celebrating.'

'What's wrong with the local?' asked Wickery, joining them. 'Give us a hand with the doors, Pop.'

The heavy doors rumbled noisily in their grooves, met with a clang, and reopened slightly. It was dark outside, and cold. Forthright shivered. 'That's a good idea of yours, Dave,' he said, as they moved towards the car. 'Tanbury's about the right distance; it'll give the old sow a thorough testing. And it's good beer at the George, too. Better than the Lion.'

'White wouldn't like it,' said Wickery. 'Joy-riding in a customer's car. He'd be mad as hell.'

'Let him — he's always mad about something. And we're not joy-riding, we're testing. What's wrong with having a drink on the way? It's our time we're working in, not his. The trouble with you, Bert, is that you're too soft with the blighter. You want to get tough. Just because he's Doris's uncle that doesn't make him Lord God Almighty, does it?'

Wickery felt his cheeks flushing, and was glad of the dark. Harry had never fully forgiven him for marrying the boss's niece. It made no difference that White had been against the marriage, had done his utmost to prevent it. In Harry's eyes Wickery had betrayed them, had gone over to the enemy.

There was a bit of the Communist in Harry, he thought.

4

'If you're set on losing your job, go ahead. I'm not. Maybe it isn't so hot, but I've got Doris to consider.' He appealed to Wells. 'Don't you agree it'd be a daft thing to do, Pop?'

But Wells wanted to talk privately with Dave; and there was no privacy to be had at the Lion. 'You're letting White get you down, Bert, like Harry said. No harm in going into Tanbury. Anyway, White won't know of it. He does his drinking at the club.'

'There's Loften.'

'Oh, him!' Forthright dismissed the junior partner with contempt. 'Loften wouldn't make anything of it. Come on, let's get weaving. You're outvoted, mate; better give in and come quietly.'

I'm always giving in, Wickery thought bitterly, as he climbed into the driving-seat of the Humber. If it isn't them it's White — or Doris. I'm fed up with other people trying to run my life.

He did not speak during the seven-mile journey into Tanbury. Wells, beside him, respected his silence. He knew that Bert had been right, that what they were doing was extremely foolish. But he comforted his conscience with the knowledge that discovery was unlikely.

Forthright and Chitty were troubled with no such thoughts. Chitty was full of his new job. 'It's a smashing place, Harry. Every gadget and contraption you can think of. And big! You could lose White's tin shack in one of the bays. There's good money to be made there, boy, for a chap that knows his way around.'

'Did you tell White you were going after it?'

'No ruddy fear! He'd have put a stopper on it if he could. Changed my half-day or something.'

The George was the largest pub in Tanbury, and popular. Unable to secure a table, the four men stood drinking at the bar. Under the influence of the beer Wickery's mood gradually mellowed, and presently he and Forthright went over to the other end of the room to play darts.

This gave Wells his chance. At fifty-five he was the oldest of the four — a thin, wiry little man with wispy red hair streaked with grey. It was his protruding eyes that had given him his nickname. In his wizened and weather-beaten face they seemed abnormally prominent. 'Does Molly know about this new job of yours?' he asked Chitty.

'Not that I've got it. I told her I was going after it, of course. But she was out when I called at your place this evening.'

'Out? Where?'

'Mrs Wells didn't know.'

The older man frowned. Sarah ought to be more strict with the girl, he thought; Molly was becoming a sight too flighty these days. But such reflections were not to be voiced before his prospective son-in-law. 'Think you'll like London?' he asked.

'I'd like any place after Chaim,' said Chitty.

It was his round. He took two pints of beer to the darts-players and stood watching them for a few minutes. 'They're pretty good,' he said, when he came back to the bar. 'Take some beating, those two.'

Wells nodded, impatient at the interruption. 'There's nothing to stop you and

Molly getting married now, is there?' he asked.

'Only cash. And we'll need some place to live. London's pretty full, they tell me.'

'You won't want much,' Wells said hopefully. 'A bed-sitter would do for a start. Needs less furniture. What about your sister?'

The young man frowned.

'Yes, Susan's the difficulty. Molly and me could have been married months ago if it hadn't been for her. On the money White pays me Susan and I can just about manage. The question is, will twenty-five bob meet the extra cost of three instead of two?'

Wells was dismayed. 'You're not thinking of taking Susan with you? That's asking for trouble.'

'What else can I do? She can't stay here.'

'Why not? She could get a job, couldn't she?'

'She could get a job in London, come to that,' Chitty said thoughtfully. 'That'd help a lot. She wouldn't have to do the housework and the cooking. Not with Molly there.'

Wells called for another round.

'I don't like it,' he said. 'It's all wrong for a young couple to start married life with a third person in the home. You want the place to yourselves. Why can't Susan get a job here and stay on at the cottage?'

Chitty put his glass down on the counter with a thump.

'Because I don't trust her. I don't trust that blighter Loften, either.'

'Loften? What's he got to do with Susan?'

'Far too much. He's always sniffing around the place when I'm not there. If Susan weren't a damned soft fool she'd have sent him packing. But he gets round her with tales about that wife of his — how she doesn't understand him, doesn't love him.' He took a long pull at the beer and came up panting. 'Bah! It makes me sick.'

Loften and Susan Chitty — that was news to Wells. He wondered if the others knew about it. 'D'you mean he tries to make love to her?' he asked.

Chitty shook his head. 'No. But it'll come to that if I don't get her away. I can't watch her all the time. Maybe —'

Wells caught his arm. 'There's Loften now,' he said. 'Just come in. Of all the ruddy luck . . . '

Chitty turned towards the bar, leaning on it with both elbows firmly planted. 'It's a free house,' he said. Noting the other's anxious expression, he grinned. 'Don't worry, Pop, I'll not make a scene. I'm not out for his blood. Not yet, anyway.'

Loften came over to them, threading his way through the crowd. He was well-dressed, not particularly good-looking. 'Have a drink?' he said, his voice soft, smooth. He seemed pleased to see them. But then Loften was always pleased to see people, always affable. An improvement on Andrew White.

'We were just going,' said Wells. 'Only dropped in for a quick one.'

He hoped the newcomer had not noticed the darts-players.

But Loften had. He called Forthright and Wickery over and insisted on all of them joining him in a drink. 'Only time

10

for a quick one myself,' he explained, lifting a well-manicured right hand to look at his watch. 'Nearly ten. I have to be in Chaim by ten-twenty. I'll have one on you fellows some other time.'

Wickery had not realized it was so late. 'We'd best be going too,' he said.

Wells and Chitty nodded, but Forthright looked sour. He wasn't ready to leave, he wanted another drink, he hadn't finished his game of darts. But he could not protest in front of Loften. He despised the man, but Loften was a link with White.

It had begun to rain, and the damp, cold air chilled them as they left the warmth of the pub. They watched Loften get into his car and drive off in the direction of Chaim, and then they walked down the High Street towards the Humber.

'Good thing we didn't leave it outside the George,' said Wells. 'Loften might have asked some awkward questions.'

'Funny he didn't offer us a lift,' said Wickery. He and Wells were ahead of the other two. He could hear Forthright's voice loud behind them, and wondered anxiously if Harry was a bit tight. Drink always loosened Harry's tongue. 'He couldn't know we had a car.'

'Didn't think of it, perhaps. Just as well, too. I don't know how we'd have got out of that one.'

'He's a rum chap,' Wickery said thoughtfully.

'I don't trust him.' Wells's tone was definite. 'Too smooth.' He wondered whether he should mention what Dave had said about Susan and Loften, but decided against it. Dave might not want it broadcast. 'Six months he's been at the garage, and we don't know a thing more about him than the day he first come — except that he don't know a back axle from a crankshaft.'

'And his wife,' said Wickery. '*She* was a bit of an eye-opener.'

'Oh, her!' The older man sniffed. 'She's a bitch of the highest order. You don't have to be told that, it sticks out a mile.'

'I wonder why they ever came to a place like Chaim. You can see they don't belong.'

They turned down the narrow, unlit road in which the Humber was parked. 'I bet she leads Loften a dance. Every time she comes to the garage it's either for money or to bawl him out,' said Wickery.

Wells remembered the last time Mrs Loften had come to the garage. He had seen Dave Chitty eyeing her, sizing her up. He wasn't entirely happy about Dave. For a young man recently engaged to a pretty girl like Molly he seemed too lukewarm in his affections, too appreciative of other women's charms.

He was suddenly aware that the voices behind them had ceased. He stopped, clutching his companion's arm. The two stood listening.

'They're not following,' said Wells.

'No. Maybe they missed the turning. Let's get the car and go after them.'

They cruised slowly down the High Street. There was no sign of the missing pair, and on the way back Wickery stopped the car opposite the turning down which it had been parked. 'No sense in chasing around,' he said. 'We'll wait here until they show up.'

Across the street a sign, faintly illuminated, proclaimed the corner building to be a pub called the Boar's Head. Wells drew his companion's attention to it. 'I'll bet they slipped in there for a quick one,' he said. 'Sort of thing Harry would do. Once he's on the booze he's never satisfied until he's had a skinful.'

He was getting out of the car when Wickery stopped him.

'Let 'em be, Pop. Harry might turn awkward if he's had a lot more to drink. You know how it takes him. They'll be throwing them out shortly — it's not far off closing-time now.'

They had not long to wait. The two men came running across the road in response to Pop's hail and clambered into the back seat. There was a pungent smell of whisky, and Chitty at least was very drunk.

'Fooled you there.' Forthright laughed stupidly. 'That'll learn you to drag me away from my beer before I'm ready.'

'Damned idiots!' said Wells, as Wickery let in the clutch. 'You won't half have a head tomorrow, drinking whisky on top of all that beer.'

Wickery made no comment. He was driving fast, anxious to be back before White. The road was straight, but the beam from the headlamps was slashed and shortened by the rain, and the single ancient wiper moved slowly and jerkily. Forthright started to sing. He had a good baritone voice, and was much in demand at social gatherings. Chitty joined in intermittently, knowing neither the words nor the tune.

Pop Wells stuffed his fingers in his ears.

'Shut up, Dave! You've got a voice like a ruddy corncrake,' he said, turning to look at the two behind. They were lolling back with their heads on the cushions and their feet propped against the front seat; but at this insult to his vocal powers Chitty struggled into a more upright position and reached forward.

'Lemme tell you  —' he began indignantly.

Forthright, without interrupting his song, stretched out an arm and caught the younger man by the collar, pulling him back on to the seat. A drunken struggle ensued, which resulted in Chitty collapsing on the floor of the car.

Harry Forthright leaned back again, content.

For a few moments Chitty remained recumbent; then he started clambering to his feet. As he did so the car began to swing round a left-hand bend and, losing his balance, he clutched wildly for support. His hand encountered Wickery's head, and Wickery braked instinctively. Chitty, impelled forward by the sudden reduction in speed, threw both arms round the driver's neck at the same time as Forthright, suddenly aware of the danger, caught him and pulled him sharply backward.

Chitty hung on. With his neck being jerked over the back of the seat Wickery took one hand from the wheel to ease the pressure on his throat. As he did so . . .

'Look out!' screamed Wells and Forthright together.

None of them saw what happened. Instinctively Wickery stamped both feet hard down on the pedals. The car lurched as it hit the verge and bounced off. There was a jarring bump; and then the car ran on for a few yards before coming to rest with its front wheels touching the grass on the opposite side of the road.

For a moment they sat, collecting their wits. Then Wickery flung open the door of the car and got out to examine the near side. Wells and Forthright followed, the latter instantly sobered.

'It wasn't only the bank we hit,' Wells said nervously. 'We ran over something.'

'What?'

'I don't know. Didn't you feel the bump?'

He ran back down the road, followed by Forthright. Wickery stayed by the car, his whole body pregnant with fear. He had seen nothing, nobody. But he had felt the bump, and he guessed what was in Pop's mind.

Forthright's voice called to him softly from the darkness.

'It's a woman, Bert. Back the car down here so as we can see.'

She lay on her face, legs sprawling, one arm bent awkwardly beneath her. There was blood on the dull grey hair and the woollen-stockinged legs, indecently exposed by the rucked-up skirt.

They turned her over gently. She was dead.

For a few moments they knelt there in the heavy rain, full of pity for the old woman and fear for themselves. Then Forthright scrambled to his feet.

'Let's get out of this,' he said hoarsely.

The others looked at him, aghast. 'We can't do that,' Wickery exclaimed. 'She needs a doctor . . . the police . . . '

'Don't be a fool, mate. She's dead, isn't she? What good can a doctor do? Come on! Let's get away before someone turns up.'

'There may be marks on the car,' Wells objected.

'We'll see to that when we get back. We've got to paint the wing, anyway.'

Wickery shook his head. 'We killed her,' he said dully. Disaster had come upon them so swiftly that he felt confused and unable to grasp its full implication. But he knew that Harry's suggestion was outrageous.

'For God's sake don't stand there arguing!' Forthright cast anxious glances up and down the road. 'Can't you see what the police'll make of this? A party of drunks, they'll say — and in a borrowed car. It'll stink to high heaven.'

'It was you and Dave who were drunk, not me.'

'What the hell's that got to do with it? We're all in this together. And how will Doris manage, with you cooling your heels in gaol for God knows how long?' He thought of Ma left on her own, and his anxiety deepened. 'Come on, Bert, blast you! Hurry, man — hurry!'

Wickery stood up as the other tugged at his arm. 'No,' he said. 'It's all wrong. We can't do it, Harry.'

'Wrong? Of course it's wrong! But — oh, hell! Here, Pop — you tell him. Maybe he'll listen to *you*.'

The little man was as confused as Wickery, but there was in him an urgent longing to escape. He felt sick and frightened — he had never seen a corpse before. He grasped eagerly at Harry's suggestion, not caring or even thinking about right and wrong. Anything to get away.

But because of the fear and confusion in his mind his pleading was frenzied and incoherent, and after a few moments he abandoned it in favour of more urgent methods. The dazed Wickery found himself being propelled by the other two towards the car, and he struggled to get free. He wanted to escape as urgently as did they. The thought of Doris left alone — dependent, perhaps, on her uncle — was torture to him. But he could not bring himself to leave the old lady, to abandon her poor dead body so callously.

He broke away and ran back to her.

The others stood undecided. They could not go without him. And yet . . .

As Wickery bent to lift the body Forthright cried out in alarm. 'Leave her alone, you fool! You'll get blood on your clothes!'

Wickery faced them, the headlights shining full on him. He had made his decision. 'Give me a hand, then,' he said. 'I want to move her on to the grass. I'm not leaving her here.'

Forthright hesitated. He knew it would be wiser not to move the body. If they were unlucky, if the accident should later be traced to them, they might then have pleaded ignorance. But there was no time for further argument. At any moment they might be discovered.

He helped Wickery to place her gently on the grass on the far side of the road, arranging the body to suggest that she had been flung there by the car. Then they left her.

Dave Chitty still lolled in the back of the Humber, asleep and snoring. Wickery drove fast to the garage. The distance was short, but during those few minutes his brain worked rapidly. In giving way to the others he had dropped no hint of his intention, which had been to telephone the police as soon as they reached the garage. But now, away from the scene of the accident and with freedom correspondingly nearer, his resolution began to weaken. There was sense in what Harry and Pop had said. No punishment, however severe, could compensate the old woman for the life they had so abruptly taken from her. And he himself had been entirely blameless. Why should he make himself responsible for the drunken behaviour of the others?

Apparently unseen, they got the car into the garage and drew the heavy doors together. 'Lucky we're away from the village here,' said Forthright, kneeling to examine the front of the Humber. 'There's no one can say what time we got back.'

Wells joined him, but Wickery stood undecided by the office door. Suppose the old woman wasn't dead after all? A doctor might save her if . . .

'Come on, Bert, blast you!'

But she *was* dead. No doubt about that. And a telephone call could be traced.

He walked over to the car.

Apart from a few scratches and smears of mud on the near-side wheel and wing there were no visible traces of the accident. No marks on the bumper or the radiator, no sign of blood. But they took no chances. They put her over the pit and washed the front with petrol, hoping to remove any tiny particles of hair or cloth or blood that might be there. Then they started to clean and polish the rest of the body.

'Damned lucky we didn't break any glass,' said Wells, as he gave a final rub to a headlamp. 'When you come to think of it, it's amazing that nothing's bent or stove in.'

Dave Chitty woke up and said he felt sick. They got him out of the Humber, and Wells took him round to the back of the garage. He swayed as he walked.

Wickery had just started to paint the wing when there was a heavy knock on the door. He was so startled that he dropped the brush. 'White!' he exclaimed.

Forthright shook his head. 'No. No car. And he wouldn't knock, he'd use his key.'

A loud voice hailed them. 'Hey, Pop! Harry! Open up. It's me — Willie.'

'Willie Trape! God!' said Wickery.

'Leave him to me,' Forthright said shortly, disdainful of the other's jittery nerves. He opened the door to admit a large and very wet policeman.

'Evening, all. I saw the lights, so

thought I'd call in to tell you the news. There's been a nasty accident on the Tanbury road.'

'Anyone hurt?' asked Forthright.

The constable took off his cap and mopped his brow. 'Old woman killed. Mrs Gooch — lives in that cottage t'other side of Witton Hall. She must have been walking home when the car hit her. Driver didn't stop, neither; didn't report the accident, anyways. First I heard of it was from the cyclist who found her.'

'There's too much of that hit-and-run business these days,' said Forthright, showing proper concern. 'As a matter of fact, we were in Tanbury ourselves this evening. Left there just after ten.' He turned to the silent Wickery. 'What time were we back here, Bert? About twenty past, wasn't it?'

Wickery nodded. There could be no turning back now. 'About that,' he agreed, uncertain why Harry was lying about the time, but with no option but to trust to his handling of the affair.

'There was no one on the road then,' Forthright said.

'No. She didn't leave the Clays' until half-past ten.' He wandered over to the Humber, where Wickery had again started on the wing, and chuckled hugely. 'Covering up the evidence, eh?'

Wickery managed a feeble grin. Forthright laughed. 'Mrs Riley's car, isn't it?' asked Trape.

'Yes. She had a nasty skid last Friday — ran into the back of a three-tonner. White promised to have it ready for her by tomorrow. That's why we're working late.'

'What were you doing in Tanbury, then?' asked the constable.

'Road testing,' Forthright explained. 'Called in at the George for a quick one. Mr Loften was there too — left a few minutes before us.' He decided to lead the conversation away from their visit to Tanbury. 'Which side of the road did you find her? I mean, which way would the car have been going?'

'Towards Tanbury, the Sergeant thinks. Though it's odd she should have crossed the road when she didn't have to.'

'Any skid-marks?'

'No. Too wet. It's still coming down in buckets. Mr White in?'

'Not yet. Shouldn't be long, though.'

'Well, tell him to keep a look-out for the car. There may be damage done to the front of it, and there's a chance the owner might bring it in later if he's a local chap.'

'We'll keep our eyes skinned,' Forthright promised him.

Wickery continued to ply his brush, wishing that the constable would leave. As Harry had said, White should be back soon. He wanted to be away from the garage before that happened.

But it was another five minutes before they got rid of Trape.

Forthright thought the interview had gone well enough; Wickery was not so sure. 'Why did you have to tell him we'd been at the George?' he asked.

'In case the police heard of it from someone else. Loften, for instance. That'd look bad. And it helps to fix the time we're supposed to have left Tanbury. They'll ask Loften, and he'll bear us out.'

'But how did you know that altering the time would put us in the clear?'

26

'I didn't,' Forthright confessed. 'But it was around quarter to eleven when we knocked the old girl down, and it seemed unlikely she could have been on the road long before that. If we could prove we were back here by ten-twenty, and if she was known to have gone out after that — well, it was a good bet, anyway.'

'It won't be so good if they find out you and Dave were at the Boar's Head.'

'They won't.' Forthright was confident. 'Dammit, why should they?'

Wells came into the garage with Chitty. The latter had sobered up considerably, but looked white and ill. He sank on to a pile of tyres and sat there with his head bowed between his hands, his elbows resting on his knees. 'I heard Willie when he called out, but I thought I'd better keep Dave out of the way,' said Wells, his face anxious. 'What happened?'

Forthright told him.

'Well, we've done it now,' said Wells. 'We can't go back on it now. But if anything goes wrong . . . '

'It won't.' Wickery wondered if Harry was as confident as he sounded. 'What

27

about Dave? Does he know?'

'I told him out back. Shook him up bad, it did.'

'So it ruddy well ought,' Forthright said viciously. 'If it hadn't been for him we shouldn't be in this perishing mess.'

At the sound of his name Chitty looked up. He was about to speak when the sound of tyres on the gravel outside caused all four men to turn and stare at the closed garage-doors. The car came nearer and then stopped, engine running, headlights shining through the cracks in the doors. A horn blared throatily.

'White,' said Forthright. As he passed Chitty on his way to open the doors he whispered fiercely, 'Clear off as soon as he comes in. Don't let him see you.'

Andrew White was a stocky, square-shouldered man with bushy eyebrows and a prominent, aggressive chin. His iron-grey moustache and hair, still abundant at forty-eight, gave him a military appearance which he liked to foster. So short was his neck that his head seemed to spring directly from his shoulders.

He got out of the car and walked with

springing steps to where Wickery was putting the finishing touches to the wing of the Humber. 'What the hell have you fellows been up to?' he barked. 'This job should have been done hours ago. I'm not paying overtime for nothing, blast you!'

'It was that front spring held us up,' said Forthright. 'It didn't fit.'

'H'm! Had her out on the road yet? Steering okay?'

'Yes. She's all right, except that the brakes need relining. Mrs Riley said to leave them.'

'The woman's a menace,' said White, frowning. 'Heard about the accident tonight?'

They looked at him, wondering how he knew. 'Willie Trape was in. He told us,' Wells said.

'Nasty business,' said White. 'Party of drunks, probably. They didn't report it, either. That won't do 'em any good when the police catch up with them.' He looked hard at Wickery. 'Or perhaps they hope to get away with it, eh?'

'I wouldn't know.' Wickery's conscience

still troubled him. He wanted to forget Mrs Gooch.

White lifted the bonnet of the Humber and felt the cylinder-block. 'How long a run did you give her?' he asked.

'Tanbury and back,' said Forthright.

'Tanbury, eh? See anything of the old woman?'

'No. She wasn't on the road till half-past ten, so Trape said. We were back long before then.'

'Were you?' There was an edge to his voice that made Wickery shiver. 'The engine's still hot.' He lit a cigarette and turned to Wells. 'Wasn't that Chitty who left just now?'

Wells nodded.

'Really?' White was almost purring. 'Most extraordinary. When Trape stopped me up the road to tell me about the accident he said he'd called in here. But there was only Forthright and Wickery here, he said; they told him you and Chitty had gone home. How do you account for that, eh?'

He barked the last word at Wells, stabbing him in the chest with a rigid forefinger. The other two stood aghast, waiting for Pop to speak. Neither could think of a sufficiently plausible answer with which to come to his aid.

'We — we hadn't gone home,' Wells said at last, recovering some of his wits. 'Dave came over queer when we got outside, so I took him round to the gents'. We were out there when Willie Trape called, and afterwards Dave thought he'd like to sit down for a bit, until he felt better.'

Andrew White looked at him admiringly.

'Hardly the way to treat your prospective son-in-law, letting him go home alone in that condition. He *is* your prospective son-in-law, isn't he?'

The little man nodded.

'Hoping to get married soon?'

Again Wells nodded.

'H'm! Well, I shouldn't have thought four pound ten a week was sufficient for that. But it's his affair, of course, not mine.'

'Dave's getting five pound ten a week,' said Wells.

'He *was*.' The last word was heavily stressed. 'But I'm afraid it'll be four ten in the future. Business is slack; too many overheads and not enough coming in. We've got to cut our costs somehow.'

They looked at him in consternation. 'You mean — you're knocking a quid a week off his wages?' gasped Wells. 'Why, you — you can't do it!'

'Oh, yes, I can.' White was obviously enjoying himself. 'And not only his, either; that wouldn't be fair. We must all do our share. Of course, officially you will continue to receive your present wages. That's what the books will show, anyway. But unofficially — ' He paused, looking at them with a slight smile on his face. 'Unofficially, you will each return a quid a week to me.'

'Like hell we will!' said Wickery. 'Why, you — '

'Shut up, Bert. Leave this to me,' said Forthright. He turned to White. 'Why do you suppose we'd be willing to do that?' he asked.

'Why? Well, it could be a form of insurance. One can insure against almost anything these days. Fire, burglary, unemployment — even accident. Yes, I think insurance describes it well enough.'

He beamed at them maliciously.

'That's no answer, Mr White. Just what are you getting at?'

The smile disappeared. 'You want it straight, eh? All right, then. You'll be paying me to keep my mouth shut. And if you don't like the idea of that, I'll inform the police that it was you four drunken fools who killed that old woman tonight. Is *that* plain enough for you?'

'You — you were there?' spluttered Wells.

'Of course I was there. My car was parked off the road, only a few yards away. You were too drunk or too frightened to notice it, I suppose.'

For some moments none of them spoke. It was Forthright who broke the silence. 'It's blackmail,' he said sternly.

White laughed. 'Your sense of values is somewhat muddled, isn't it? Having committed manslaughter, what right have you to cavil at blackmail? You can consider yourselves damned lucky to get off so lightly, my lads. And if you don't like it — well, just say so, that's all.'

He opened the office door, and then paused.

'One other thing. I'm behind with my book-keeping, Bert, and I'd like Doris to take on her old job again. She won't want any wages, of course. A labour of love, eh? Tell her to start in the morning.'

Wickery took a step forward, his fists clenched. 'You damned well think again!' he shouted. 'She's not coming.'

White glared at him. 'It'll be very unfortunate for you if she doesn't,' he said. 'You'd better persuade her. Or would you rather I did it for you?'

Wickery would have rushed him then, but the others caught hold of his arms and held him back. 'Knocking the swine down won't help,' said Forthright.

'A very sensible remark — though crudely expressed,' White agreed. 'Tempers may be a little short this evening, but I shall expect more civility in the future.' He yawned. 'Well, now — I think that covers everything, doesn't it? I'm for bed.'

They did not hurry as they walked

down the road towards the village. They did not notice the rain. All their thoughts were on the scene just ended. But when Wells started to accuse Forthright of being responsible for their predicament Forthright cut him short.

'All right, all right, blast you! How the hell was I to know that the swine was there? And you can shout your perishing head off, but we'd be a ruddy sight worse off in gaol. Nor I didn't notice you were all that keen to stay and face the music. Once you'd got the idea there wasn't no holding you.'

'There must be *something* we can do,' Wickery said desperately.

'Nothing short of murder. But I'm sorry about Doris, mate. You got a rough deal there. She won't like going back to the garage.'

'She'll hate it like hell. What the devil am I going to say to her? Tell her the truth, I suppose.'

'Cut that out.' Forthright was alarmed. 'I know Doris. I wouldn't put it past her to go to the police.'

Wickery knew that was true. With her

hatred of her uncle and her passionate regard for the truth, Doris might prefer to see her husband dealt with by the law rather than knuckle under to White. I might prefer it too, he thought. I was a fool to listen to Harry; I ought to have done what I knew was right.

But he had no choice now; to confess would involve the others. 'What about the money?' he asked. 'How do we explain that?'

The same problem had occurred to Wells. Even if he kept nothing back for beer and tobacco, Sarah would still have to go short on the housekeeping. It would take a damned good story to keep Sarah quiet about *that*.

'Tell 'em what White said — that business isn't too good,' Forthright suggested. 'Say it's only temporary, that he's promised to make it up to us later. With interest. That'll give 'em something to look forward to.'

'I suppose we couldn't quit?' asked Wells. 'Get another job?'

'You think White would let us go? Be your age, Pop. He's on to a good thing and he knows it.'

'What would he be up to, parking in that rain?'

'A woman, of course. What else?'

'Blast Dave!' said Wickery. 'If it hadn't been for him we wouldn't be in this mess.'

'You can't blame a chap for something he does when he's drunk,' said Wells. Bewildered and unhappy, he still felt it his duty to defend Chitty. And Dave had a nasty temper. If he thought the others had their knife into him there was no knowing what he might not do.

They reached the cottage in which Harry Forthright lived with his invalid mother. It stood by itself, away from the village and about two hundred yards from the garage. Fruit-trees shielded it from the road, and behind it was the forest.

'We've got to stick together,' said Forthright, as he pushed open the garden gate. 'Don't you chaps try anything on your own. And don't forget that we're still free, even if we *are* going to be short of cash. That's worth a ruddy sight more than a quid a week, isn't it?'

# 2

## The Months Between

Chaim village lay south of the road which led eastward to Tanbury and westward to Rowgate. North of the road was the forest, much depleted by frequent inroads on its timber, but still possessed of some grandeur. It was thickest to the east, where, about half a mile from the village, stood White's garage; a solid, red-brick structure with showroom and offices to one side, and over these a four-roomed flat in which the proprietor lived. On a concrete base in front of the building stood a row of petrol-pumps; to the left was the yard, with scrap-heaps of empty tins and drums, piles of worn-out tyres, a derelict chassis or two. But the clearing had been cut from the forest, and the forest still hemmed it in. It was a damp and gloomy spot in winter.

To Doris Wickery it had seemed

gloomy even in summer. 'You'll never know how thankful I am to be away from that dreadful place,' she had told her husband on their first evening of married life. 'This cottage may be small, but at least it's a home.'

'Sounds as though you married me just to be quit of the garage,' said Bert. 'Or could there be another reason?'

'There could and there is,' she reassured him, demonstrating it. After a while she said, 'I suppose it wasn't the garage, really. Just Uncle Andrew. It's queer, isn't it, that one can hate one's own flesh and blood?'

'He's not your flesh and blood,' he pointed out. 'Only your uncle by marriage. And everyone else hates him, so why not you?'

'I think it's his eyes,' she said. 'The way he looks at you. It's — it's possessive, somehow, and rather disgusting.'

'It's his damned bad temper that gets my goat,' replied her husband. 'That and his meanness. Grudges every farthing he spends. And fancy keeping all that money under his bed, just because he can't bear to pay bank charges on it! One of these days somebody'll pinch the lot — and serve him ruddy well right!'

Doris nodded. 'That's why he didn't want us to get married,' she said. 'Because of his meanness, I mean. It wasn't that he objected to you; he'd have been the same about any man. He couldn't bear the thought of losing a free cook-cum-housekeeper-cum-secretary-cum-clerk.'

Wickery grinned. 'He was on about that this morning. Said maybe, after you'd settled down to married life, you might care to work for him again. He hinted he might even be prepared to pay you a small wage.'

'And what did you say to that?'

'Nothing doing, I said. Having got myself a wife, I aim to keep her.' He squeezed her slim waist. 'I don't believe in married women going out to work. Makes them a darned sight too independent.'

Doris returned the squeeze. 'I haven't been married long enough to know about that, darling. But if I *do* have to help out financially — and Uncle Andrew doesn't pay you a lot, does he? — it won't be at the garage. Nothing on earth could make me go back there.'

★　★　★

Bert Wickery recalled this conversation as he let himself in at the cottage door. But he dare not weaken now. Doris would have to do it — she'd just *have* to. And because he knew that with every minute that passed he *was* weakening, he went straight upstairs to where she lay awaiting him in the big double bed.

Doris thought he was joking when he told her. Only when he came nearer and she saw his expression did she realize that this was no joke. And even then she could not believe that he had actually agreed to White's demand.

'But you said yourself I'd never have to go back there,' she pleaded unhappily. 'I don't mind going out to work if we're all that hard up, darling. But not with Uncle Andrew. I just *couldn't*.'

He sat down wearily on the bed, not

41

looking at her. 'We haven't any choice,' he said miserably.

Despite her bewilderment, her hatred of what he was asking her to do, her heart ached for him. She leaned across and touched his hand softly. 'What is it, darling? What's wrong? Tell me.'

He shook his head.

'I can't. It isn't only me — the others are in it as well. We're in a jam, Doris — a hell of a jam.' He gripped her hand and squeezed it. 'Maybe, when we've had time to think, we'll find a way out. But until then — well, we'll have to do as White says, blast him!'

'And that includes me?'

'I'm afraid so.'

'Is it — are the police after you?' she asked anxiously.

'No. At least — well, they could be. But it's White we have to worry about.' He turned to face her. 'It wasn't my fault, Doris. I've done nothing wrong, really. I was just unlucky enough to get mixed up in it.'

Doris started work at the garage the next morning. Her uncle was affable, too affable at times; but he did not spare her. He dismissed the daily woman who had looked after him for the past year, and in addition to her office work Doris cooked his meals and cleaned the flat and made his bed. She found the atmosphere in the garage even more depressing than it had been before her marriage. The men worked silently and without enthusiasm. Although she had been a favourite with them, they showed no pleasure at her return. Almost, it seemed to Doris, they resented her presence there; and after a few days, when she had had time to appreciate her uncle's attitude towards them — just as though they were slaves, she thought — she sensed the reason for their resentment. They were ashamed that she should be a witness to their degradation.

Even George Loften seemed to have caught some of the gloom that now pervaded the garage. Loften had not joined her uncle in partnership until about six months after her marriage, but she had met him once or twice on her infrequent visits to the garage to see her husband. He had seemed quite a pleasant man, she thought, and most courteous. Bert didn't trust him, said he was the 'smarmy' type; but then Bert mistrusted any man who took pains with his appearance. Doris sometimes wished he were a bit more of the 'smarmy' type himself.

Loften did not ignore her as did the others; but whereas hitherto he had always made her aware of her youth and prettiness, now he hardly seemed to notice either. Doris guessed he was having trouble with his wife again, and felt sorry for him. He couldn't have much of a home life, poor man, with a wife like Elsie Loften.

It was not until the county police called at the garage on her second day there that she heard about Mrs Gooch. They did not stay long, and their inquiries were of a routine nature. But after they had gone Doris sensed her husband's relief, and guessed something of what had happened. The knowledge terrified her, the more so because when she tried to voice her suspicions to Bert he lost his temper and told her not to meddle. It was the first time he had ever spoken roughly to her; and although he apologized later he offered no explanation, and his guilty secret lay like a barrier between them. If it did not break their love, it made them awkward and uneasy in each other's presence. They shared no confidences. At home the radio blared unceasingly in the evening, obviating the necessity for conversation. It was a relief to go to bed, even though sleep did not come easily to either of them. Night brought an escape from reality.

★   ★   ★

Dave Chitty pushed the bacon aside and reached for the teapot. 'I'm not hungry,' he said. 'Cup of tea's all I want.'

His sister eyed him, noting the symptoms. But she removed the unwanted plate in silence. Dave had a nasty temper. He could be particularly unpleasant after a thick night.

He gulped the tea down noisily. It was hot and sweet, and eased the dryness in his throat. But it could not still the throbbing in his head or quell the rumbling of his stomach. 'You'd better eat something, even if it's only dry toast,' Susan advised him, after a reverberating belch. 'You can't do a day's work on an empty stomach.'

'I know what I can do. I don't need you to tell me.' But he took the toast and buttered it, and began to eat. He felt slightly better, and recalled uneasily what he could of the events of the previous night. It wasn't much. All that had happened after leaving the Boar's Head was a complete blank. His knowledge of it depended on what Pop had told him, and even that was blurred in his memory. Something about having knocked down an old woman on the way back — killed her, Pop had said . . .

Sweating, he took another draught of tea. That was a nasty business. Still, he wasn't driving, he was just a passenger in the car. No one could blame him, thank the Lord! And, from what Pop had told him, it seemed that they had come out of it all right. They had got away . . . no one had seen them. He remembered walking home across the fields, feeling like nothing on earth . . . stumbling up to bed . . .

He turned to his sister. 'Where the hell did you get to last night?' he asked.

Susan flushed. 'I was out.'

'You're telling me you were out! It had gone half-past eleven by the time I got back, and you weren't home then. Where were you?'

It never occurred to her to question his right to ask. He had always bullied her, tried to run her life. 'I was sitting with old Mrs Quayles while Annie was at the pictures,' she said.

'What? Until gone twelve?' He scowled at her. 'You can't come that lark with me. You were out with Loften, weren't you?'

'For a while, yes. He picked me up in his car and we went for a spin. But I didn't realize it was so late.'

'I bet you didn't! Too ruddy well occupied, eh? You want to watch your step, my girl, or you'll find yourself in trouble.'

'There's no need to be insulting, Dave,'

she said, goaded into defending herself. 'George Loften knows how to behave himself, and so do I. There was nothing like that. We just talked.'

'What about?'

'His wife, mostly. You know they don't get on.'

That's his fault, thought Chitty, recalling the glamour of Elsie Loften. I bet I could get on with a smasher like that, given half a chance. The knowledge that he would never have that chance made him irritable, and he said, 'That's just a line. You ought to know better than to fall for it.' But he had lost interest in his sister, and the venom had gone out of his voice.

'You'll be late,' said Susan.

As he walked over the fields to the garage his thoughts were more concerned with the future than with the past. The accident to Mrs Gooch was an unreality, but the new job in London offered vast possibilities. For one thing, he and Molly could get married. He wasn't madly in love with Molly, but she was a good-looker and had what it takes, and it wasn't a bad thing to have a wife to come home to of an evening.

I'll tackle White this morning, he decided. Maybe he'll let me go at the week-end, so's I can start at the new place Monday. But the sight of Doris Wickery seated at the typewriter in the outer office made him pause. He looked at her in astonishment.

'What are you doing here?' he asked.

'Working,' she said listlessly. 'Uncle needed some help.'

'Did he, though. Well, he's going to need some more very shortly. I'm giving notice — got a job in Town.' He jerked his thumb towards the inner office. 'Old man in?'

His cheerfulness puzzled her. Bert had said they were all involved. 'Have you seen the others?' she asked.

'Not yet. Why?'

'I think you'd better speak to them first,' she said. She did not know why.

Chitty frowned. Had there been trouble about that business of last night? Doris wouldn't know, of course, but . . .

'Did they say they wanted to see me?'

'No. But I think you'd better.'

He went through to the workshop at the back. The other three were there, and misgiving deepened as he looked at them. Their gloomy faces foretold trouble.

It was Forthright who told him.

Chitty was filled with anger. 'You mean the swine saw the accident, and now he's blackmailing us?'

'Yes.'

'He hasn't told the police?'

'Of course not. As long as he keeps his trap shut he's four quid a week to the good. *And* he's got Doris back — for nothing.'

'But what about my new job?'

Forthright shrugged his shoulders. 'You've had that, chum. Forget it.'

Chitty tried to think calmly, to control his anger. He had to have that job — he just *had* to. To spend years — perhaps the rest of his life — in that God-forsaken hole . . . and at even less money than the little he had been getting before . . .

'I didn't get out of the car,' he said slowly. 'White can't have seen me — he couldn't even know I was there.'

'He saw you leave the garage,' said Forthright. '*And* he saw the state you were in.'

'That doesn't prove anything.'

'It doesn't have to prove anything. If you don't pay your whack White'll get tough. We're taking no risks, my lad.'

'But it's damned unfair,' he cried angrily. 'I wasn't driving; I wasn't even in the front of the car. Why the hell should I suffer because Bert didn't look where he was going? If you ask me —'

'Shut up!' Wickery stepped forward, his fists clenched. 'You've got a nerve to complain, damn you! Don't you understand that if it hadn't been for your drunken fooling in the back of the car the accident would never have happened? It's you and Harry that's responsible, not me. And yet you stand there bleating —'

Forthright caught him by the shoulders and swung him sharply round.

'Cut that out.' There was an ugly look on his face as he confronted the angry Wickery. 'I wasn't that drunk, and you know it. I'm getting a little tired of you and Pop trying to put all the blame on me. Dave's right — if you'd driven at a reasonable speed there might never have been an accident. You were taking a risk you had no right to take.'

'I was driving fast because we were late. And whose fault was that, damn you? Yours and Dave's. A couple of ruddy drunks who don't know when they've had enough — that's what you two are. If Pop and I —'

'Thieves falling out?' White stood in the doorway, eyeing them with some amusement. 'Not a very edifying spectacle. And if you don't want your — er — misfortune to become too widely known I suggest you confine your quarrelling to a more private place.' His tone sharpened. 'I won't have it here, anyway. I pay you to work, not to talk.'

'Pay us, do you?' Chitty snapped. 'I thought it was us had to pay you.'

White stared at him coldly. 'You don't approve of the arrangement?'

'Like hell I don't!'

'Perhaps you would prefer the alternative?'

'I'd prefer anything that doesn't mean

paying good money to a damned rat like you,' said Chitty, beside himself with rage.

Without a word White turned and walked out of the workshop. As the crisp sound of footsteps on concrete ceased and they realized he had gone into the office, Forthright said urgently, 'Go after him, you fool. Do you want to land us all in the can?'

Chitty stood irresolute. Fear was eating into his anger, but pride forbade an apology. 'I'm not grovelling to a swine like White,' he declared. 'I'll see him in hell first.'

'He'll see you in gaol, you mean,' said Wickery. 'You and the rest of us. Go on, blast you, stop him!'

'You don't have to grovel, Dave.' Wells tried to speak calmly. He was as worried as the others, but he knew from experience how stubborn Chitty could be. You couldn't drive him, he had to be led. 'He won't expect you to apologize — just tell him you're willing to pay what he asks. It won't be for long — we'll think of something. But we daren't let him go to the police. They'd give us a heavy sentence — White would make it sound as bad as he could, you know that. And us not reporting it makes it worse, see?'

Sullenly, Chitty said that he did see. With an angry look at the others he stalked off to the office, Wells's gently urging hand at his back. 'Damned young fool!' said Forthright. 'Who does he think he is, trying to ditch us like that? Another bleat out of him and I'd have knocked his block off.'

'You got to make allowances,' said Wells, returning from seeing Chitty safely into the office. 'All he knows about the accident is what we told him. It's not as real to him as it is to us.'

When Chitty came back they asked him what White had said. He glared at them and went out to the yard without answering. Forthright would have followed, but Wells stopped him. 'Leave him alone, Harry. Give him time. He's pretty sore.'

'We're all sore,' growled the other. 'It's no worse for him.'

In that he was wrong. Whereas he and

Wells and Wickery had settled homes and a fixed way of life, Dave Chitty had always been restless. He wasn't content to continue as he had begun; he had ambitions. He wanted to marry Molly Wells, but she was all he wanted from Chaim. For the rest, he wanted a more exciting life in a big town, a better job, more money. To the other three White's blackmail meant the loss of all luxuries, a tightening of the belt; but it did not affect the manner of their lives. To Chitty it was the end of everything he had envisaged.

As days lengthened into weeks and months his bitterness increased. At the garage he was sullen and morose, flaring occasionally into violent outbursts of rage, but otherwise taking little notice of his companions. The day's work over, he would go home, silently eat the meal Susan often had great difficulty in providing (the pound a week he gave White came out of the housekeeping money; he was not going to curtail his own spending) and then go off to the pub. Even there he did not mix freely with the company in the bar, but sat alone, drinking his beer and brooding over his misfortunes. On the rare occasions he drank with friends a quarrel usually resulted.

Susan was not sorry to be without him in the evenings. Her brother's behaviour both worried and frightened her. Dave had offered no reason for giving her less money, and she attributed it to his heavy drinking. But what had caused the change in him she did not know and was too frightened to ask. She did ask Loften. But Loften seemed no better informed than herself, and was preoccupied with his own domestic affairs. His wife had left him; and although she returned a month later, their reconciliation was more in the nature of an uneasy truce. 'We may share the same house, but we've had it as far as marriage is concerned,' he told Susan on one of his increasingly frequent visits; and added, when Susan protested at his easy acceptance of the fact, 'No point in flogging a dead horse.'

Molly Wells was both hurt and incensed by her fiancé's behaviour. He came to see her seldom, and sometimes a whole week passed without their meeting. He was moody and quarrelsome, making no lover-like approaches. There was no further talk of marriage. Molly decided that he was cooling off, that he no longer wanted to marry her. He denied this; but when she left off wearing her engagement ring he did not appear to notice the omission.

The next time they met she handed the ring back to him.

'What's this for?' he asked. 'You breaking it off?'

'It looks like it, doesn't it?' she said tartly. 'If you can't be bothered to take any notice of me, there's others as can. You're not the only fellow in Chaim, Dave Chitty.'

She had hoped that this would reignite the spark that now seemed to be missing in him. But Dave made no further protest. He stood scowling at the ring for a moment. Then he thrust it into his pocket and walked off.

Hurt and bewildered, Molly went home crying.

'I'll have a word with him,' her father

promised her, distressed at her obvious unhappiness. He knew well what was wrong with Dave, but he could not explain it to Molly. Dave was so eaten up with self-pity that he had no thought or consideration for anyone else. Not even for Molly. 'It's not that he doesn't love you, dear — I'm sure of that. It's just that — well, he's upset because he didn't get that job in London. He'd set his heart on it, you know — couldn't talk about anything else. But he always reckoned you and he would be married first.'

'Don't you dare say a word to him,' cried the girl. 'If his precious job means more to him than I do, then I'm glad I found it out before I married him.'

'How did Dave come to lose that new job?' asked Mrs Wells, after Molly had gone upstairs. 'That evening he came back from London he called in to see Molly, and he told me he'd got it. It was all fixed, he said. What went wrong?'

'I don't know,' said her husband. 'Dave kept quiet about it — just said it was off. But it's upset him proper, no doubt of that. And I don't like him and our Molly falling out. It's a shame.'

'He could try elsewhere, couldn't he?' the woman persisted. 'There's other jobs.'

'I suppose so. Perhaps he has. Dave doesn't talk about himself much.'

He shied away from the topic as quickly as he could. Dave Chitty's troubles were too closely linked with his own for him to wish to discuss them with Sarah. She had seemed to swallow the story he had told her as to why there was less money coming in. But one never knew with women.

'She'll take it badly,' said Mrs Wells. 'I hope to goodness she doesn't get into trouble, the way girls do these days.'

'Molly's got her head screwed on right,' said her husband. 'She won't do anything foolish.'

But he was not so sure of this when one evening some weeks later he saw his daughter getting out of a car at the end of the lane. It was obvious that neither Molly nor the driver wished to be recognized. Their leave-taking was hurried.

As the car backed and turned Wells

recognized it. A deep anger filled him, and he grabbed the girl roughly by the arm as she came abreast of him.

'Ouch!' she cried, startled. 'You didn't half give me a fright, Dad.'

'I'll give you more than that, my girl, if I ever catch you with White again. What the hell do you think you're playing at, going out with a man like him?'

'I'm not playing at anything.' She tried to sound haughty and indignant, but her voice was not properly under control. 'Mr White very kindly offered me a lift back from the pictures. Nothing wrong in that, is there?'

'There might be. Is this the first time?'

'No. But there's no need for all this heavy-father business. He's a very nice gentleman, and he's always behaved quite properly.'

'You tell that to Dave,' Wells said grimly.

'I'll not tell Dave anything. Dave and me are through; I'm free to do as I please. Why shouldn't I go out with Mr White if he asks me?'

'Because I'll beat the living daylights

out of you, that's why. White's got only one use for women, and I won't have him trying it on you. Get me?'

'Yes. But really, Dad, I —'

'You do as I say, Molly. Your ma and I have given you a pretty free hand, but this is where I put my foot down. You'll have no more to do with Andrew White.'

'But suppose he offers me a lift, as he did tonight? He's your boss, Dad. No sense in offending him.'

'You let me worry about that,' said Wells.

As they walked the few yards to their home she said sadly, 'It's not much fun for me, Dad, without Dave. I used to look forward to him taking me out, even if we didn't go anywhere in particular. But now — well, it's so *dull*. You can't blame me if I want a bit of fun now and again.'

He pressed her arm gently. 'I'm not blaming you, my dear. You enjoy yourself all you can, so long as it isn't with White. He's out. And don't worry about Dave. He'll be back.'

'I'm not worrying,' she said. 'He can drink himself silly for all I care.' As they turned in at the gate she added, thinking aloud, 'A car's so much nicer than a bus. I hate buses. And I hate waiting for them, too — particularly on a cold evening after the pictures.'

'Maybe,' said Wells. 'But buses are safer.'

Worried, he mentioned the incident to Wickery and Forthright. 'I don't think she'll do it again,' he said. 'I scared her good and proper. But she's young and high-spirited — and White's not a bad-looking chap, even though he's old enough to be her father. And then there's the glamour; him having a car, and money. She feels flattered like.'

Wickery nodded. 'She misses Dave, I expect. Why not speak to White?'

'What's the use? According to Molly, all he's done is to offer her a lift now and again. No harm in that, he'd say. And no more there isn't; it's what he may be planning that worries me. You know what a nasty bit of work he is. He hates our guts, doesn't he? Suppose he's aiming to get at me through Molly, same as he got at you through Doris?'

'I don't think he hates us. He just likes kicking people around and watching 'em squirm,' Forthright said bitterly.

'I'll make him squirm if he tries any of his tricks on Molly,' said Wells. 'Settle him once and for all, that's what I'll do.'

Loften came into the workshop, and the discussion ceased. But later Wickery took Wells aside. 'Did you mean what you said about White, Pop?' he asked. 'About settling him if he got fresh with Molly?'

'Of course.'

'What would you do?'

'Do? I don't know. I hadn't got around to thinking about that. Hope I won't have to, neither.'

'No. But if you do?'

'Well — beat him up, I suppose.'

'You'd have a job. He's younger than you, and a damned sight bigger.'

'Oh, well . . . ' He stared at Wickery, perplexed. 'What's biting you, Bert? You got something up your sleeve?'

The other hesitated. Then he said, 'I've had enough. I'm through with paying blood money to White, damn him!'

'Any special reason?'

'Doris. She's in the family way.'

Wells thought this over. 'You mean you'll need more money for the kid?'

'Yes. We're in debt already. By the time Doris has got all the things she needs there'll be nothing over to live on. And that's not all. In a few months she'll have to stop working here — and what's White going to say about that?'

The little man looked his dismay. 'Phew! That's a stinker, isn't it? That's real tough. Poor Doris! She'd have been so pleased about the kid, too.'

'She's still going to be pleased. She doesn't know about the money, and she isn't going to. She's going to stop work, and she's going to have the baby. And she's going to have everything she needs for it, too.'

'How are you going to manage that?'

'Look, Pop. It's over a year now since the accident. What can White do if we just draw our pay and then refuse to hand him his quid?'

'Go to the police, like he threatened.'

'Can he? We've been a pack of fools, Pop, to go on paying him for so long. He can't split on us now — not a year after it happened. He'd be what they call an accessory, which is just about as bad as doing the job yourself. He'll kick up rough and try to throw his weight about, but I don't think he'll go to the police. If he does he'll land himself in gaol along with us.'

Wells thought this over, his brow creased in concentration. 'It sounds all right,' he admitted. 'But he's a fly character. We'd be taking a big risk, I reckon.'

'Oh, yes, there's a risk,' Wickery said impatiently. 'But isn't it worth it? Harry and I think so, anyway.'

'You've spoken to Harry?'

'Yes. He's all for it. He's fed up with staying at home every evening, never being able to play darts or have a drink. And then there's his Ma. The doctor says she'll never get well if she stays here. Harry's got to take her to live at the seaside, he says, if she's to have a chance. That's what she needs — sea air. And that cottage of theirs is damp as hell.'

'What about Dave?'

Wickery shook his head. 'Dave's going to be tricky. He'd agree, of course — he hates White as much as any of us, but — ' He hesitated, frowning. 'Harry thinks we might go a bit further than what I suggested. He says he'll need capital if he's going to move, and he wants to break into the garage and try to get back some of the money White owes us. I don't like the idea myself, however much I could do with the extra cash. Particularly if Dave's with us. Dave's the sort of chap who might ruin everything.'

'You can't leave him out,' said Wells. 'You and Harry may have it all planned, but you can't do nothing without me and Dave being in on it. We agreed to that, didn't we? Not that I'm saying I like the idea; I'd want to know a lot more about how you was going to work it before I'd make up my mind.'

'We haven't got it planned — we've just talked about it, that's all. And we weren't aiming to do anything without you. But Dave — well, we'll see.' Wickery had guessed how it would be. He had warned

Harry that they couldn't have Pop without Dave. 'The main thing is to get cracking. There isn't much time — not for me, anyway. The kid won't wait.'

# 3

## The Way to Freedom

It was hot in the Forthright cottage. Bert Wickery loosened his tie and then sorted the cards in his large, capable hands, the knuckles of which were accentuated by grease and grime from the garage. Slowly he counted the probable tricks, pausing at eight and searching for another.

'May as well risk a bundle,' he said.

Chitty laughed unpleasantly. 'Quite a gambler, aren't you? Doris'll be wondering what's happened to all her matches, the way you splash 'em around. Maybe you wouldn't shout so loud if it was real money we were playing for.'

The others made no comment. They played the hand listlessly, their thoughts elsewhere. The ticking of the clock on the mantelpiece and the slur and snap of cards collected and laid down were the only sounds in the room. As the last trick was played Wickery leaned back in his chair with a sigh.

'Solo doesn't seem to be my game,' he said. 'This is the third week we've been playing, and I still haven't got a bundle.'

Chitty pushed his chair back noisily and stood up. 'It's no good without money,' he said impatiently. 'You chaps all overbid your hands. There's no sense to it.'

Wells edged a finger round the inside of his collar. 'Phew! It's hot in here. Mind if I open a window, Harry?'

'Go ahead,' said Forthright. He went over to the radio and tuned in to the Light Programme. A burst of applause filled the air. As it died away a woman began to sing, her voice lush in the sentimentality of a popular song. Forthright came back to the table and began to shuffle the cards. 'You playing, Dave?'

'No. I've had enough. I'd rather talk about what's going to happen to White.'

'There's a long while to go before we pack it in,' Wickery pointed out. 'We may as well play cards as twiddle our thumbs.

As for White — I thought that was all settled.'

'Not for me it isn't. I think we ought to do him in. And Harry agrees with me, don't you, Harry?'

Forthright did not answer, but went on shuffling the cards, avoiding the three pairs of eyes now focused on him.

'Well?' demanded Wells. 'Do you, Harry?'

'I don't know. There's a lot in what Dave says. If we take this money and then stick our toes in we're leaving White a free hand. Bert says there's nothing he can do; but he's a crafty devil, and he won't take it lying down. He's safer dead, and that's a fact. But murder . . . well, I don't know about that.'

Wickery rounded on them, distrust and apprehension in his eyes. 'You cut that out, all of you. When this thing started we were just going to refuse to pay him his damned quid. Then Harry had this idea of trying to get back some of the money he owes us. I didn't like it, and I still don't like it; but if that's what you want, all right. But murder!' He shivered. 'God, no!'

'It's just talk — they don't mean it.' Wells tried to reassure him. He didn't much care one way or the other what happened to White, but he didn't want Bert upset. Not at that stage. 'If it came to the point they couldn't kill a man in cold blood any more than you could.'

'Oh yes, I could,' said Chitty. 'It'd be dead easy. And there's no question of cold blood where White's concerned. Every time I look at the swine my blood boils.'

Forthright nodded. 'I feel like that too,' he admitted. 'When I hand over his blasted quid I want to poke him on the snout instead. At first I used to tell myself it was a sort of justice on us — his blackmailing us because of Mrs Gooch, I mean. But not now.' He sighed. 'It'd do me a power of good to knock his ruddy block off.'

Wickery tried to pull himself together. The plot was getting out of hand. What had begun as a simple stand against White's tyranny was developing into a major crime. If he didn't stop it . . .

'There's to be no murder and no funny business,' he said with all the firmness he could muster. 'Unless that's understood right now you can count me out. And if you try to carry on without me I'll warn White.'

'It wouldn't be because you're related by marriage, I suppose?' Chitty's tone was calculatingly insolent. 'The dear wife's uncle, and all that?'

Wickery controlled his temper. 'I've put up with a good deal from you, Dave, but I'll not stand much more of it. You know damned well that I've suffered more from White than any of you. I just don't happen to like murder, that's all.'

'Bert's right,' said Forthright. 'Murder's a nasty business — we'd best leave it alone. We'll just take the money and then, come Friday, refuse to pay him his blasted quid.'

'You're sure he still keeps the money in his room?' Wells asked Wickery.

'Doris says so. It's in a metal box under his bed.'

'How much do you think there'd be?'

'I don't know. I didn't like to ask Doris

too many questions, in case she smelt a rat. But several hundred quid, I imagine.'

'Do we take the lot?'

Wickery frowned, hesitating. 'Yes, that's a point. If we take more than he owes us it'll be stealing. I don't like that. But the box will be locked — we wouldn't be able to open it in his room. Too dangerous.'

'You fellows make me sick,' exclaimed Chitty. 'What is this, a Sunday school outing? Of course we take the lot — and anything more we can lay our hands on.'

'Hear, hear!' said Forthright. 'If we're going to do the job don't let's be squeamish about it. The amount won't make any difference if we're caught. White owes us a damned sight more than two hundred quid, or whatever it is we've paid him.'

'Well, when do we get it?' Chitty demanded. 'I'm sick of all this talk.'

'We could make it next Tuesday,' said Forthright. He turned to Wickery. 'Okay by you, Bert?'

'Yes — if you and Dave give me your word that you'll leave White alone. Not otherwise.'

They made their promises, Forthright good-humouredly, Chitty with an ugly scowl on his face. Much as he disliked the proviso, it was the fact that Wickery had made it that irked him most.

'How do we get into the garage?' asked Wells. 'We've got to fix that.'

'We've got to fix a lot of things,' said Forthright. 'I'm aiming to get hold of a key. It's the safest — What's that?'

As the others stared at him he stood up, switched off the radio, and listened. Then he walked to the door and opened it, peering into the dimly lit hall. There was no one there.

'I could have sworn I heard someone out here,' he said nervously. He went through the hall to the front door, which was unlocked. The cool air bathed his face, but the night was dark and he could see no one. A few cottage lights twinkled distantly in the village, but there was no beam from a torch, no lights of a car. For a moment he stood listening; then he closed the door and went back to the warm sitting-room.

'Who was it?' Wells asked anxiously.

'No one.' He sat down and picked up the cards. 'Did any of you chaps hear it?'

'Hear what?'

'A noise. As though someone was in the hall. And I thought I heard the front door close.'

'D'you mean to say it wasn't locked?' asked Chitty. 'That's ruddy careless, I must say! Anyone could have walked in and listened to what we were saying.'

'It never is locked,' Forthright answered curtly.

Wickery tried to laugh. 'Forget it — you're giving me the jitters. You must have imagined it, Harry — none of us heard it, anyway. And who — '

He started nervously at the sound of tapping on the ceiling.

'Ma,' said Forthright. He went quickly from the room, and the others sat silent, listening to his hurrying feet on the stairs and the low murmur of voices above them that followed. Wickery picked up the pack and began to build a house of cards. Wells watched him, surprised that his hands should be steady enough for such a task. 'How d'you think Harry expects to get hold of a key?' he asked.

'Ask White for it, I shouldn't wonder,' Chitty said sarcastically.

Wickery's victory on the fate that was to be White's had given him an unusual sense of elation, of importance. He was no longer merely the originator of the plan, he was shaping its execution. Even the formidable Forthright had submitted to his wishes. 'Not getting the wind up, are you, Dave?' he asked casually, placing another card on the growing pile.

Such a suggestion from the man he most despised was too much for Chitty's self-control.

'You mind your own ruddy business,' he shouted. He brought his fist down on the table with a crash, and with a little sigh the house of cards collapsed.

Wickery cupped his hands and slid the cards together.

'If I'd had my way, Dave, you wouldn't be here,' he said. 'A chap who can't control his temper is a dead loss on a job like this.'

Harry Forthright came clattering down the stairs. He went over to the radio and knelt in front of it, twiddling the knobs. Wells swore under his breath.

'We forgot to switch it on again,' he said.

Forthright stood up as the sound of music gradually swelled in volume. 'Yes. It doesn't matter tonight, but it would next Tuesday. A mistake like that could have busted us.'

'What did Ma say?'

'Not much. Why had we switched off the radio, and for us not to talk so loud. She thinks we're arguing about the cards.'

'If you ask me I think this alibi idea of yours is ruddy well daft,' said Chitty, still bristling with anger and spoiling for a quarrel. 'Fancy pinning your faith on an old woman like Ma!'

'You think of something better, then,' growled Forthright.

Wells hastened to his defence. He had his own doubts about the proposed alibi, but now was not the time in which to air them. If matters were to go forward smoothly it was up to him to keep the peace. Dave was already at odds with

Bert. It wouldn't do to have Harry upset also.

'I suppose it's all right using Ma the way we aim to,' Wickery said doubtfully. 'It doesn't seem fair, somehow, getting her to tell a lot of lies.'

'That's okay, mate.' Forthright sounded confident. 'They won't be lies to Ma. She's made up her mind that we can't play cards without arguing, and nobody's going to make her believe otherwise. That's because she thinks cards are wicked, you see.'

'But she can't hear us. Not with the radio on.'

'She thinks she can — and that's good enough for Ma. It's only when the radio stops that she really listens for us. She's getting a bit fanciful, Doctor Foley says. He says she sort of lives in two different worlds at once: the real world, same as us, and another that's full of people we can't see and voices we can't hear. She gets the two mixed sometimes.'

'It must be them other voices she's confusing with ours,' Wells suggested.

'That's what I think. Anyway, if the

police ask her whether we were here Tuesday she'll swear solid she could hear us. They won't get any change out of Ma.'

'We've only got your word for that,' said Chitty.

Forthright ignored him. 'Don't you get Ma on your conscience,' he said to Wickery. 'She'll be okay. All that worries Ma is our playing cards. She takes a poor view of that.'

'We can pack it up after next Tuesday.'

'No. We'll have to carry on for a week or two, or it'll look suspicious.'

Chitty laughed.

'Suspicious, eh? That's rich. Are you kidding yourselves that White won't know it's us as robbed him? Not even after we refuse to pay him his money on Friday? You must be crackers!'

'He may know, but he can't prove it,' said Wells.

'He can put the police on to us. They'll do the proving, don't you worry.'

'Listen,' said Wickery. 'Try and get this into your thick head. White can't tell the police he suspects us without giving them a reason. And what would that be? That he's been blackmailing us? Not on your life! He can't even tell them about Mrs Gooch; they'd nab him as well as us. We're sitting pretty, I tell you — unless you go and make a fool of yourself.'

What's happened to Bert, wondered Wells. Perky as hell, and full of confidence. Looks like this business is doing him a bit of good. 'There's one thing White could do,' he said. 'He could write an anonymous letter to the police telling them it was us run over Mrs Gooch.'

'They wouldn't take much notice of that, Pop. It isn't evidence. If they couldn't pin it on us a year ago they're not likely to be able to do so now. The only new bit of evidence they could find would be at the Boar's Head — and that's something White doesn't know about.'

'Bert's right,' said Forthright. 'It sounds okay to me.'

'It didn't yesterday,' said Chitty. 'You agreed with me it would be safer to kill the swine. And so it would. There'd be no need then for all this palaver about what he may or may not do. He can't do a damned thing when he's dead.'

'That may be so, but — '

'And what's more,' Chitty continued, ignoring the interruption, 'you fellows haven't got the guts of a louse. Money — that's all you think about. Get back the money and you're satisfied. Well, it doesn't satisfy me. White's given us all these months of hell; now I want to give *him* hell. If we're not going to kill the swine at least let's give him a damned good hiding, something to remember us by.'

There was a glint of approval in Forthright's eye, and even Wells did not dissent. Alarmed, Wickery said hastily, 'Cut that out, Dave. You promised — '

'All right, all right. A chap can say what he thinks, can't he? No harm in that. It makes my blood boil to think of White getting away with it, us just taking what's ours by rights and him not a penny the worse. I want to hurt him good and hard.'

'So do I, if it comes to that. But I know White. It's going to drive him crazy, knowing it was us took the money and him not able to do a thing about it. It'll hurt him a damned sight more than a hiding would.'

'You're scared,' Chitty taunted him.

'That'll do,' said Wells. 'There's been enough of this bickering. You'd do better to keep a civil tongue in your head, Dave, and try to help instead of hindering.' He turned to Forthright. 'You know, Harry, it seems to me that even if White holds his tongue the police are still going to be suspicious of us. Are you sure that alibi's going to be okay?'

'The ruddy thing's so full of holes it'll damned well sink itself,' growled Chitty.

'Such as what?' Forthright demanded. The alibi had been his brain-child, and he felt bound to defend it.

'Well, your Ma might come downstairs and find us out.'

'She never comes downstairs. She can't, not without help. She just bangs on the floor with that stick of hers.'

'There you are, then,' exclaimed Chitty triumphantly. 'She bangs, and you don't answer. What then?'

Forthright scowled. It was a flaw, and he knew it. But Wickery came to his aid.

'You can't expect miracles,' he said. 'You can't prove something that isn't true. We've got a sporting chance that Ma will swear we were here all Tuesday evening, and that's about as near to the perfect alibi as we can hope to get. If Harry goes up to see Ma just before we leave there's nothing much can go wrong, is there?'

'You never know,' said Chitty. His bad temper seemed suddenly to have left him. 'Why shouldn't some of us stay here? No need for us all to go.'

'And who's to stay?'

'We could draw lots for it.'

'It wouldn't work,' said Forthright. 'The fellows who stayed here would have a pull over the others. If things went wrong they'd be sitting pretty — they couldn't have done the job themselves, but they'd know who could. I'm not suggesting any of us would split, but — well, if the heat's on you never know which way a chap will jump. Let's leave it the way it is.'

'Why not do it before ten o'clock, while White's still at the club?' suggested Wells.

'No go. Too many people about, for one thing. And it's not late enough to rule out the chance of someone calling here while we're away.'

The chimes of Big Ben boomed out from the radio. Forthright got up and switched it off, leaving the note suspended in air for a brief moment before it finally collapsed. They had become so used to talking above the noise that its abrupt cessation intensified the silence.

'Twelve o'clock,' Forthright said unnecessarily, checking his watch. 'Three-quarters of an hour to go before we pack up. Come on, let's have another game of solo. We've done enough talking for one night. Okay, Dave?'

'Okay.'

As Wells and Wickery walked home together after parting from Chitty at the bridge, Wells said, 'Do you think it'll work out?'

'I don't see why not. So long as Dave keeps his head, there's nothing much can go wrong.'

'Dave's more wind than purpose. Harry's the chap you want to worry

84

about. He doesn't say much, does Harry, but I know how he feels. I don't envy White if Harry gets the chance to do him a bit of no good.'

'We'd all like to take a swing at the blighter,' said Wickery. 'But if either of those two lets us down I'll — oh, hell! Let's drop it.'

★ ★ ★

Because their decision had not been taken suddenly, but had matured during several weeks of careful and often heated discussion, the increased tension among the men at White's garage was not as noticeable as it might otherwise have been. But the tension was there. Doris Wickery, for one, noticed it. The sullen, hangdog look had gone from the men's faces; it had been replaced by a nervous expectancy. The animosity that had flickered constantly between them and White for the past year was still there; but now it seemed more vital, as though it had received a rejuvenating shot in the arm. Where before it had smouldered it now blazed. Yet there was no open rebellion in word or act, nor did the men cluster in groups as they had been wont to do in the past.

Doris noticed the change, and wondered. 'What's happening at the garage?' she asked her husband one evening. 'You all seem — well, different.'

'How d'you mean, different?'

'I don't quite know. It's difficult to explain, but — well, it's as though you were waiting for something to happen. You seem on edge, somehow. Not just you, darling — all of you. That trouble you had with Uncle Andrew — it isn't over, is it?'

'I don't know what you're talking about,' Wickery said nervously, dismayed by his wife's intuition. 'There's nothing different as I know of. You're imagining things.'

'Perhaps,' she agreed sadly. 'Wishful thinking, I suppose. But I'm worried, Bert. I can't go on working here much longer. You realize that, don't you?'

'I'll talk to White,' he promised. 'It'll be all right.'

White himself seemed to have caught some of the tension. He was even more abrupt than usual in his orders, more scathing in his criticism. Had they not known that his days of tyranny were nearly over the men might have been goaded into open rebellion. Perhaps White was surprised that they were not.

Only Loften seemed unaffected. Since his wife left him he had been gloomy and ill-tempered, and her subsequent return had apparently done nothing to cheer him up. 'If she's such a regular bitch I wonder he doesn't finish with her for good and all,' Forthright commented one day to Wells. 'I wouldn't let any woman muck my life up. And he doesn't seem stuck on her, either. He can't say more than a few words to her without cussing.'

'He's changed a lot since he first come here,' said Wells. 'I wonder how our little picnic next Tuesday will affect him?'

His cottage being so near to the garage, Forthright always went home to lunch. A woman from the village came in during the morning to prepare it and to keep an eye on his mother; but she left at midday, and Forthright liked to assure himself that the old lady lacked for nothing. Forty-two and still unmarried, he was closer to his mother than are most men.

On the following Wednesday he went home as usual to eat his lunch and read his paper. But he found difficulty in concentrating on the news, and his mind kept returning to Andrew White. Despite what he had said the previous evening about murder, he would have no compunction in killing the man. The world, thought Forthright, would be better off without White. It became, therefore, a question of safety. Like Wickery, he had no desire to put his head in a noose. If their alibi was strong enough, if there was no risk, it seemed to him that White's death was eminently desirable. There would then be no complications, no need to try to anticipate the man's reactions. But if the police did not accept their alibi, if something went wrong . . .

He had become so immersed in his thoughts that he did not hear the front door open or the soft footsteps in the hall.

A light tap on the sitting-room door made him leap from his chair, his heart pounding.

'I'm sorry if I startled you,' said Susan Chitty, staring at him, a troubled look in her grey eyes. 'I've brought some eggs for your mother from Mr Iverson. He called in with them yesterday evening, and I said I'd bring them up.'

He thanked her, angry with himself at having let his nerves betray him. We'll have to keep a tight hold on ourselves, he thought, if we're to get through this next week without letting anyone know that something's afoot. He was still more worried when he learned from Wickery that Doris had already queried their behaviour. 'If Doris puts two and two together after next Tuesday I suppose it's not so bad,' he said. 'You can see she keeps her mouth shut. But with anyone else it'd be a different story.'

It was Chitty's behaviour that they feared most. He was as quarrelsome and as unpredictable as before, but the anticipation of his coming freedom had loosened his tongue. When he drank he no longer drank alone. If he were, in some unguarded moment, to hint at what they were planning . . .

But Chitty was no fool. What was to come meant too much to him to throw it away. He watched his tongue carefully and drank more sparingly. He was tempted to seek out Molly Wells, to make it up with her, to hint that in a little while he would be a man with money and a decent job away from Chaim, that they could get married as soon as she pleased. But he knew that Molly loved him, that she would be unable to resist spreading the good news among her friends. Better to say nothing, better to wait. It would not be long now.

But this bridling of his tongue, the need to keep a check on his normally ebullient nature, made him all the more nervy and irritable in the safety of his own home. He did not bother what Susan might say or think. Although he would have been surprised had anyone suggested that he was not fond of his sister, he did not really consider her as a being with thoughts and an entity of her own.

90

She had always been dependent on him, had always given way to his wishes. Her friendship with George Loften was about the only independent action she had ever taken; and that it had persisted was due to Dave's absence from home of an evening. Had she had more companionship from her brother she would not have needed Loften. But she had no other friends; and Loften, with his smooth tongue, his courtesies, his ability to draw her out of her shell, and his flattering interest in all she did and said and was, had become closer to her than her brother had ever been.

Although Dave Chitty's mind was now centred mainly on the freedom he was about to enjoy, the new and fuller life that awaited him, he gave some thought also to the deed that was to bring about this desired change. Despite his belligerent attitude towards the others and his expressed desire to kill White, he was not quite certain that, should the lot fall to him, he would be able to commit murder. Like many highly strung people, he had a vein of cowardice in him — cowardice that was more mental than physical. At times — usually after White had been particularly sarcastic or unpleasant — he debated with himself the means he would adopt. Should he beat White's brains in with a spanner, or should he strangle him with his hands? It would depend on his mood of the moment, he thought. But even if he did neither, at least he'd give him a damned good hiding.

It was on the Friday that Forthright made his bid for a key to the garage. He and Loften were working on a car under the lean-to outside. It was a cold day, and the main doors were shut, the small inner door closed but not locked.

'This perishing cold eats right through one,' said Loften, blowing on his fingers. 'We ought to have a brazier out here.'

'We ought not to be working out here at all in this weather,' grumbled Forthright. He began searching among his tools, then in his pockets. 'Blast! I've left my ignition spanner on the bench. I'll nip in and get it.'

He walked round to the garage door and pushed it. It did not move.

'Someone's released the catch,' he said. 'Can I borrow your key, Mr Loften?'

'If I've got it.' Loften searched his pockets, 'I think that's the one,' he said, tossing it to Forthright. 'Try it, anyway.'

'Thanks.'

He went into the garage, to reappear a few moments later. As he walked the few yards that separated him from Loften he stumbled; the key slipped from his fingers, and both men saw it drop through the grating that covered an old disused drain.

'Blast!' said Forthright. 'I'm sorry about that, Mr Loften. It's this damned cold. My fingers feel like lumps of ice.'

Loften nodded sympathetically. 'Not your fault,' he said. 'It's not important — I never use the damned thing. White always has the garage open of a morning long before I get here.'

As he told the others later, Forthright was surprised at how easy it had been and how calmly Loften had accepted the loss. 'He never suspected a thing. Only bad moment was when the key teetered on the edge of the drain. I thought it wasn't going to fall in, and I couldn't shove it with my foot. Loften was watching.'

'What would you have done if it *had* stuck?' asked Wells. 'He'd have noticed you'd swapped the keys.'

'No, he wouldn't. I'd have picked it up and given him back his own key. But it would have wrecked our plan for getting into the garage. I couldn't have tried again.'

They felt more confident now that this first and vital step had been successfully negotiated. 'Roll on, Tuesday,' said Chitty, his little eyes gleaming behind the thick lenses. 'I can't wait to know what it feels like to handle a decent-sized wad of dough!'

# 4

## End of a Tyrant

As the sitting-room door opened the three men jerked their heads nervously towards it. Above the noise of the radio they had not heard Chitty's footsteps in the hall.

His face was set and grim, his voice unusually restrained. 'Well, he's back,' he said. 'Been back just over half an hour.'

'Lights out?'

'Yes.'

Pop Wells sighed. Forthright looked at the clock. 'Twenty-five past ten. If we leave here at eleven that should give him time to get to sleep.'

The cards were on the table, but they had not used them. The moment they had waited and planned for was now too close for pretences. Wickery cleared his throat noisily.

'Got the pieces of paper ready?' he asked.

'Yes. They're in my pocket with the key.'

Chitty was walking restlessly about the room. As he passed the fireplace he threw his half-smoked cigarette into it, took a dirty pair of gloves from his pocket, and put them on. For a while he stood looking at them, flexing his fingers. Then he drew off the gloves, stuffed them hurriedly into his pocket, and resumed his restless pacing.

'Sit down, man,' said Wells. 'You make me nervous.'

Chitty grunted, but sat down. 'Let's have a drink,' he said. 'It's cold out.'

Wickery had seen the bulge in the other's hip-pocket. 'We want to go easy on the booze,' he cautioned. 'One of us is going to need a steady head tonight. *And* a steady hand.'

'You worry about yourself, mate. Mine are steady enough. Come on, Harry, fetch it out.'

Forthright looked at him. Then he leaned back in his chair and reached behind him to the cupboard.

'Beer, eh?' said Chitty, accepting the proffered bottle. There was a slight *plop* as he unscrewed the top and tilted the bottle over the glass. 'I could have done with something stronger. However, here's how.'

Forthright looked inquiringly at the others, but they shook their heads. Wickery could not resist a dig at Chitty. He knew it was foolish, but he had suffered much from Chitty's tongue during the past year.

'We don't need Dutch courage,' he said.

Wells frowned. Even Forthright looked apprehensive. But Chitty either did not hear or for once chose to ignore the challenge. He continued to pour the beer steadily down his throat.

Wells sighed with relief and licked his thin lips. 'Go through the details again, Harry,' he said. 'I want to make sure I've got 'em right.'

They were to leave the cottage by the back door, said Forthright, and take the track through the woods. It wasn't completely screened from the road, but it was sufficiently far from it to make detection unlikely. When they arrived at the garage he would put Loften's key in the lock, and they would then each draw one of the four pieces of paper he had prepared. *NO* was written on three of these, *YES* on the fourth. They were then to separate and go into the forest by different routes, far enough to enable any one of them to make his way to and from the garage without the knowledge of the other three. 'It's only a few minutes' walk to the garage from here — we should be in our places by ten past eleven, and it'll be about a quarter past when the chap who's drawn the *YES* goes into the garage. After that it's up to him.'

'Except that there's to be no killing — and no bashing, either,' said Wickery, looking at Chitty.

'Yes, yes. We know all about that,' Forthright said testily. 'Leave the key in the lock when you come out, and hide the cash-box under the back of the junk-heap in the yard. Nobody'll think of looking for it there, and it'll be weeks before that pile is shifted.'

Chitty put his glass down on the table with a thump. 'You mean we're not taking the money with us?'

'No. Too damned risky. The police might search us — *and* our homes. We'll leave it hid until the heat's off. It'll be safe enough.'

'How long do we have to wait?' asked Chitty. 'I don't want to hang around here for weeks. I want to get cracking.'

'You'll wait until it's safe,' said Forthright. 'Certainly a week or two. We've got to carry on as before — unless White sacks us. If you start chucking money around the police will want to know where it came from.'

'Fair enough,' said Wells. 'What next?'

'Well, after the money's been hid the chap goes back to his place in the forest. We'll all wait until the church clock strikes a quarter to twelve, and then we'll meet again behind the garage. I'll collect the key from the door, and we'll come back here. We've got to be back before midnight — the radio shuts down then.'

Wickery was surprised at his own

calmness. His only worry was that either Chitty or Forthright might do something foolish. He hoped that it would fall to him or Wells to go into the garage. White was a sound sleeper, and he'd have had plenty to drink. There shouldn't be any danger. And, much as he hated White, he lacked Forthright's and Chitty's leaning towards violence. All he wanted now was the money to ease the financial strain on Doris and himself. Compared to that, revenge was unimportant.

Wells found himself sweating. Maybe that was due to the heat of the fire — but he knew he was afraid. He hated White and he needed the money, but the thought of going into the dark garage, of climbing the stairs to the flat above, filled him with fear. Suppose White was not asleep, was waiting for him? And, even if all was well, he would have to rummage under the bed, defenceless, completely at White's mercy if the man should wake.

Pray God, he thought, don't let it be me!

'Why not draw lots now?' asked Chitty.

'It'd save us having to use our torches in the woods.'

'I thought of that,' said Forthright. 'But even if we didn't say a word our faces would give us away. I bet we'd all know at once who was going to do the job. And we don't want that.'

'Why not? We can trust each other, can't we?'

'Perhaps. But it's better if we don't have to.'

'We'll have to face each other when we get back,' Wells pointed out.

'Yes, I know. But we'll have got used to the idea by then, and the job will be over and done with.'

'Time we were on our way,' said Wickery. 'It's nearly eleven.'

They got up slowly. Now that the time had come there was a sudden lack of eagerness. They were setting out on a criminal enterprise, however justified they considered that enterprise to be; deliberately putting themselves outside the Law. We'll always have tonight on our consciences, I suppose, Wells thought uneasily. Just as well we shan't be seeing so much of each other. Harry and Dave will be leaving Chaim, and Bert and I will be in different jobs. We couldn't go on as before, not even if White gave us the chance.

He tried to fix his mind on the thought that the money was theirs, that it wasn't stealing. But, although that comforted his conscience, it did not still his fear. With a guilty sense of shame at invoking the aid of his Maker in such a project, he began saying to himself, over and over again, 'Oh, God, don't let it be me! Oh, God, don't let it be me!'

Chitty was thinking of the weapon he would take with him up the stairs. One of those heavy spanners, perhaps, or a wrench. He wouldn't use it if White kept quiet, but he wasn't going to be caught napping. If the swine woke up he'd let him have it. No point in being squeamish *then*.

In imagination he heard the sickening, squelching thud as the heavy weapon descended on White's defenceless head, and shuddered. Pop was right, it wouldn't be all that easy to kill a sleeping man. Not even a man he hated as much as he hated White. His thoughts switched to the money. Several hundred quid, Bert had said. That was a tidy sum, maybe a hundred each. But he didn't like the idea of leaving it on the junk-heap. Better to force the lock and share the cash out right away. He'd a good mind . . .

His little eyes glittered as a brilliant idea occurred to him. None of them knew exactly how much the box contained. If he had to do the job, why shouldn't he abstract a hundred or so and leave the rest to be shared out later? The others wouldn't know; and wasn't the chap who took all the risks entitled to a major share of the perks?

Well, here's hoping, he thought. I don't know as I'm over-keen on doing the job, but I could do with that extra hundred.

They put on their gloves, tested the torches, and went out through the back door and along the track to the garage. They walked quickly, without speaking. Forthright wondered about the radio. It was a reliable set — but suppose it went wrong tonight? Suppose there was a long break in the transmission; would Ma call out, or knock on the ceiling? Suppose she had one of her bad turns, or suppose someone called at the cottage? It was late for callers, but one never knew. He had impatiently rejected these same doubts when they had been raised by the others, but he could not reject them now. He was glad when they reached the garage and the need for action superseded his fears.

No light was showing, no one moved on the road. He took the key from his pocket and fitted it in the lock, making sure that it turned easily. Then he went back to the others.

Without a word each in turn selected a folded slip of paper from his outstretched hand and went off into the forest. Wickery took the right-hand track. Wells and Chitty followed the main path towards the ridge known locally as the Swan's Neck, and after a few yards forked right and left respectively along little-used tracks leading into the heart of the forest.

The remaining slip of paper clutched tightly in his gloved hand, Forthright turned and walked back along the way they had come. If I'm one of the lucky ones, he thought, I can keep an ear cocked for that radio.

His hands felt hot and uncomfortable in the unaccustomed gloves, but they did not tremble as he clumsily unfolded the paper and switched on his torch.

★  ★  ★

The chiming of the church clock brought both relief and anxiety to the four men. The job was over. There had been no alarm, apparently no hitch. Now they had to await the consequences.

They assembled quietly and quickly behind the garage, and, after Forthright had collected the key from the door, walked in silence back towards the Forthright cottage. Half-way there Chitty stumbled and fell. Pop Wells helped him to his feet. 'Hell!' exclaimed Chitty. 'I've lost my ruddy glasses.'

He knelt down and groped with his hands on the path. The others did likewise, not wishing to use their torches. It was Wickery who found them. 'I'm afraid they're broken,' he said, handing the frame to Chitty. 'Both lenses gone.'

Chitty swore softly. He was almost blind without his spectacles. 'That means I'll have to go into Tanbury tomorrow to see the oculist.'

Tomorrow, thought Wickery. Tomorrow's going to be rather different from the days that have gone before. I'll be glad when it's over.

The cottage was as they had left it, the radio still playing. They filed into the sitting-room and stood around awkwardly, blinking at the light. 'Hadn't you better see that Ma is all right?' asked Wells. He caught sight of his face in the mirror over the fireplace, and hastily smoothed down the ruffled wisps of hair.

Forthright shook his head. 'She'd wonder why. I never do, not unless she knocks. What about a game of solo? We've got to do something for the next half-hour.'

'Count me out,' said Chitty. 'I can't see without my specs.'

'About those specs,' said Forthright. 'If anyone asks, say you broke 'em on the way home tonight.'

They sat down at the table. Wells cut and Forthright dealt. As he watched the pile accumulating in front of him Wickery said quietly, 'There's blood on the cards.'

Forthright flushed. 'I scratched my hand looking for Dave's specs,' he said. But he did not offer his hand for inspection.

Nobody made any comment, and he continued dealing. After a few hands Wickery said he wasn't going to play any more — he didn't feel like it.

He kept thinking of Doris. When the news broke she was certain to ask some very awkward questions — and how was he to answer her? And how to explain the money when they collected it? Doris liked her uncle no more than he did, but she would certainly disapprove of what they had done.

It was as Forthright was gathering up the cards that the knock came.

They looked at each other and then at the clock. A quarter past twelve — too late for any ordinary caller. At a nod from Forthright and with a sinking feeling at the pit of his stomach Wickery, who was nearest the door, opened it.

Molly Wells stood there, blinking at the light. 'I'm sorry,' she said. 'But Mum's had one of her turns. She asked me to come and get Dad.'

Wells stood up. 'No sense in chasing after me at this hour,' he grumbled. His wife's turns were notorious in the village. They occurred without apparent cause, usually at times most inconvenient to others. For that reason she received scant sympathy from her family. 'What can *I* do?'

But he was secretly relieved at the summons. He would be glad to get away from the others. 'I was just coming, anyway,' he said.

Molly looked at Dave, and then away. 'I didn't mind the walk,' she said. 'I don't often get out of an evening nowadays.'

After she and her father had gone the three men talked desultorily, killing time. Chitty would have liked to have walked home with Molly, but he knew she would not have been pleased had he done so. In her father's company they would have had nothing to say to each other. I'll get her alone in a day or two, he thought, and put things right. No sense in going on like this. Not now.

At a quarter to one they went upstairs to say good-night to Ma. It was a habit they had formed. Looking at her as she lay in the bed she so seldom left, Wickery wondered anew how anyone so frail and shrivelled could still live.

'And about time too!' said the old lady. 'Sitting there all night, playing cards and smoking! What good does it do you, eh? That's what I want to know.'

Wickery confessed that it did them no good at all. 'We'll probably give it up, Ma,' he said. 'Dave here says he's fed up with solo, and Doris doesn't think much of being left alone so long.'

'Nor I don't wonder, either,' said Ma. 'Where's Mr Wells?'

'He went home quarter of an hour ago,' said Forthright. 'Molly came for him. Mrs Wells had one of her turns.'

Ma Forthright nodded sagely. 'Cards always lead to trouble,' she said. 'Always did and always will.'

Wickery wondered whether she might not be right on this occasion.

*  *  *

Wells called for Forthright on his way to work the next morning. He had no liking to face alone the trouble that he knew lay in store for them. 'He may not find out until later that the money's gone,' he said. 'But when he does there's going to be one hell of a flaming row!'

White had not unlocked the garage doors when they arrived, and they walked up and down to keep warm, speculating aloud on what was likely to happen. Ten minutes later Loften drove up in his car. 'White must have had a thick night,' he said, as he joined them. 'He's usually an early riser. If you hadn't lost my key, Harry, we could have let ourselves in. Brrh! It's cold.'

As the minutes passed, and still there was no sign of White, Wells and Forthright grew silent.

'What's happened to Chitty and the Wickerys?' asked Loften. 'They're late too.'

Forthright explained that Chitty had broken his spectacles the previous evening and had gone into Tanbury to have them repaired. 'He's as blind as a bat without them,' he added.

'You're telling me!' said Loften. 'Remember the last time he lost them? A chap with eyesight like his ought to keep a spare pair handy.'

When Wickery arrived he too expressed surprise that the doors had not been unlocked, and avoided the eyes of his workmates. Wells thought he looked haggard, as though he had had a sleepless night. I hope he hasn't had trouble with Doris, he thought. Doris is a damned sight too inquisitive. *And* too clever.

'Where's Doris?' asked Loften.

'She's sick. I made her take the day off. That's why I'm late.'

At half-past eight, half an hour after they were due to start work, Loften began to look worried. 'What the hell's up with White? He's never been as late as this before.'

'Maybe he's sick too,' Wickery suggested.

'Perhaps. Damn you and that key, Harry. It's the first time I've ever needed the ruddy thing, and now I haven't got it.'

'I'm sorry, Mr Loften. I couldn't help it.'

'No, no — of course not. But it's a blasted nuisance, all the same.' He sounded irritable, and Wickery wondered if he'd had another row with his wife. 'If White really is sick he'll be needing a doctor.'

'He could telephone.'

'Not if he's too ill to come downstairs. And if he isn't, why hasn't he opened the doors? Damn it, we'll have to do *something*. Can't hang around out here all the morning.'

They banged heavily on the garage doors and, when no response was forthcoming, walked round the building examining the windows. The latter were all closed except one.

'That's his bedroom,' said Forthright, pointing to the open window.

'White!' shouted Loften. 'Hey, White! Are you all right?'

There was no reply.

112

They returned to the front of the building. While they were discussing the matter Willie Trape passed on his bicycle, and Loften called him over and explained their predicament.

Constable Trape looked doubtful. 'You think we ought to break in?' he asked.

'If we can. Mr White may be seriously ill.'

'Why not get a ladder from the village?' Forthright suggested. 'Climb up to his bedroom window.'

It took some time to fetch the ladder. With it came a few idlers. Excitement was scarce in Chaim, and news of the locked garage promised well.

'You'd better go up, Mr Loften,' said someone. But Loften hung back. 'Not me. I don't like ladders,' he said. 'You go, constable.'

Nothing loath, the constable mounted the ladder. From below Forthright, Wickery, and Wells watched him in an ever-increasing agony of mind. Forthright, glancing at Loften, noticed that the latter was eyeing him curiously, and tried to compose his features.

Willie Trape reached the ledge and peered in through the open window. For a few seconds he remained motionless, a broad blue posterior atop of pillar-like legs. Then he jumped back, knocking his head against the top frame of the window. There was a gasp from those below as he made a desperate grab at a rung above him and hung there, suspended by one hand; then, with a rapidity amazing in so bulky a man, he was down the ladder and had turned a scared face towards the spectators.

'He's been murdered!' he cried. 'Mr White's been murdered! He's lying on the bed with his head smashed in and blood all over the place!'

# 5

## No Pieces to Pick Up

Doris Wickery sat in the outer office of the garage and listened to the police moving about upstairs. Her husband was with her, and Willie Trape — the latter looking both uncomfortable and important at the same time. This was Constable Trape's first contact with murder, and he was inclined to resent the intrusion on his peaceful everyday existence. His chief consolation was the prestige he would undoubtedly gain through his connection with the investigations now in hand.

Loften, Forthright, and Wells were in the garage. The big doors were shut, a policeman was on duty outside. A few idle spectators, mostly women and children, stood on the gravel gazing morbidly at the garage. Murder had hitherto been something that one read about in the newspapers, something not quite real. Rather like the cinema. And now here it was on their own doorstep.

Forthright and Wells avoided each other. They knew how essential it was that they should discuss the murder, that at any moment the police would start to question them. Well, they could cope with the police; it was not the police who worried them. Wickery was the danger now. No killing, he had said, or the alibi is out. Would he stick to that, or would he play along with them? Yet despite their uncertainty, their fears, each was reluctant to broach the topic.

Wickery had told Loften the truth when he had said that Doris was sick that morning. She was sick most mornings. But her husband's insistence that she should not go to the garage had surprised her. He had said nothing on previous occasions.

'Uncle will be furious,' she had protested. 'And there's nothing really wrong with me.'

'You stay here,' he had said firmly. 'I'll deal with White.'

116

She had done as he had wished, since it was unusual for Bert to dictate to her; but as the morning wore on her anxiety deepened. Why had Bert been so insistent that she should stay at home on that particular Wednesday? Could it have any connection with his odd, almost detached manner of the past few days?

She arrived at the garage shortly after the county police.

Doris felt no grief, no sense of loss, over her uncle's death; it was the manner of his death that worried her. Bert had always disliked her uncle; and since that memorable night when he had told her she would have to return to work at the garage she had watched his dislike grow to something stronger, something akin to hate. And he had acted so strangely of late . . . and why had he wanted her to stay at home that morning? Surely he could not have known that Uncle Andrew was dead unless . . .

She looked at him, standing forlorn and anxious by the office door, and shuddered at the direction in which her thoughts were heading. She was almost glad when he went out, leaving her alone with Trape.

The policemen came downstairs and into the office. They looked at her curiously; and one, whom she took to be the Inspector by the deference, almost humility, accorded him by Constable Trape, asked her identity.

'I'm Mrs Wickery. Mr White was my uncle.'

'What other relatives had he?' asked the Inspector. He was a tall, rather forbidding-looking man with a long, thin face. 'My name is Pitt, Mrs Wickery. Detective-Inspector Pitt.'

Doris said she thought there were no other relatives.

'Had your uncle any particular enemies?' he asked, sitting down.

'He wasn't a popular man,' she said slowly. She must be careful. If Bert was a — but she must not give him away, no matter what he had done. Not until she had had a chance to talk with him, at any rate. 'I wasn't over-fond of him myself. But I can't think of anyone who disliked him enough to . . . to . . .'

'Dislike isn't quite the same thing, Mrs Wickery,' he said drily. 'However, I take it that you can't suggest a reason why anyone should wish to murder your uncle?'

There was the money, of course, the cash-box he kept under his bed. She had seen it dozens of times when sweeping the room. Should she mention that? If Bert . . .

'No,' she said, as firmly as she could.

He eyed her speculatively, pulling with forefinger and thumb at his lower lip. Then he began to ask further questions. He wanted to know so much about her uncle, and she herself knew so little. Finally he asked, almost casually, 'Were you and your husband at home last night, Mrs Wickery?'

'I was. My husband was out playing cards. He got home about one.'

The grey eyebrows lifted slightly. 'One, eh? Rather late, wasn't it?'

'No, not for a Tuesday. That's about the usual time.'

'It's a sort of regular fixture, is it, this card party?'

'Since they started it, yes. But that was only a month ago.'

'They?'

'My husband and the other men from the garage. Not Mr Loften, of course, or my uncle.'

They fell silent. Doris wondered whether the Inspector was thinking what she was thinking — that those Tuesday night card-parties might have had a more sinister purpose behind them. Bert never had been one for cards. When she had expressed surprise that first Tuesday he had said that he must have some relaxation and that he could no longer afford to play darts at the pub. It had sounded reasonable at the time — but had it been true? If only, she thought unhappily, I could talk to Bert. But it would have to wait until they got home; there would be little privacy at the garage.

She was alone now. Constable Trape had been sent on some errand; George Loften and the Inspector were in the inner office. She became aware that she could hear their voices, could even distinguish something of what they were saying. The communicating door, she saw, was ajar.

Doris did not hesitate. She got up from her chair and tiptoed across the room, keeping a watchful eye on the door to the garage. If she could learn something of what was in the Inspector's mind, or of what Loften had to tell him, it might help Bert.

It might also, she thought, help to decide her own course of action.

The Inspector was speaking.

'You say he kept this box in his room, Mr Loften. How much money would it contain, do you think?'

'I don't know.' That was Loften's voice. 'Quite a tidy sum, I imagine.'

'A hundred pounds?'

'Oh, more than that. More like two or three hundred.'

Her attempt to keep that piece of knowledge from the police had not been very successful, thought Doris. She had meant to find out first if it was still there, or if Bert . . .

'Who else would know about this money?' asked the Inspector.

121

'Goodness knows. I don't suppose he broadcast the information. Mrs Wickery, of course. Possibly some of the men — or possibly not. I just don't know, Inspector.'

'No, sir, I suppose not. Now — this visit of his to the club last night. You say he had dinner there every Tuesday? Quite a lot of people would know about *that*, eh?'

'I imagine so. We all knew here, anyway.'

'And at what time would he return?'

'There again you've got me beat. We didn't see much of each other out of working hours. Couldn't the club help you?'

'They would know when he left,' said the Inspector. 'When did you last see Mr White?'

'Six o'clock yesterday evening. That's when we knock off.'

'And what did you do after that, sir?'

'Me? I went home for dinner, and then ran into Tanbury for a drink at the George. On the way back I called in to see a friend, and stayed there rather later than I had intended. It was nearly one o'clock when I got home.'

'Can you let me have the name and address of this friend, sir?'

There was a slight pause. Then Loften said, 'I don't really see why that is necessary, Inspector. If you don't mind, I'd rather keep it to myself.'

Another pause. Doris imagined the Inspector's gaze fixed on the other man's face as it had been fixed on hers, and wondered if Loften felt as uncomfortable as she had done.

'I see.' Inspector Pitt's voice was cool, unemotional. 'Well, I've no right to press you for that information, Mr Loften. But it might help us both if you were to give it.'

'How? How does it help me, for instance?'

'You're a partner in this business, sir, so I presume you have a key to the garage. You knew about the money White kept in his room, and you're unable to provide an alibi for the time the murder was committed. Does that add up to you the same as it does to me, Mr Loften?'

'If you're trying to make out that I had

anything to do with White's murder — '

'I didn't say that, sir.'

'No, I know you didn't. But you damned well suggested it. And you're wrong about the key, too. I *did* have one; but last Friday one of the men — Harry Forthright, it was — accidentally dropped it down a drain. Damned good thing he did, too, if you ask me. It helps to put me in the clear.' He paused, but the Inspector made no comment. After a while Loften went on, 'As for this friend of mine — well, if you must know, I visited a lady. Miss Chitty, the sister of one of the men here. Nothing wrong in it, of course; but it doesn't do to spread these things around. I wouldn't have stayed so late if my wife had not been away for the night.'

'Thank you, Mr Loften. And, by the way, I understand Mr Chitty hasn't turned up this morning. Did you know about that?'

'Yes. He's gone into Tanbury to get his glasses fixed. He broke them last night.'

'Who told you that?'

'Harry Forthright. This morning, while we were waiting for White to open the garage. He and Wells were here before me.'

'I see. About that key, sir — I suppose there's no doubt that it *was* lost?'

'Oh, absolutely none. I saw it happen. Tell me, Inspector — at what time was White killed?'

'Somewhere around midnight, sir, according to the medical evidence.'

'And you've no idea who did it? No fingerprints, or anything like that?'

'It's early days yet, Mr Loften,' the Inspector answered evasively. 'My chief concern at the moment is how the murderer got into the garage. That's why I was particularly interested in that key you lost. Would any of the men have one?'

'No. Only White and myself.'

There were sounds of movement in the room, of a chair being scraped along the floor. Doris went back to her seat at the office table.

Loften came out shortly after and went into the garage. Inspector Pitt stood in the doorway and looked at her. 'Did you know your uncle kept money — a lot of money — in his bedroom?' he asked.

'Yes, of course.'

'You didn't mention it.'

'No.' And then, because she felt nervous under his fixed stare, 'Has it been stolen?'

'Probably. It's not in his room, anyway.'

Her husband came in from the garage. He gave her an anxious look, and Doris wished she could have spoken to him. But Inspector Pitt took him into the inner room, and this time the door was firmly shut.

Wickery was nervous — more, he was thoroughly scared. He was no longer fighting to escape a few years in gaol, but to save his life. It did not help to know that his nervousness must be apparent to the Inspector.

It did not go too badly at first. They had rehearsed it so often that even in his present state of mind he found himself answering the questions promptly and easily. Routine stuff first: how long had he been employed at the garage, his relations with White — things like that. Then came the more detailed questioning: when had he last seen White; what had he been doing the previous evening? He rattled it off glibly, and felt better.

There came a pause while the Inspector consulted his notebook. Then he said, 'This card party of yours. I understand it's a regular Tuesday night fixture. Been going on for about a month, hasn't it?'

'That's right.'

'What made you start it?'

They had not anticipated that. He sought for a convincing answer, and found none. 'I — well, I don't know, exactly. It seemed cheaper than going to the pub.'

'Was it your idea?'

'Partly mine. I don't remember which of us suggested it first.'

'I see. Fond of cards, Mr Wickery?'

'Not particularly. But it makes a break, gives one an evening out.'

It sounded stupid, he thought; but the Inspector had already changed the subject, was asking about the money. Yes, said Wickery, he had known it was there. 'Everyone knew. Everyone at the garage, that is. D'you think that was the motive, Inspector? Robbery?'

127

Inspector Pitt looked at him. 'How did you know the money had gone?' he asked curtly.

'I — well, I didn't really.' He could feel the warmth seeping up from under his collar and flooding his cheeks. I must look as guilty as hell, he thought. 'It was the way you put it. You wouldn't have asked about the money if it was still there, would you?'

'Perhaps not.' The Inspector sounded pleasantly matter-of-fact once more. 'Did you walk home alone last night?'

'Well, Dave Chitty was with me as far as the village. But alone after that, yes.'

'I gather it was on the way home that Mr Chitty broke his glasses?'

'That's right. He fell over while we were crossing the field.'

It was Wells's turn next, and then Forthright's. Their interviews went on much the same lines as Wickery's. Both admitted that they had known about the money and that they had disliked White, and both gave the vaguest possible reasons to account for their sudden interest in cards.

But as Forthright was leaving the office the Inspector stopped him. 'I'm told Mr Chitty has gone into Tanbury to have his spectacles repaired,' he said.

'Yes. He broke them on his way home last night.'

'So Mr Loften told me. He says you mentioned it to him this morning while you were waiting for White to open the garage.'

'That's right.'

'Before Mr Wickery had arrived,' added the Inspector. 'Now, doesn't that strike you as odd?'

Forthright knew that something was wrong, that he was being led into a trap. But he could not see where the danger lay.

'I don't understand, Inspector.'

'Don't you? If Chitty broke his spectacles *after* he had left your house last night, how could you know about it this morning — before you had seen Wickery?'

Forthright drew a deep breath. It had been a stupid blunder, he thought, and so unnecessary. But he had tremendous confidence in himself; and, apart from a silent prayer of thanksgiving that it had been he and not one of the others who had been so neatly trapped — they would probably have confessed on the spot, he thought — he was not unduly alarmed.

He laughed. 'I see what you mean, Inspector. Yes, it would look a bit odd, wouldn't it? Well, Mr Loften must have been mistaken, that's all. I certainly spoke to him about Dave, and I know I got the news from one of the other two — but it couldn't have been Wells, could it, because he wouldn't know? I suppose that what happened later got us all a bit mixed up about this. However, it seems pretty obvious that I must have spoken to Mr Loften about Dave's spectacles *after* Wickery arrived, and not before. Otherwise — well, how could I have known they were broken?'

'That's what I was wondering,' said Inspector Pitt.

As he left the office Forthright knew that the policeman was still watching him. I was a damned fool, he thought angrily, to drop a clanger like that. I talked myself out of it, but it's bound to leave a doubt in the man's mind. He nodded curtly to Doris and went through to the garage, wondering how much to say to the others. No point in putting the wind up them — they were jittery enough already — but they had to be warned.

But Loften was there. And Loften gave him no option.

'Did the Inspector ask you about Dave's glasses, Harry?' he said; and when Forthright nodded he went on, 'I must say, I couldn't understand what he was getting at. Not until afterwards, when I'd had a chance to think it over. Tell me — how *did* you know this morning that Dave had broken them?'

'Bert told me, Mr Loften.'

'But you told me about it before Bert arrived.'

Here goes, thought Forthright. If I can convince Loften he was wrong, maybe he'll help me to convince the police. 'That's what the Inspector seemed to think,' he said casually. 'Got the idea from you, I suppose. But, as I pointed out to him, you must have been mistaken.' He

131

turned to Wickery. 'It *was* you told me about Dave, wasn't it?'

'Yes,' said Wickery.

'That's right,' Wells agreed, uncertain of the point at issue but anxious to confirm any statement made by the other two. 'I was there. I heard him.'

Forthright smiled. 'You see, Mr Loften?'

Loften looked from one to another of the three men. Then he too smiled. 'I see very well,' he said, and went back to the office.

Forthright gazed reflectively at the closed door. 'I hope we're not going to have any trouble with *him*,' he said. 'That'd be the last straw.'

When he went home to lunch that morning Wells went with him. 'What's all this to-do about Dave's specs?' asked the little man, as they took the track they had used the previous night. 'I don't get it.'

Forthright told him. 'It's not important in itself,' he said. 'It doesn't prove anything, and it's our word against Loften's. But it's made that damned Inspector suspicious.'

132

'He'll go through our alibi with a tooth-comb,' Wells said unhappily.

'Let him. It'll get him nowhere.' Forthright stopped. 'This is where Dave fell over on the way back last night. He must have tripped over that root. Perhaps we'd better pick up the pieces before the police do it for us. Now we've told them he broke his specs in the field it wouldn't look too good if they found the glass here.'

They searched diligently for some minutes, but there was no glass visible. 'This can't be the place,' said Wells.

'But it is. I know this damned path backward. And Bert said both lenses were broken when he picked them up, so there ought to be plenty of glass around. Come on, let's have another look.'

But although they got down on their hands and knees and scraped the soil with their fingernails, the second search was no more successful than the first.

'What's the meaning of that?' asked the bewildered Wells, as he stood up and brushed the dirt from his trousers.

'I don't know. But as the cops can't

have been here first — we'd have seen them from the garage — it looks to me as though Dave was lying.'

'Lying? How could he be lying? You saw his specs afterwards, didn't you? You saw they were broken?'

'They were broken all right. What I mean is, he didn't break them here. He just wanted us to *think* he did.'

Wells was about to protest again when footsteps sounded on the path behind him, and he turned. It was Wickery, looking harassed and distraught.

'I meant to come with you,' said Wickery, 'but I had to see to Doris first. She's gone home.'

'Didn't she want you to go with her?'

'Yes. But I thought it was important that I should have a talk with you two first.'

Wells and Forthright looked at each other, but said nothing. The three men walked in silence to the cottage, and while Forthright was upstairs with his mother Wells told Wickery of their fruitless search for the broken lenses. 'Harry seems sure it was the right place,' he said, 'but I can't help feeling he's wrong. Why should Dave want to pull our legs over a thing like that?'

Wickery said nothing. His brain registered the information and stored it away, but at that moment it had something bigger and more vital to cope with than a few pieces of broken glass. When Forthright returned Wells looked at him expectantly. Forthright frowned. He knew they had to have it out with Bert, that time was pressing; but he knew, too, that it wasn't going to be easy.

His reluctance to broach the matter made his voice harsh.

'Well, Bert?' he asked. 'How about it? Are you with us, or aren't you?'

'I gave the right answers to the Inspector, if that's what's worrying you,' Wickery said tonelessly.

Wells breathed a sigh of relief. Bert wasn't going to be awkward, after all. But Wickery soon shattered his complacence. Fists clenched, he turned on them furiously.

'I wish to God I knew which of you three devils killed White! Didn't I say, over and over again, that he wasn't to be touched? And didn't you agree — all of you, even Dave? Do you think I'd have had any part in it if I'd known this was going to happen?'

'Take it easy, Bert.' Wells put a friendly hand on the other's arm. 'The chap what done it may not have meant to kill him. But if White woke up and recognized him — well, he had to do something about it, didn't he? It's unfortunate, but —'

'Unfortunate!' Wickery shook his hand off impatiently. 'That's a damned cool way to describe murder, I must say! And don't give me any of that tripe about not meaning to do it. Of course he meant it; why else did he take that spanner upstairs with him? And now I'm expected to lie, to risk my neck to save *his*, damn him! Why the hell should I?'

'One of us killed White, Bert, don't forget that. One of us four. If you go to the police you'll give us all away, yourself as well. You wouldn't want to do that.'

'It seems to me you don't object to White being killed,' Forthright said contemptuously. 'All you're worried

136

about is your own ruddy neck. That's right, isn't it?'

'No, damn you, it isn't! And even if it were, what difference does that make?'

'A hell of a difference. Personally, I'm damned glad White *was* killed — he's better out of the way. But I don't wish to swing for him any more than you do, and that's why I'm going on with this the way we planned it. It's our only hope. And if you don't appreciate that then you're a bigger fool than I thought you were.'

'I'm a fool, all right,' said Wickery. 'I ought to have guessed, the way you and Dave kept harping on murder, that you weren't going to stick to what we'd agreed.'

Forthright's face flushed angrily. He took a step forward. 'Are you saying I killed White, damn you?'

Wickery did not move.

'You or Dave,' he said. 'It wasn't me, and I don't think it was Pop.'

Wells looked anxiously at Forthright. In this mood Harry could be dangerous. 'I think it'd be best  —' he began, slipping between them. But Forthright pushed him aside. He went up to Wickery and stood facing him, fists clenched, unshaven chin thrust pugnaciously forward.

'You'd better get this straight, Bert Wickery.' His voice was even and controlled and coldly menacing. 'I say I didn't kill White. Do you believe me? Of course you don't — no more than I believe you. All your silly prattle about how one of us is risking your blasted neck doesn't cut any ice with me. For all I know it's just a lot of hot air to conceal the fact that it was *you* who killed White. Yes, you,' he said fiercely, as Wickery opened his mouth to speak. 'Who'll get White's money? Doris, as like as not. You had the strongest motive of all of us to get rid of him, and you know it. I'm not saying you *did* kill him; but you can cut out all that sanctimonious humbug; it gets you nowhere as far as we're concerned. At some time or another we're all going to protest our innocence, and none of us is going to believe the others. And certainly none of us is going to believe *you*.'

For a few moments Wickery confronted

him, his face working. Then his whole body seemed to sag. He shuffled wearily to the table and slumped into a chair, burying his face in his hands.

'It isn't only me,' he said brokenly. 'There's Doris — and the kid. It's what's going to happen to them that worries me.'

'Nothing'll happen to them if you pull yourself together,' said Forthright, relieved. Until the last week or two, when Bert had begun to assume a disquietening air of authority and purpose, he had never failed to impose his will on the other. He was glad to see that he could still do so. 'Believe me, mate, our only chance is to carry on the way we planned it. There's more at stake now, but the risk of discovery's no greater. White's murder doesn't upset our alibi in any way. So long as that hangs together, we're safe.'

'So's the murderer, blast him,' said Wickery, sitting up. 'That's what gets my goat — that we've *got* to shield the swine, whether we like it or not. Well, just let me find him out, that's all. I'll soon settle his ruddy hash for him.'

'You're not likely to do that,' said Wells.

'We took care of that when we planned it.'

'I'm not so sure,' Wickery retorted. 'What was all that about Dave's spectacles? If there are no bits of glass where he's supposed to have broken them, that means he was lying, doesn't it? Well, there's only one reason I can think of why he'd need to lie about a thing like that.'

Wells hurried to the defence of his prospective son-in-law.

'That's unfair, Bert. You can't say things like that about Dave when he's not here to defend himself. It ain't right. And didn't we agree not to snoop on each other, not to try and find out who done the actual job?'

'We were discussing robbery then, not murder,' Wickery said sternly.

Forthright banged his fist on the table. 'Who cares about agreements, damn it? I'm not interested in whether Dave killed White — that's his affair. But it's *our* affair if he bust his specs in White's room. We gave him an alibi, didn't we? So if the police find the pieces of glass and can trace them to Dave, we're *all* sunk. If Dave's been scattering clues around the place, he's no right to keep it secret from us.'

'What do you suggest we do, then?' asked Wells.

'Do? Why, ask him, of course.'

Knuckles rapped loudly on the front door. Forthright went into the hall, to return with Inspector Pitt and a uniformed constable.

'They want to see Ma,' he explained. 'Don't go, you two. I'll be down in a minute.'

★ ★ ★

Ma Forthright brushed the wisps of grey hair from her forehead and surveyed the two policemen shrewdly.

'You'll have come about the murder, I suppose,' she said, in response to the Inspector's apology for intruding. 'My Harry's been telling me.'

'That's right, ma'am. Just a few questions I'd like to ask you.'

'Well, I shouldn't have thought an old body like me could help much. Still, I'm glad to see you; I like new faces, even policemen's. Folks don't bother to visit me now; they think I'm that near me grave I'm not worth the trouble. And what with me eyes being bad — well, if it weren't for the wireless I don't know what I'd do with meself all day.'

'It's a great boon to invalids,' Inspector Pitt agreed. 'And it was partly on account of the radio that I've called to see you.'

'I've got me licence, if that's what you're after,' she said sharply.

The Inspector laughed. 'I'm sure you have, ma'am. No, it wasn't the licence. It's just that, with Mr White being murdered last night, we like to know where everyone was at the time. Your son, for instance.'

'Don't you go suspecting my Harry. He's no murderer — he's a real good man, is Harry. No woman ever had a better son. He's looked after me since his father died — eighteen years ago, that was — and never a grumble. Many's the time I've told him he ought to get married; but not him. 'You and me's got on well enough together all these years, Ma,' he'd say. 'We don't want another woman butting in now, do we?' Real unselfish, that's what he is. There was a time about a year ago — no, longer than that it'd be, nearer fifteen months now — when the garage wasn't doing too well and Mr White had to reduce his wages. But *I* wasn't allowed to suffer; if anyone went short it was Harry.'

The old lady closed her eyes. She loved to talk, and it was seldom she had a fresh listener. But she soon tired. 'I'm afraid this is rather a strain on you,' the Inspector said kindly. 'If you'd prefer to wait — '

'I'm all right,' she said. 'There's a lot more life in me than people think. Harry's going to get me away to the sea soon, and I'll be a different woman there, the doctor says. What was it you wanted to know, Inspector?'

'Just about last night, Mrs Forthright. If your son was here, as he says. He tells me he and his friends were playing cards until quite a late hour.'

'And so they were. I don't hold with card-playing meself, but you men have to have your pleasures, and I dare say it's better than the pubs. And they're a nice lot, I'll say that for them, even if they do get a bit heated now and again. Young Dave Chitty, he's rather wild at times. But the other two, Bert Wickery and Mr Wells, they're real steady-going fellows.'

'They were here the whole evening?'

'They were. I didn't see them, of course, but I could hear their voices above the wireless. It was close on one when they left — they came up to say good-night to me, same as they always do of a Tuesday. Not Mr Wells — he'd gone about twenty minutes before; his wife had one of her turns, poor thing. Molly — that's his daughter, you know. Such a pretty little thing. I wasn't altogether sorry when she and young Chitty broke off their engagement, because she deserves a really *good* husband — Molly came to fetch him.'

'Did you see or hear *her*, Mrs Forthright?'

'No. Molly's quiet, you don't hear her much. But I heard voices in the hall — just before half-past twelve, that was — and footsteps on the path, and I

144

reckoned it was one of them going home a bit early.' She coughed violently, and Pitt waited anxiously for the paroxysm to pass, fearful of the harm it might do her. I ought to have insisted on her son staying in the room, he thought. Odd that he preferred not to. Is that a sign of guilt — or innocence?

The coughing ceased. 'You — you won't be able to blame any of those four for Mr White's murder,' the old lady wheezed. 'They didn't like him, none of them; but they couldn't have killed him, could they?'

'Mr White seems to have been rather unpopular, by all accounts,' remarked the Inspector.

'So I'm told. I never met him meself.'

'Well, I'll be getting along. Many thanks for your help, ma'am; if your son and his friends were here all yesterday evening, that makes it easier for us.' He nodded to the constable, and the two men walked to the door. As they reached it the Inspector turned and said, almost casually, 'Of course, you can't be expected to know whether they were *all* here the *whole* evening. Just going by their voices, you wouldn't have missed one if he'd slipped out for a while.'

Ma Forthright thought this over.

'That's true,' she agreed. 'But ask Harry. He'll know.'

Pitt said he would do that. He thanked her again, apologized for disturbing her, and went downstairs to where the three men awaited him.

'Your mother looks a very sick woman, Mr Forthright,' he said. 'I hope this interview hasn't been too much for her. I cut it as short as I could.'

'She's tougher than she looks,' said Forthright. 'But thanks all the same.'

The Inspector asked the way to the Loftens' house. Forthright took him to the door and pointed it out. It lay only a hundred yards down the main road, away from the garage.

'I hope the old lady proved helpful,' he said, as the Inspector took his leave.

'Yes, I think she did,' answered the other. 'Very helpful.'

Forthright closed the front door behind the two policemen and stood listening to

146

their footsteps fade away down the garden path. Then he turned to Wells and Wickery, who had followed him into the hall.

'I wonder what he meant by that last crack?' he asked uneasily.

# 6

## The Growth of Suspicion

Detective-Inspector Pitt was not normally an imaginative man, but it seemed to him that the Chittys' front parlour was filled with a secret and sardonic mirth. It was so small that he could almost see it hugging itself. Is it generally so amused, he wondered, or is it laughing at something in particular? Me, for instance? The room was clean and neat and unlived-in, the furniture poor in quality but rich in variety. Perhaps that's the answer, he thought — and imagined he heard the little room chuckle in appreciation of his discernment. 'So much care and attention lavished on me, and what do I give in return?' it guffawed. 'Nothing. I'm a parasite, I don't earn my keep. She comes in to dust and clean and polish, but nobody *uses* me. Nobody ever sits in the chairs, nobody *does* anything in here. It's money for jam, chum, money for jam!'

Inspector Pitt, who had been gazing idly round, promptly sat down in a threadbare armchair, which squeaked loudly in protest and tilted him alarmingly to port. Undaunted, the Inspector righted the list, produced notebook and pencil and laid them in a threateningly business-like manner on the oak-veneered table, and made a mental grimace at the room. That'll larn it, he thought — and immediately stood up, ashamed of his rather childish behaviour. He was glad there had been no one to witness it.

Susan Chitty returned from attending to something in the kitchen. She felt nervous and awkward in the presence of this rather forbidding-looking man. One didn't meet many strangers in Chaim.

'I haven't come across your brother yet,' he said. 'I was hoping to find him here.'

'He's not back from Tanbury,' she answered. 'He had to go to the oculist about his glasses.'

She could be quite good-looking if she

spent a bit of money on herself, thought the Inspector. Nice features, and a good figure if you liked them thin.

'He wasn't at home yesterday evening, was he?'

'No. He was playing cards at Mr Forthright's place.'

'And at what time did he come home?'

'Soon after one — about a quarter past, perhaps.'

'Is he usually as late as that?'

'Yes, on a Tuesday he is.'

Her manner was half defiant, half frightened. She answered his questions as though somewhere there must be a hidden trap she had to avoid; and all the time she was fidgeting with her hands or moving restlessly where she sat. The slightest noise from outside seemed to startle her. A bad case of nerves, thought Inspector Pitt. Am I as terrifying as all that?

He tried to put her at her ease. 'It doesn't sound as though your brother is likely to be much help to me,' he said, 'but I'll have a chat with him later, just in case. I feel I know him quite well already;

wonderful how everyone knows everyone else's business in a small place like this. Isn't he engaged to Mr Wells's daughter?'

'He was,' Susan said doubtfully, his friendliness calming her fears. 'I think they broke it off.'

'I'm sorry.' His tone matched his words. 'Had they been engaged long?'

'Just over two years.'

'Too long,' said Pitt. 'I'm a firm believer in short engagements. Speaking as a confirmed bachelor, of course.'

She smiled slightly. A pity she doesn't do it more often, he thought. It makes her almost beautiful.

'They couldn't really afford to get married,' she volunteered. 'My brother's not one for saving, I'm afraid.'

'Few of us are these days, miss. I suppose the slump at the garage may have put him back a bit, too? I'm told Mr White had to ask them all to take lower wages. Just over a year ago, wasn't it?'

The smile left her face.

'I — Dave doesn't take me into his confidence much,' she said truthfully. 'I don't know.'

Inspector Pitt did not labour the point. 'My main reason for calling — apart from seeing your brother, of course — was to ask about Mr Loften,' he said. 'I understand he was here yesterday evening?'

'Yes.'

'What time did he leave, miss?' As the girl hesitated he added, 'I'm not trying to pry into your personal affairs, you know. I merely want to find out where everyone was.'

She flushed. 'Mr Loften and I are merely good friends, Inspector. There's nothing for you to pry into.'

'No, of course not. But you haven't answered my question.'

'He arrived about ten o'clock and left at ten minutes to one,' she said, the flush deepening. Her eyes avoided his.

'I see. Well, that seems to dispose of that. Thank you, miss.'

The front door slammed, and a moment later Dave Chitty came into the room. His cheeks were flushed, and he had obviously been running. 'Good Lord, Susan!' he cried breathlessly. 'Have you — '

He stopped suddenly as he caught sight of the Inspector.

'This is Detective-Inspector Pitt, Dave,' said the girl. 'Inspector, this is my brother.'

'Oh!' The expression on Chitty's face hardened. 'You'll have come about the murder, I suppose.'

'That's right, sir. How did *you* hear of it?'

'I got off the bus at the garage. They told me there.' He looked anxiously from one to the other, then slumped into a chair. The springs creaked noisily, and Pitt smiled to himself, recalling his former fancies. The room will be laughing the other side of its face soon, he thought. 'Was it me or my sister you wanted to see?' Chitty asked.

'Both, sir. I'm just trying to pick up all the information I can.'

'You won't get any here. Susan was at home, and I was out playing cards,' said the other. '*And* I've got three good witnesses to prove it,' he added defiantly.

'Yes, sir. Your friends told me about that. But I'd like your own version, if you don't mind.'

Chitty gave it. Like his friends, he was word-perfect. Facts and times both corresponded exactly with the versions given by the others.

'Thank you, Mr Chitty. You'd make a good witness. But about these spectacles of yours. Broke them on the way home last night, didn't you?'

'Yes. We took the short cut across the fields, and I caught my foot in a rut or something. Damned annoying. I can't read a word without them.'

Looking at the man's eyes, Pitt believed him. Their natural smallness was accentuated by the half-closed lids. 'Could you show me where you broke them?' he asked.

Dave was not prepared for this. It had never occurred to any of them that the police might be interested in such an apparently unimportant incident. And there had been no one at the garage to warn him; only Loften and the police.

'I don't think so,' he said slowly. 'I could show you the field, of course. But it's a fair size and — well, it was

154

pretty dark, you see.'

'Let's have a look at the field, then,' said the Inspector.

As Chitty had said, it was a fair size; about ten acres of pasture, with a well-defined track crossing it diagonally and forking right and left some hundred yards before it reached the Tanbury road. 'Did you keep to the track?' asked Pitt, as he and Chitty stood looking at it over the low blackthorn hedge.

'That was the idea, of course,' said the other. 'But it was dark and we kept wandering off it. That was how I came a cropper,' he added, with what he considered to be a touch of genius.

Pitt left him there, having other calls to make in the village, and Chitty climbed the stile and began to walk across the field towards the garage. He was puzzled and worried by the Inspector's interest in his spectacles. What had the others been saying?

'Hullo, there!' said Molly Wells. 'You look a bit down in the mouth. Worried you may lose your job?'

He had been vaguely aware of an

approaching female figure. Now, as he looked at her, appreciating her fresh young beauty, he remembered suddenly that the obstacle to their marriage no longer existed. He was free again, free to take a new job and to marry and leave Chaim. And they would have all the money they needed.

Impetuously he caught her hands in his. She looked at him, surprised by his action. It had taken all her courage to address him; and she had only done so, swallowing her pride, because she had thought to detect, during the past week or two, an added interest in his eyes at sight of her. She had not expected a rebuff, but neither had she been prepared for such loverlike enthusiasm.

'Molly,' he said; and then again, 'Molly.'

'What's the matter, Dave?' She did not draw her hands away.

'Nothing's the matter,' he said, excitement mounting within him as the prospect began to take shape. 'Not now. Let's get married, Molly. Soon.'

'Well, really!' She slipped her hands out

of his and stepped back, looking at him in astonishment mingled with delight. 'You break off our engagement, ignore me for months, and then — '

'It was you who broke it off, not me. Not that I blame you, of course.' He seized her hands again and drew her to him. 'I've been a brute and a fool, Molly, but I've never stopped loving you. Here!' He fumbled hastily through his pockets and triumphantly produced the ring. 'Put this on again, eh?'

'You haven't been drinking, have you?' she asked anxiously.

'No. Sober as a judge, that's me.' He drew her closer. 'Will you marry me, Molly? Will you?'

'I'll have to think about it. I'm not going to be bullied into marrying you after the way you've treated me.' It was a weak, instinctive protest against the clamour of her heart. She loved him, but pride told her that she must not capitulate too readily. 'What would we do for money, anyway? When I marry I want a proper home, with my own furniture and — and things. I'm not going to pig it in one room, my lad.'

'You wouldn't have to,' he said. 'I've got money — enough, anyway. More than you think, perhaps. And now that White's dead I can — ' He stopped, suddenly realizing what he was saying. 'I've always wanted to get away from here, you know that; and now's a good time to make the break. I'll get a better job — in town, somewhere. What do you say, Molly?'

'You had a better job in town offered you once before, Dave — remember? Why didn't you take that?'

'I — they changed their minds,' he lied.

But already he was returning to reality. He was involved in a murder — perhaps it might not be so easy to leave Chaim. And if things did not go well, if their alibi was proved to be false . . .

Molly saw the doubt in his face, felt it in the reduced pressure of his hands on hers. She had not meant to deter him with her arguments, but rather to spur him on. Fearful that by her quibbling she might have lost something she greatly desired, she pressed closer to him.

'I'll marry you if you really mean it,

Dave,' she said softly, hiding her face against his jacket.

The presence of her pliant body within the circle of his arms momentarily banished doubt and fear. He put one hand under her chin and tilted her face so that he might kiss her.

'Of course I mean it,' he declared between kisses.

She drew away from him, laughing happily. 'You choose a fine place and time for love-making. I must say! Half the village can see us.'

'Who cares?' He kissed her again.

'Not me,' Molly confessed.

With their arms around each other's waist they walked slowly and blissfully to the end of the field. For a few moments they stood there, locked in an embrace — until, from across the top of the hedge, Dave saw the garage. Memory returned to him, and he drew away from the girl.

'I ought to be getting back to work,' he said.

Molly ran most of the way home. She burst into the living-room, cheeks flushed, eyes dancing, and threw her

159

arms round her mother in an ecstatic embrace.

'Oh, Mum, I'm so happy! Dave's just asked me to marry him! He says it was all a mistake our breaking it off, and he still loves me. And he's going to leave Chaim and get a job in London, and he's got quite a lot of money saved up, he says, so he can't have — ' She stopped. For the first time she noticed the tall man standing by the window. She drew away from her mother, abashed.

'This is Inspector Pitt, Molly. He's come about Mr White being murdered,' said Mrs Wells.

She made it sound as though he had come about the rent.

Pitt smiled at the girl. She thought he looked nice when he smiled. 'Rather a grisly subject on such a happy day, eh? It seems I have to congratulate you, Miss Wells. Who's the lucky man?'

'Dave Chitty,' she said, blushing.

'Oh, yes. He works at the garage, doesn't he?' Pitt frowned thoughtfully. The girl's announcement made the question he had to ask her all the more tricky. 'You knew Mr White, didn't you, miss?'

'Only slightly.'

'Oh.' There was a pause. 'I was given to understand that you knew him rather better than that. Been out with him in his car, haven't you?'

'Well, yes.' Molly looked anxiously at her mother, seeking advice. Mrs Wells said nothing. 'He — he gave me a lift home once or twice, that's all.'

'You wouldn't know anything about his private affairs? No idea who might have killed him, and why?'

'No,' Molly said firmly. But she was relieved when he turned his attention to her visit to the Forthright cottage the previous evening. There she was on firmer ground.

When the girl had left the room Mrs Wells turned indignantly on the Inspector. 'Who's been telling you tales about Molly?' she demanded. 'There never was anything between her and White. Why, he's old enough to be her father! She's been in love with Dave Chitty for years. They were all set to get married over a year ago, only . . . '

'Only what?' asked the Inspector, as she paused.

'Well, they had a tiff. You know what young people are, always blowing hot and cold.'

'Yes, indeed. You'll be pleased to see them married, then?'

'I most certainly will. So will my husband. It's worried us a lot, knowing the way Molly felt about Dave, and him acting so queer.'

'Queer? How queer, Mrs Wells?'

She had been so set on heading him off from Andrew White that she had not thought where they were going. 'Oh, just queer,' she said, intentionally vague. 'Avoiding Molly, breaking off the engagement. But I dare say he was worried about him not earning enough to get married.'

'I see. But didn't your daughter mention just now that he had money put by? Enough for them to marry on?'

She shuffled uneasily. 'Young people exaggerate,' she said. 'Dave Chitty isn't one for saving.'

'So his sister told me. And he's quite a heavy drinker, I believe. That runs away with the money.'

'He doesn't drink that heavy,' she answered. She wished she knew what he was driving at. With a murder on his hands he couldn't just be making polite conversation, he must be after *something*. But what? If she knew that it would be easier to answer his questions.

'What sort of a man was White?' he asked.

'I hardly knew him myself,' she said. 'But he wasn't popular in the village. Too much of a snob.'

'What about his employees — your husband, for example? What did *he* think of him?'

'None of them liked White,' she said grudgingly. 'He wasn't an easy man to work for.'

'I suppose it didn't help when he cut their wages,' the Inspector said thoughtfully. 'You must have felt the pinch a bit during the past year.'

'It was longer than that,' she said. 'But we managed.'

'Unusual for wages to go down nowadays,' he said. 'The trend's all the other way. Didn't their union have something to say about that?'

'None of them belongs to a union.'

He stood up, reaching for his hat. 'Well, I mustn't sit here gossiping; I'll be on my way. Good luck to your daughter — and thank you. You've been a great help.'

Have I? she wondered, as she watched him walk briskly down the garden path. I wish I knew how.

★ ★ ★

They met at Forthright's cottage that evening, after the garage had closed. It was an uncomfortable meeting. Until the gathering was complete they avoided the topic that obsessed their minds. There was no friendliness, no confidence. They sat eyeing each other with mistrust and suspicion, reading guilt in every twitch of a facial muscle, in every awkward movement of head or hand or foot.

When Chitty arrived, late as usual, Wickery scowled at him. But Forthright gave him no chance to speak.

'There's no point in starting a slanging match,' he told them. 'White is dead and one of us killed him, and that's all there is to it. Bert thinks it was Dave or me. Well, let him — that's what I say. I've got my own suspicions, come to that. But none of us can prove a damned thing, so what's the use of accusing each other? If we hang together' — Wickery flinched at this unfortunate choice of words — 'and try and keep one jump ahead of the police, there's no reason why we shouldn't be all right.'

Looking at them, he realized he was voicing a policy that all, himself included, would find it hard to follow. Apart from Pop's almost paternal affection for Dave — an affection which might prove awkward, and which Forthright suspected was not reciprocated — there was no real comradeship to bind them. They had never been more than acquaintances, thrown together by a common trade. Each of us would shop the others, he thought, if he knew them to be guilty — particularly if by doing so he could save his own skin.

It was not a comforting thought.

'United we stand, divided we fall,' quoted Wells. He tried to sound cheerful, but his words had a mournful, last-ditch ring, and he could not keep the fear out of his voice.

Wickery said nothing, but sat contemplating his shoes. Chitty, with Molly fresh in his mind, looked the least concerned of the four.

'I didn't kill White,' he said defiantly. 'I might have done if I'd had the chance, but I didn't. It wasn't me who went into the garage last night.'

None of them took any heed of his denial. It was a foregone conclusion that he would make one.

'Even if we knew which of us done it, it wouldn't help much,' said Wells, speaking mainly for Wickery's benefit. Harry had said he could handle Bert, that Bert hadn't the guts to stand out against the rest of them. But Wells wasn't so sure. Bert's sense of grievance was strong; if he could name the murderer with certainty he might still go to the police. 'They'll never believe we didn't plan to kill White, that it was an accident. If one of us hangs we all hang.'

'Cheerful devil, aren't you?' said Forthright.

'What about the money?' Chitty asked impatiently. All this palaver, he thought, was a waste of time. White was dead, and good riddance to him. Either their alibi worked or it didn't; there was nothing they could do now to improve on it. 'When do we collect?'

'Not yet,' said Forthright. 'I told you we'd have to wait a bit. That's still more important now that White's dead. The police won't give up so easily.'

'But I want to be off,' Chitty protested. 'Molly and I aim to get married soon.'

'We can't help that.' Forthright was annoyed at the other's persistence. 'You kept her waiting long enough; a few more weeks won't make much difference.'

Wickery spoke for the first time.

'You're a lot of ruddy fools,' he said slowly. 'There won't be any money.'

They stared at him. Chitty swore blasphemously and stood up. Wells put a restraining hand on his arm.

'What the hell are you getting at?' Forthright demanded. 'If that's meant to be funny it doesn't make *me* laugh.'

'One of you double-crossed the rest of us when he murdered White,' said Wickery. 'He deliberately put us in a spot that may cost us our lives. And if he could do that do you think he wouldn't hesitate to double-cross us over the money as well? You can bet your bottom dollar that it isn't there, that he bagged the lot for himself, the swine.'

There was a stunned silence. Then Chitty pushed his chair away so that it fell with a crash. 'We'll soon settle *that*,' he said grimly, and made for the door.

Forthright barred his way. 'Don't be a fool, Dave. Do you want the police to *know* we killed White?'

But for once Wickery supported Chitty.

'There's not much risk,' he said. 'They'd never think we would try to recover the money from under their very noses. Probably there'll be no one about; and even if they catch us we can say we needed a bit of scrap from the dump.

That sounds reasonable enough — we've done it before. I reckon we ought to find out where we stand, if only to know just how big a rat one of us is.' And as Forthright moved slowly away from the door he added, 'But I don't think Dave ought to go alone. One of us had better go with him.'

'Meaning what?' Chitty demanded angrily.

'Meaning that I don't trust you, Dave — you nor the rest of them.'

'All right,' said Forthright. 'You go with him.'

To the two who remained the time passed slowly. Wells said he thought Wickery was putting the wind up them unnecessarily. Bert used to be such a cheerful chap, he said, and now he was morbid and suspicious of everyone. He ought to get a grip on himself or he'd go to pieces completely. Of course the money was there. None of them was the type to play such a low-down trick on his pals.

Forthright was not so optimistic; nor was he surprised at the change in

Wickery. 'He's a good sort, but he lacks guts. He's scared, Pop — scared stiff. And hell! Who can blame him? When I think what may happen to us I'm scared myself.'

'So am I,' Wells admitted.

When the two men returned there was no need to ask the result of their mission. The expression on their faces was enough.

'Not a brass farthing,' said Chitty. 'Not even the perishing box.'

'Are you *sure?*' asked Wells.

'We practically moved the whole ruddy scrap-heap from one side of the yard to the other,' said Wickery. 'You've had the money, Pop.'

'What do you mean by that, blast you?'

'Nothing personal. Just a manner of speaking.' Wickery slumped wearily into an armchair. 'But there it is, the money's gone. One of you three is a pretty wealthy man right now — damn you!'

He had spoken quietly at first, but the last two words were uttered with such venom that even Forthright was startled.

'Cut that out, Bert,' he said sharply.

'Stop trying to whitewash yourself! As far as I'm concerned you're as likely to be guilty as Pop or Dave. *More* likely, in fact.'

'Hear, hear!' said Chitty.

For some minutes they argued furiously, each vying with the others in his attempt to divert suspicion from himself and to cast it elsewhere. They were now, as Wells pointed out, without money, without a job, and in danger of being hanged. And whoever had let them in for all that *deserved* to be hanged!

A loud banging on the ceiling quietened them. Forthright ran upstairs. While he was gone the others sat silent, eyeing each other malevolently.

'She was a bit fussed,' said Forthright when he returned. 'Didn't like the way we were shouting.'

'Maybe we'd better clear out,' Wells suggested. 'Talk it over when we've cooled off a bit.'

'Not yet,' said Wickery. He turned to Chitty. 'You've been opening your big mouth quite a lot this evening, Dave. Suppose you open it just once more and tell us where you *really* broke your glasses last night?'

Chitty flushed. 'What's biting you now, damn you? Didn't you see me fall? Why, it was you who found them, blast it!'

'The frame, yes — but not the lenses. Harry and Pop looked this morning, and there was no sign of any broken glass.'

'Well, what of it? They must have looked in the wrong place.'

Forthright shook his head. He was angry with Wickery for having raised the matter so abruptly and at such a time, when their tempers were frayed and there was little likelihood of getting Dave to own up. He had meant to speak to Dave quietly, and alone. 'No, Dave. I know every inch of that path — I couldn't be mistaken. You never broke those glasses where you said you did. They must have been broken before.'

'Here, what the hell is this?' Chitty stood up, banging his fist angrily on the table. 'Wasn't it you who was all for us getting together and no questions asked? Stop snooping, can't you? Leave me alone.'

'We're not snooping — not in the way you mean, anyway,' said Wells evenly. 'We're not trying to fix you, or anything like that. But we must know where you broke those specs, Dave. It's important.'

'I don't see why.'

'Then you're a damned fool,' said Forthright. It was too late now for niceties and soft soap — they'd have to bludgeon it out of the fellow. 'Come on — where *did* you break them?'

Chitty hesitated, looking from one to another of the grim faces watching him so intently. He seemed about to speak, but Wickery's bitter tongue did not wait for him.

'You broke them when you murdered White, didn't you? And you left the broken glass in White's room, you stupid fool, so that the police could find it and convict the lot of us. And then you have the nerve to stand there and say you don't think it's important. You ought to be shot!'

It was too much for Chitty. He caught Wickery a terrific buffet on the cheek, sending him sprawling; and then they were on the floor, fighting grimly. Chitty had his hands round the other's throat by the time Forthright managed to drag him clear.

'You damned idiots!' stormed Forthright, as he and Wells stood between the two combatants. 'What the hell's come over you both?' He turned to Chitty. 'Bert had no call to speak like that; he deserved a hiding, and he got it. All the same, he's not the only one who thinks you may have broken those glasses in some place which is going to look mighty suspicious. And if you did then we've a right to know where it was. We're all in this together, don't forget.'

But Chitty was past argument or reason. His beady eyes, red-rimmed, glared at them balefully.

'Go to hell, the whole boiling lot of you. But I'll tell you what *I* think. Maybe I was in favour of White being killed, but so were you, Harry; and for all Bert's sissy talk I bet he was as keen as the rest of us to see the end of the swine. You and Bert planned this job between you, Harry, and it was you who wrote on the pieces of paper; dished 'em out, too. There's been some funny business somewhere, if you ask me, and you two devils are at the bottom of it. Pop and I are just a couple of suckers. Well, I'm not going to be a sucker any more. From now on you can count me out — I'll look after myself, thank you. But I didn't kill White, and if anyone tries to frame me I'll know how to deal with him. So look out!'

The door slammed behind him. Pop wiped the sweat from his brow.

'It's been too much for him,' he said. 'I'm not sure it isn't getting to be too much for all of us.'

'Rot,' said Forthright. 'But he's a ruddy young fool, and unless someone knocks some sense into him he'll wreck the whole damned show.'

'I don't mind having a bash,' Wickery said.

'You? That's just about what you *would* have, my lad. He looked like giving you one this evening, anyway.'

'The police were searching the field this afternoon,' Wells said thoughtfully. 'The one where Dave's supposed to have bust his glasses.'

'Well, they won't find anything there.'

'No. But doesn't that look as though Dave *didn't* kill White? I mean, if the cops had found his broken lenses in White's room, why should they be looking for them in the field? It wouldn't make sense.'

Forthright stared at him. 'You're right!' he exclaimed. 'Why the devil didn't you mention that before?'

'I don't know. With all this rumpus about the money, I suppose I just forgot.'

Wickery was gazing intently at Forthright, watching him as he paced jerkily up and down the room. 'I suppose there *wasn't* any funny business with those pieces of paper?' he said softly, almost as though he were asking the question of himself.

But Forthright heard him. He stopped his pacing and stood over the seated Wickery, his manner threatening.

'First Dave, then you,' he said fiercely. 'I've had just about enough of this. You know damned well there wasn't any funny business. There couldn't have been — you chose your own piece of paper, didn't you? I didn't force you to take it.' His eyes narrowed. 'And since you're so free with your accusations, Bert Wickery, let me ask you this. How was it you knew the money wouldn't be under the scrap-heap, eh? Was it because you'd put it some place else, somewhere where only you could find it?'

'Now it's you who's being foolish,' Wickery said disdainfully. 'You know damned well I was only guessing.'

'Do I? I'm not so sure. And here's something else I'd like to know. Why were you late getting to the garage this morning?'

'Because I was trying to prevent Doris from coming with me, that's why. I wanted to spare her.'

'Spare her from what?' Forthright sounded triumphant. 'How did you know there'd been a murder?'

Wickery flushed. 'I'm going home,' he said. 'I've had enough of this. Maybe I was wrong to start accusing Dave, but at least I had a damned good reason. You're just being offensive for no reason at all.'

He felt tired and spent as he crossed the fields to the village. Pop was right, he thought, we can't keep this up much longer. The realization that his ordeal was not over for the day, that Doris would be waiting at home to question him, caused his spirits to sink still lower.

I'll slip into the pub for a drink, he thought. Maybe that'll bolster me up a bit.

The landlord was pleased and surprised to see him. 'Over a year since you been in, Bert,' he said. 'The darts team's never been the same without you and Harry Forthright. One from bottom of the league, we are.'

Wickery smiled listlessly. 'I'll have a whisky, Sam,' he said.

'Whisky, is it? Gone off the beer?' He put the glass on the counter and reached for a siphon. 'Nasty business, this murder. How's it going to affect you chaps at the garage?'

'We don't know yet.' Wickery added a splash of soda and sipped the whisky appreciatively, feeling its warmth inside him. 'I expect Mr Loften will carry on.

For a bit, anyway.'

The landlord leaned across the counter.

'The police come to see me this afternoon,' he said confidentially. 'Asked quite a lot of questions, they did, about you and the others up there. How often was you in the pub, did you drink a lot — things like that. But I told them. Haven't set foot in the place for over a year, I said; only Dave Chitty. But the other three — gave it up just like that, I said. Even resigned from the darts club.' He frowned. 'A pity about Dave. I did what I could for him, but there's no denying he comes in most nights. Not that he drinks heavy, mind you; just reg'lar. I told them that.'

'Thanks for trying to help, Sam.'

'Think nothing of it, lad.' The landlord laughed. 'I told 'em,' he said again. ' 'If I had to rely on them chaps for a living,' I said, ' I'd be out of business in two shakes of a duck's rudder.' ' A glass banged impatiently in the public bar. 'All right, I'm coming.' He grinned at Wickery, leant across and gave him a friendly pat on the shoulder. 'Keep your pecker up, son. And give my love to Doris.'

As Wickery had expected, Doris was waiting for him. He noticed that her cheek, not her lips, was proffered for his kiss.

'Where *have* you been?' she asked anxiously. 'I've been worried sick about you.'

'I'm sorry. But the others wanted to talk over this wretched business, and I couldn't very well refuse.'

'*They* wanted! How about me? Do you think *I* didn't want to discuss it with you?' She sniffed. 'You've been drinking, Bert.'

'I dropped in for a quick one on the way home. It's been a hell of a day; I felt I needed something to buck me up.'

She looked at him thoughtfully for a moment. Then she shrugged her shoulders. 'I'll get your supper,' she said. 'It's ruined, of course, but I suppose it's still eatable. There's nothing else, anyway.'

He had no desire for food. The whisky, he decided, had not done its job; all he wanted was bed and sleep. But he had to eat something, if only to calm Doris. He was glad that the fish was burnt; he could pick at it without her remarking on his lack of appetite.

Doris picked up her knitting. She did not speak again until he pushed his plate away and reached for the tea-pot. Then her fingers gradually slowed, and she said, looking at him with a flush on her cheeks, 'Bert! Who do you think killed Uncle Andrew?'

'I don't know.' He stirred his tea slowly and steadily, his eyes fixed on the steaming liquid. 'Hadn't we better leave that to the police? It's their job, not ours. We've nothing to go on.'

'Have they? Anything to go on, I mean?'

Wickery shook his head. He wished he knew the answer to that question.

The needles started to click again. 'The Inspector was here this afternoon,' said Doris.

That shook him. 'The Inspector? What did he want?'

'He asked me whether you'd had your wages reduced during the past two years.'

'Why did he want to know that?'

'He'd heard that trade had been poor

at the garage last year.'

'Oh. Well, I can't see what that has to do with White being murdered,' he said, partially relieved. 'What did you tell him, anyway?'

'The truth, of course. I said your wages had stayed the same ever since we got married, and that he could look at the books if he didn't believe me. They would tell him all he wanted to know about wages and trade, I said.'

'That was fair enough. Did he seem satisfied?'

'I don't know. Of course, I didn't mention you'd been paying back some of your wages to Uncle every week. I didn't think that was necessary,' said Doris, her head bent over her knitting.

Wickery swallowed hard. 'What do you know about that?' he asked hoarsely.

She looked at him then.

'I'm not a fool, Bert. I've known all along you were paying Uncle to keep him quiet about something. I kept the books, don't forget. You were still getting the same money, but you were giving me less. It wasn't very difficult to work out.'

'You never mentioned it,' he said miserably.

'I didn't want to worry you. I've only brought it up now because I'm frightened.' Her voice took on a shriller note. 'That Inspector is on to something, Bert. He wouldn't ask questions about your wages unless he thought they had some connection with Uncle's murder. And I want to know why. Because he's right, isn't he? There *is* some connection?'

He did not answer. He took up the spoon and mechanically began to stir the tea again. Doris put down her knitting and went over to him, kneeling on the floor at his side.

'Listen to me, Bert,' she said desperately. 'We're in this together, it's not fair to keep me in the dark. If there's trouble I want to know about it. I've a *right* to know.'

He shook his head. 'I'm sorry, Doris. Something went wrong, I admit that. But I told you before, it's not my secret.'

'Remember the night you came home and told me I'd have to go back to work at the office?' she asked. 'Uncle made you do that, didn't he?'

He nodded.

'It was that night old Mrs Gooch was killed by a car on the Tanbury road. They never found the driver, did they?'

Something seemed to snap inside his head. He pushed back his chair and sprang up, so that she fell sideways.

'For God's sake stow it, Doris! I've had just about all I can stand for one day. Stop badgering me, can't you?' He stamped across the room and flung himself into the one armchair. 'Questions, questions, questions! Even at home I don't get any peace. Why the hell can't you leave me alone?'

For a few moments she lay where she had fallen. Then she dragged herself wearily to her feet, using the table for support, and went back to the hard chair on which she had been sitting. As his anger died he saw that she was crying, quietly but copiously.

His shame was so great that he could not speak. Then he went over and put his arms round her tear-racked body. She neither welcomed nor repulsed him.

'I'm sorry, darling,' he murmured. 'I don't know what came over me, I didn't mean to hurt you. It's just that — well, anyway, I'm sorry.'

He began to kiss her quietly — her forehead, her cheeks, her wet eyes. Presently she shuddered and clutched his arm.

'It's all right,' she said haltingly. 'It — it doesn't matter.'

'But it does matter,' he persisted. 'God knows what made me break out like that. I wouldn't hurt you for the world — you know that.'

Gently but firmly she pushed his encircling arms away. Then she stood up and faced him. There was no colour in her cheeks, but her eyes were red.

'I'll not ask any more questions,' she said, 'except one. Bert — did you kill Uncle Andrew?'

Tense and expectant, she awaited his reply.

'No,' he said slowly. 'No, I didn't kill him. I don't even know who did.'

# 7

## The Menace from Without

Although White's flat had been sealed off
by the police, the garage was open for
business on the Thursday morning.
Custom at the pumps was brisk. People
from miles around found occasion to visit
Chaim that day and to stop at the garage
for a close-up of the scene of the murder.
But they found the staff singularly
uncommunicative, and were sent on their
way with their thirst for information
unquenched. Nor did the reporters fare
much better. The mechanics refused to
talk, either of the murder or of themselves, becoming abusive and sometimes
threatening when persistence was carried
too far. Only Loften received visitors with
civility. He welcomed the trade which,
although maybe only temporary, was now
pouring in, causing him to send urgent
requests to the petrol companies for

further supplies. But even Loften was evasive and unhelpful when pressed for information.

'Ruddy vultures,' muttered Chitty, as he watched the cars queueing for service at the pumps. 'What do they expect? Blood in the petrol?'

The others felt somewhat ashamed of their conduct of the previous evening, and among themselves had offered and accepted grudging apologies. They appreciated that, however much truth there might have been in some of the accusations levelled, a certain amount of unity was essential if they were to defeat the police endeavours to discover White's murderer. Even the loss of the money was tacitly ignored for the time being. But when apologies were offered to Chitty he scornfully rejected them; he seemed quite unrepentant of his behaviour, and pointedly ignored his workmates. Only to Wells did he condescend to talk, and even to him his conversation consisted mainly of abuse of the other two. Wells tried to patch up the quarrel, explaining that none of them now believed he had broken his spectacles in White's room. Chitty said he couldn't care less what they believed — from now on he was looking after his own interests. He didn't need help or advice from anyone, least of all from a couple of tricksters like Forthright and Wickery.

Inspector Pitt arrived at ten o'clock, bringing with him a stout, red-faced man in tweeds. Pitt and Loften went into the office, but the stout man did not accompany them. He wandered idly about the garage, periodically coming to a halt near where one or the other of the mechanics was working. It seemed that the men themselves, rather than their jobs, were what interested him. He made no attempt to engage them in conversation, but stood staring at them sheepishly; and when Chitty rudely told him to ' — off' he scuttled away into the yard and remained there out of sight until the Inspector reappeared from the office and took him off in the police-car.

'Who the devil was the fat bird?' asked Wickery. 'Didn't look like a police-officer to me.'

'Nor me,' Wells agreed. 'More like a farmer.'

'I've got an idea I've seen him some place before,' Forthright said slowly. 'Damned if I can remember where, though.'

He was still puzzling over the fat man when Jack Iverson, a neighbour of the Chittys, called in on his motor-cycle. Forthright spotted him in the queue outside the pumps and went over to speak to him.

'Thanks for the eggs you sent up last week, Jack,' he said. 'Darned good of you. Ma doesn't care much for meat, but she's a real glutton when it comes to eggs.'

'Think nothing of it,' said the other. 'There's more when she wants 'em. I meant to bring them up myself and have a word with the old lady — I know how she likes people popping in to see her — but the missus wasn't feeling too good that evening, so I took 'em next door. I thought Dave could hand them over in the morning.'

'Susan brought them to the cottage.'

'Yes, I know. She had her hat and coat

on and said she was going past your place, so she took them with her.' He eyed the long queue of cars with interest. 'Looks like murder's good for trade,' he said. 'If you had one a week maybe you'd all make your fortunes. How are the police making out? D'you think they'll get the chap who done it?'

'I wouldn't know. They ask a lot of questions, but they don't give much away.' Forthright spoke slowly, his mind busy with another problem. Something Jack Iverson had said . . . 'Is the missus better?' he asked.

'Oh, yes. Nothing to it, really. Nothing that a night's sleep wouldn't put right.'

'Which evening was she queer?'

The other thought for a moment. 'Tuesday week — the evening Susan took the eggs.'

'Susan brought them midday on the Wednesday,' said Forthright.

'Did she? Well, I saw her set off with them Tuesday. About nine-thirty, it was. But maybe she changed her mind and didn't go for her walk.'

'I dare say,' Forthright agreed. He did

190

not wish to arouse the other's curiosity.

It was not until an hour later that he was able to talk to Wells and Wickery alone; but when he told them of his conversation with Iverson they looked puzzled. 'I don't get it,' said Wells. 'What's biting you?'

'Jack said Susan left about nine-thirty Tuesday evening to bring the eggs up to my place; Tuesday week, I mean, not last Tuesday. But she didn't bring them — not till the next day.' He paused, and added weightily, 'Remember I said I thought someone was in the hall? That could have been Susan.'

'But she'd have come in. She wouldn't wait in the hall.'

'She might — if she heard what we were talking about,' Forthright said.

Pop Wells's eyes popped even farther.

'Good Lord! You think she overheard us planning to kill White, and was too frightened to let us know she was there?'

'Yes.'

'Just a minute,' said Wickery. 'We weren't planning to kill White, Pop, only to take the money. Remember?'

191

The little man flushed. 'Of course I remember,' he said testily. 'It was a slip of the tongue. You're too damned touchy, Bert, that's what's the matter with you.' He turned back to Forthright. 'Would she have told Dave, d'you think?'

'No. They're not very close, those two. More likely she's kept it to herself. I thought she was a bit odd when she called on the Wednesday. Sort of scared.'

'We'll have to speak to her,' said Wickery, trouble reflected in his watery blue eyes. 'If you're right, Harry, we're in a bigger mess than ever.'

They decided that Wells should leave early for lunch, bringing Susan back to the garage with him on the pretext that Dave wanted to see her urgently. Dave did not go home to lunch, but was in the habit of wandering off into the woods on fine days to eat his sandwiches there. With any luck they could tackle Susan without her brother's knowledge. In his present mood Dave might turn ugly if he found they had sent for Susan without first consulting him. If Susan *had* been at the cottage Dave would have to be told eventually; but they hoped that the seriousness of the news would swamp any protests he might wish to make about the manner in which it had been obtained.

They were unlucky. Chitty did not go into the woods to eat his lunch, but sat in the garage. When he saw Wells and Susan arriving he put down his bread and cheese and went out to meet them. Forthright and Wickery, uneasy in their minds, thought it best to leave it to Wells.

'Thank the Lord Loften isn't here,' muttered Wickery. 'If we're in for fireworks at least we can keep them private.'

'What are you doing here, Susan?' asked Dave. 'Anything wrong?'

The girl looked from him to Wells. Something in the latter's face warned her not to ask questions. Bewildered, she shook her head.

'I brought her up, Dave,' said Wells unhappily. 'I — we — there's something we feel we ought to discuss with her.'

'We?' said Chitty, frowning. 'Who's 'we'? Why wasn't I told about this? Damn it, Pop, you've no right — '

'Wait, Dave.' Wells saw Forthright and Wickery coming out to join them. 'This is something real serious — honest it is. If you hadn't been in such a black temper about last night we'd have spoken to you first; but you might have refused, and we knew it couldn't wait, and so — '

He paused, as Chitty turned, still scowling, to confront the two men behind him.

'Well?' he demanded truculently. 'What have you two devils been cooking up now?'

'You're a fool to carry on like this, Dave,' said Forthright. 'We apologized for what we said, didn't we? What the hell's biting you?'

'You are,' said Chitty. 'I want to know why you chaps sent for my sister without asking me first. Damned cheek, I call it.'

'Call it what you like,' Forthright answered impatiently. He had not found it easy to apologize, and Chitty's curt rejection of his peace overture was difficult to swallow. 'Maybe you'll think differently in a moment. I'm going to ask your sister a question — any objection?'

And as Chitty stood irresolute Forthright turned to the girl. 'Did you call in at my place Tuesday night last week with some eggs from the Iversons?' he asked.

The girl's face was white and set. 'I — I brought them Wednesday,' she said. 'You were having lunch.'

'I know. But you called Tuesday night also, didn't you?' And as the girl did not answer he said softly, 'How much did you overhear, Sue?'

Tears began to well from her eyes as she looked at the grim faces of Wickery and Forthright, at the unhappy Wells, the puzzled, angry Dave. Then she broke away from them and ran into the garage. She leant against the wall, hiding her face, her body shaking spasmodically as she cried.

Wells went after her. He put an arm round her, trying to comfort her.

'What the hell is all this in aid of?' demanded Chitty.

Forthright told him. Chitty swore fluently. 'You mean Susan heard everything?'

'Not everything, perhaps. But enough.

Why didn't she come in, otherwise?'

'We'll find out,' the other said grimly.

If Susan had meant to keep her secret she made no effort to do so now. Faced by an angry, almost threatening brother, her defences were down. Yes, she said between sobs, she had gone into the cottage without knocking, and was about to open the living-room door when she had heard their voices raised in what seemed to her like angry argument. She had not meant to listen, only to wait until the argument was over. 'But you spoke so loud I couldn't help hearing,' she said.

'And just what did you hear?' asked her brother.

'Well, that you were going to rob Mr White the next Tuesday and that you'd been paying him money because of Mrs Gooch.'

'Did you understand *why* we had been paying him money?'

'Not at first I didn't. But afterwards I remembered about the accident, and I supposed it was because you'd killed her and Mr White had found out.'

Chitty turned to the others. All the

antagonism had gone out of him. It was as though he were appealing to them not to hold him responsible for his sister.

Susan had stopped crying. She, too, looked at her brother's companions — half fearfully, half defiantly.

'Why didn't you come in afterwards?' asked Wickery.

'I was too frightened. You all sounded so — so different, somehow. I just wanted to get away as quick as I could.'

'But you could have told Dave afterwards, when he got home.'

No, she couldn't, thought Wells. She was probably even more afraid of Dave than she was of us. He felt sorry for the girl; it was no fault of hers that she had become involved in their troubles. She was to be pitied rather than blamed.

'There's no real harm done,' he said. 'Susan'll keep her mouth shut. The police won't suspect she knows anything, so they won't try to get at us through her.'

Chitty nodded, relieved. 'They've already had a talk with her,' he said. 'They won't bother her again. You didn't tell them anything then, Susan, did you?'

'No.'

'Good. Well, you'd better get home. We don't want Loften to find you here — he'll wonder what's up.'

But Susan did not move. There was fear in her whole demeanour — in her eyes, in the way her body, pressed against the wall, shrank away from them. But there was something else as well; an almost desperate defiance, that finally conquered the fear and made her say, her voice almost a whisper:

'Why — why did you kill him?'

Watching her closely, Forthright had guessed it was something of that sort which was troubling her. 'You heard what we planned,' he said. 'We didn't mean to kill him, you know that.'

'Yes,' she said. 'But why did you?'

It wasn't easy to explain, but he tried. Her eyes were fixed intently, searchingly, on his face, as though to make certain that what he was saying was the truth.

'So you see,' he concluded, 'we don't know why he was killed or even who killed him. It was one of us, of course

— that's all we can say for certain. But which one . . . '

He shrugged his shoulders.

Her eyes left his face, and in turn she looked at the others. She stood more upright now. Defiance had ousted fear.

'You didn't like him, did you?' she said. 'None of you. Dave was always saying how you hated him.'

'That's got nothing to do with it,' Wickery said impatiently.

The snake writhed on Forthright's arm as he raised it wearily to his head. It wouldn't do to get impatient, to antagonize her. 'I think you'd best leave us to sort it out,' he said quietly, trying to sound matter-of-fact. 'When we know who did it — well, that'll be different. But until then we want to keep our mouths shut. Otherwise it means that three innocent people will suffer just because the fourth lost his head or his temper; and you wouldn't want that. So you mustn't breathe a word about this, Sue; not to the police, not to anyone. You appreciate that, don't you? Not to *anyone*.'

She did not answer. The frightened, troubled look was back. And suddenly, looking at her, Forthright began to sweat. He said, trying to sound casual, 'Of course, you haven't told anyone yet, have you?'

'Yes,' she said. 'I told George Loften.'

There was a stunned silence.

'Loften!' exclaimed Wickery. 'Heaven help us!'

'You — you — ' Chitty's face was purple with rage. Forthright saw his arm come up, and moved to protect the girl. But the arm dropped. Spluttering and swearing, Chitty subsided into impotent, silent fury.

Susan did not appreciate fully the harm she had done. Although her brother had never yet harmed her physically, alone with him she might not have ventured to speak in defence of herself. But the presence of the others gave her momentary courage.

'Why shouldn't I tell him?' she asked. 'We're friends, aren't we? He met me when I ran away from the cottage. I was frightened to death of what I knew you were planning to do, and when he asked me what was wrong I just told him. I couldn't help myself. I had to tell *someone* — and he happened to be there, and he said he wanted to help me, and — and — well, who else was there to tell?' She spoke quickly, the words tumbling after each other as though she feared that were she to stop she might never get them out. 'You've no right to accuse me, I haven't done anything wrong. I was only trying to help, to stop you from doing such a wicked thing. And then — then you killed him,' she cried hysterically. 'Why — you're murderers!'

She uttered the final accusation in surprise, as though realizing for the first time the enormity of their crime.

'We're not murderers, and we're not accusing you,' said Forthright. 'What did you tell Loften?'

'What I heard you say. That you were going to break into the garage and rob Mr White.'

'Did you tell him about Mrs Gooch?'

She nodded. Now that she had had her say her body felt limp, drained of all energy. She slumped against the wall, crying quietly.

The men ignored her. They had known themselves to be in great danger, but they had never contemplated the possibility of anything like this.

'Loften!' said Wickery again. 'Of all people she had to tell Loften!'

'Why hasn't he said anything?' asked Wells, perplexed.

'I don't know,' said Forthright. 'But we'll soon find out. Here he comes now.'

Loften stopped the car in the yard and walked towards the garage. The men waited for him, watching him, half expecting that, with their new knowledge of his power over them, they would see some difference in him. Susan Chitty alone took no interest in his approach. She was still leaning against the wall, her face buried in her hands.

As Loften entered the garage his footsteps slowed. The grim, expectant faces of the four men, the presence of Susan, must have warned him that the secret was out. But he gave no sign. 'No work to do?' he asked, not unpleasantly.

'What's Susan doing here?'

It was Forthright who answered for them.

'She's just told us you know about us,' he said quietly. 'We want to know where we stand, Mr Loften.'

Loften frowned. 'So that's it, eh? Well, you had to know sooner or later, I suppose, although I'd hoped to straighten it out in my own mind first. Quite a problem, isn't it? One can't just ignore murder.'

'But we didn't aim to murder him,' Wells said eagerly, his wizened face even more lined than usual. 'Susan told you that.'

'Maybe. But he's dead, isn't he?'

There was no real answer to that. Wickery cleared his throat. But his voice was still hoarse as he said, 'But what are you going to do, Mr Loften? You can't leave us in the dark.'

'Can't I? It seems to me, Bert, that you fellows have got the wrong idea about this. I don't owe you anything. Damn it, man, you're still at liberty, aren't you? Doesn't that tell you I've said nothing to the police as yet?'

That 'yet' silenced them for a moment. It had been spoken quietly enough; but such was its potential for danger that it seemed to grow in volume, echoing round the stone walls of the garage until it filled their ears and minds, drowning the other words Loften had spoken.

'Why haven't you?' asked Forthright. He felt he had to say something. Anything to banish the sound of that 'yet.'

'I don't know. Maybe because Susan's a friend of mine and I feel I've let her down; my promised help turned out to be rather a flop. Maybe because you're not bad chaps, really; I gather White treated you pretty shabbily, more or less drove you to it. Maybe because I didn't think much of White myself, or maybe because I can't afford to lose all my mechanics at one go. I could give you dozens of reasons — but none of them means much. Not when you compare them with murder.'

'But that's just what it wasn't — murder, I mean,' Wells put in eagerly. 'It was an accident, Mr Loften, honest it was. You know us — you know we wouldn't do a thing like that.'

'Murder or manslaughter, it's still a pretty nasty crime,' Loften said. 'With Mrs Gooch, that makes two deaths chalked up to you fellows.'

Wickery thought the conversation was developing along the wrong lines. 'We're grateful to you for giving us a chance,' he said, 'but what happens next?'

'God knows! I wish to blazes Susan hadn't dragged me into this. Why the hell should *I* have to decide what's to become of you?' He kicked irritably at a nut, sending it skidding and rolling across the garage floor. 'Well, I'd better hear what you have to say, I suppose. I'll come round to your place this evening, Harry, and we'll talk it over. But get this clear — I'm not making any promises, mind. Dave, you'd better run your sister home in my car. The rest of you might do a little work for a change.'

But their minds were too full of the horror of their position to deal adequately with work. The mere mechanical acts of tightening a nut, changing a wheel, cleaning a sparking-plug — these were possible; but with anything requiring precision, patience, or skill they found themselves repeatedly at fault. After a while they gave up trying. When Loften was about they went through the motions of the work, making a pretence of being absorbed in their job; but when he was in the office or engaged elsewhere they abandoned their pretence and gave themselves up to speculation on the future.

'We're worse off now than when White was alive,' said Wickery. 'At least he couldn't have had us hanged for murder.'

'You should grumble! Getting our own back on White was your bright idea,' Chitty reminded him. He was as morose and irritable as before, but some of the fire had gone out of him. The magnitude of their present predicament seemed partially to have stunned him. 'Any ideas for dealing with this little lot?'

Wickery kept a tight hold on his temper. A row with Dave might relieve his feelings, but it wouldn't improve their position. 'Don't let's start on that lark again,' he said evenly. 'If you hadn't got drunk and half strangled me when I was driving — if Harry hadn't persuaded us not to report the accident — there's just no end to it. The question is, what do we do about Loften? He's the menace now.'

'Get rid of him,' Chitty suggested. 'What's one more murder among friends?'

The others looked at him askance, uncertain whether he was serious or not. Wells decided that he might be.

'That's a damn' fool thing to say, Dave. Loften's done us no harm. We don't want any more talk of murder — there's been enough of that already.'

'I don't trust him,' Chitty retorted. 'He'll cause trouble, you wait and see.'

'Loften's not the only menace,' said Wickery. 'There's Susan. Are you proposing to do away with her as well?'

Chitty scowled, but said nothing. Loften had come out of the office and was watching them. Perhaps he guessed that they were discussing him, for during the rest of the day he was in the garage more than usual.

Just before they knocked off Willie

Trape rode up on his bicycle. He nodded cheerfully to Wickery, who was working on a customer's car in front of the garage.

'Where's Pop?' he asked.

Wickery jerked his thumb towards the back of the garage. 'In the workshop,' he said.

Both Wells and Forthright were momentarily disturbed by the sight of the police uniform. Then they saw Willie's beaming face and relaxed.

The constable had not come on business. 'Sorry about tonight, Pop,' he said. 'I shan't be able to make it.'

Wells looked at him in bewilderment. Then he remembered that Willie had been due to come round to his house that evening for a game of chess. They were neither of them good players, but they enjoyed a game.

'A pity,' he said. 'We'll fix another evening later.'

'What's the matter? Are they working you too hard?' asked Forthright.

'Not exactly. But you remember that accident on the Tanbury road, when old Mrs Gooch was killed?'

Forthright swallowed. 'Yes,' he said.

'Well, it seems like they're raking that up again. Of course, they never did catch the fellow that done it; but it's over a year since it happened, so what chance have they got now?' He sighed. 'Still, if they want a further report, a further report they'll have to have.'

'Didn't you make one out at the time?'

'Yes. But it seems — ' The constable broke off and smiled deprecatingly. 'Sorry, Harry, but this is something I'm supposed to keep under my hat. Official business, understand?'

'That's all right, mate,' Forthright hastened to assure him. 'Nothing to do with us.'

Wells added agreement. But I wish to God, he thought, now thoroughly alarmed, that it *wasn't* anything to do with us!

# 8

## Unknown Witness

Loften was punctual. There was a slight smile on his face as he entered the living-room and saw the four men awaiting him. Forthright wondered if it was the smile of the tiger; or perhaps he was contrasting his own appearance, immaculate as always, with theirs. None of them had slept much the previous night, and their haggard, harassed countenances showed that the strain was beginning to tell. Only Forthright had shaved; his was the only pair of eyes that met the newcomer's squarely.

'Well — where do we start?' Loften asked pleasantly, with none of the irritability he had shown that afternoon. Wells felt relieved. It was going to be all right, he thought. 'It's you fellows who have to do the talking. I'm here to listen.'

'I don't know as there's much for us to

say,' answered Forthright. 'You know what we planned to do, and how it turned out. We're in your hands, and that's about all there is to it.'

'I still can't understand why you had to kill White,' said Loften. 'At least, I can see that you're better off without him; but it seems such a monumental risk to take. Leaving out all question of right and wrong, it just doesn't seem worth it.'

'But we keep telling you, Mr Loften — we don't understand it ourselves,' Forthright said earnestly. 'We don't know how it happened or who killed him. That's the devil of it.'

Loften looked his astonishment. 'Come now, Harry — you can't expect me to believe that. You were all in it together, weren't you?'

Forthright hesitated. Was it wise, he wondered, to let Loften have all the details? So far, if he chose to turn against them and inform the police, it was his word against theirs — provided, of course, that Susan could be persuaded to keep her mouth shut.

'Only one of us was actually in White's

room,' he said slowly. 'And the way we fixed it we don't know which one of us it was. Susan told you we didn't plan to kill White, so you can guess it hit us pretty hard when we heard next morning that he was dead. You see, even if we wanted to we couldn't split on the fellow that did it. That's why we've had to back each other up and hope that the police can't pin it on us. If they do we're all for the high jump; all of us, not just one.'

Loften appeared to think this over. 'How did you work it?' he asked.

It was not a casual question — there was genuine interest behind it. But Forthright was still wary.

'I'm sorry, Mr Loften, but that's something we'd rather keep to ourselves. For the present, anyway.'

'You mean — until you know whose side I'm on, eh?'

'Yes.'

Loften shrugged. 'Please yourselves. Only don't misunderstand me if I say it sounds phoney.'

The others had so far taken no part in the conversation. It had been agreed beforehand that Forthright should act as their spokesman. But Wickery, now more at ease and impatient at so much verbal fencing, decided to ask a question that had been puzzling him.

'If you knew what we were up to, Mr Loften, why didn't you try to stop us?'

'I did.' The smile returned as he noted their astonishment. 'Not successfully, I admit; but I tried. I was handicapped, though; I couldn't speak to you openly without involving Susan — which I'd promised not to do. What's more, I didn't know all the details of your plan. I knew it was fixed for some time Tuesday night, but that was about all. For some reason or other I made up my mind you'd try to break in at the back — crooks usually do, I believe.'

Chitty scowled. He didn't relish being called a crook, particularly by Loften. He muttered a few blasphemous oaths to relieve his feelings, but softly, so that Loften should not hear.

But Loften heard the sound of his voice and paused. 'Yes?' he inquired politely.

'Nothing,' said Chitty.

213

'You didn't say anything to White?' asked Wells hastily. He sat next to Chitty.

'No. I thought I'd catch you red-handed, so to speak. But it didn't come off.'

'You mean — you were actually there Tuesday night?' asked Wickery.

'I was. I hung around near the eastern end of the garage, at the back, from ten-thirty to twelve-fifteen; and perishing cold and tired I was, too, by the end of it.'

'And you didn't see us?'

'No. If I had I'd have stopped you. That's what I was there for. But I never heard a sound.'

The men looked at each other. It seemed impossible that Loften had not seen at least some of them, or at any rate heard them. True, it was a dark night, and he had stood at the far end of the garage; but even so . . .

As if reading their thoughts he said, 'I did think I saw a light in the woods at one time. But it disappeared almost immediately, and I wasn't keen to go haring off into the dark. Thought I might miss you. I suppose that was you?'

214

'Probably,' said Forthright, still being cautious.

'I couldn't see anything out of order when I had a final look round,' said Loften. 'How the devil did you get in?'

Was it possible, wondered Forthright, that Loften had not seen through their trick to get hold of the key? 'We'll leave that for the moment, if you don't mind,' he said.

'As you wish.' But it was not, thought Wickery, as Loften wished. No doubt he had expected a complete surrender. This attempt by Forthright to withhold essential details, to retain some fragments of the shield with which they had hoped to protect themselves (and which Susan had so rudely shattered), obviously riled him; not, Wickery suspected, because of his interest in the details themselves, but because it lessened his hold on them.

And suddenly Wickery realized, with a feeling of dismay, that what Loften wanted was power — the thrill of having the four of them completely under his thumb. That was why he had not given them away to the police, why he might never do so. Despite his affability, his apparent willingness to hear their side of the affair, they had given him a big stick, and he intended to use it. Only when necessary, of course, only when they didn't dance to his tune. But what sort of a tune was he going to play? Loften, thought Wickery, could be as dangerous as White. He hadn't got White's biting, vicious tongue, perhaps, or his brutality; but he was probably just as cunning and just as ruthless.

'I decided Susan must have got the day wrong,' Loften was saying, once more urbane. 'Either that, or you'd abandoned the idea.' He took a cigarette and lit it, flicked the still burning match into the grate, inhaled deeply, and added through a haze of smoke, 'Until White was found murdered, that is. That shook me, I can tell you.'

He did not look at all shaken at that moment. Because a smile would have been out of place, he surveyed them gravely, trying to impress them once more with the immensity of their crime and his own dilemma; but Wickery, with his new-found intuition, knew that he was thoroughly enjoying himself.

Chitty said suddenly — but slowly, as though he was trying at the same time to appreciate fully the import of his words — 'So Susan was lying when she told the Inspector you'd been with her all the evening? You lied too, didn't you? You weren't at our place, you were hanging around the garage.'

Loften flushed angrily, shaken out of his complacence.

'Of course we were lying — you damned well forced us to. If I'd told the police I was at the garage they'd have wanted to know why, wouldn't they? That would have cooked your goose properly, my lad — even Susan hadn't the heart to do that, and she's as truthful a person as any I know.'

'It wouldn't have done *you* a lot of good, either,' said Forthright. He was beginning to feel easier.

'Why not? If you're suggesting the police might have suspected me of the murder you're forgetting I hadn't a motive. There was no Mrs Gooch in my case, and no blackmail.' He leaned forward, impatiently stubbing his cigarette into a metal ash-tray. 'I'm damned if I know why I should submit to all this questioning. It's you fellows who have to account for yourselves, not me.'

Forthright got up lazily and went to the cupboard, from which he produced a quart bottle of beer. Wells noticed with surprise that there were other bottles in the cupboard. How does Harry manage it? he wondered. Damned if *I* can afford to keep beer in the house.

There was a slight *plop* as the top was unscrewed. A wisp of smoke curled lazily from the mouth of the bottle. 'Beer, Mr Loften?' asked Forthright, as the golden liquid gurgled into a tilted glass.

'No.' Loften was annoyed. He lit another cigarette — hurriedly, as though he needed it to steady his nerves. Forthright passed the full glass to Wells and picked up another. 'I didn't come here for a booze-up. And it seems to me that you chaps are taking this a damned sight too calmly. Well, you're not out of the wood yet, not by any means. I tell you frankly, if I hadn't given my word to Susan you'd all have been in the can by now.'

'If you'll forgive my saying so, Mr Loften, somehow I can't believe all that blah about Susan,' Forthright said, handing Wickery his beer. 'What was the real reason for keeping your mouth shut?'

Loften pushed his chair back and stood up, banging his fist on the table so that the glasses rattled and beer slopped on to the table.

'You keep a civil tongue in your head, Forthright, or we'll close this meeting here and now,' he shouted furiously. 'I didn't come here to be insulted.'

Wells looked anxiously at the two men. They had agreed to let Harry run their party, but wasn't he carrying things a bit far? Loften still had the whip-hand; if Harry got him properly rattled he might use it. Unconsciously he ran a finger round the inside of his collar. Chitty noticed the gesture and shuddered. It seemed to him symbolic, so that his own collar was suddenly tight and had in imagination already become a hempen rope.

He gulped down a mouthful of beer. The gas rose up and choked him, and he belched noisily.

'I don't think Harry meant to be rude, Mr Loften,' he said awkwardly. Apologies didn't come easily to Chitty, and he hated Loften for his association with Susan and his new power over them. But he hated still more the feel of that rope. 'We all know you're trying to help us, but I think — '

Wickery gripped his arm. 'We're not interested in what you think. Let Harry speak for himself.'

Chitty shook his arm free with an oath. 'I've a right to say what I think, haven't I?'

Loften looked pleased. This was better. Once they fell out among themselves they'd be easier to handle. He sat down and almost beamed at them.

But Forthright wasn't finished yet. 'Just a minute, Dave,' he said, and turned to Loften. 'If you put us in the dock, Mr Loften, we'll see that you're called as a witness for the defence. How would you like that?'

Only Wickery guessed what he was at. Loften was as bemused as the others.

'What the devil are you talking about, man? Me a witness for the defence?'

'Why not? You've just told us you were at the garage Tuesday night, that so far as you know we didn't go near the place. What better defence could we have?'

Loften digested this in silence. He leaned back in his chair and looked from one to the other of the four men. The wooden chair tilted dangerously, balanced on its back legs as he thrust out his legs and stuck his hands into his trouser-pockets.

I wish he'd fall and break his blasted neck, thought Wickery.

'You want to think it out a bit more carefully, Harry.' Loften's tone was genial. 'My evidence wouldn't help you much after Susan had had her say; she lied to the police, but she wouldn't lie on oath. Don't make any mistake about *that*. I'd certainly admit that I didn't see you; but the fact that I went up to the garage expressly to stop you from breaking in would just about dish you, I imagine. Particularly as I'd also have to admit that I was only watching the rear, not the front.'

Harry's trump card doesn't seem to have got us anywhere, Wickery thought dismally. He decided it was time he took a hand.

'You wouldn't look too good yourself,' he suggested, falling back on the line of thought that had prompted him to plan the downfall of Andrew White. 'You knew a week in advance what we were planning to do, but you didn't say a word either to White or to the police. And it's two whole days now since White was killed. The police are going to ask you a lot of awkward questions, aren't they, if you start blabbing now?'

Loften took his hands from his pockets, drew up his legs, and leaned forward with a business-like air.

'It'd be damned tricky,' he agreed frankly. 'I'd look a ruddy fool, if no worse. Mind you, I wouldn't let that stop me if I thought I'd be right to speak out, but I admit that's one reason why I'm inclined to take a lenient view of what you've done. I know White was being bloody-minded, and I'm willing to take your word that his death was some sort of an accident. So if you chaps are prepared to be reasonable I'll do what I can to help you.'

They felt mentally dazed. It had come so suddenly, so unexpectedly, that they could not quite believe it. Forthright took a long pull at his beer; Chitty leaned forward for the bottle and helped himself. Wells, unable to keep the relief out of his voice, and speaking solely because he felt somebody ought to say something, said, 'What happens if the police arrest us? How do we stand with you then?'

'Call me as a witness for the defence, as Harry suggested,' Loften said with a smile. 'Let's hope it doesn't come to that, however.'

Wickery, naturally more suspicious than the others, was puzzled. What exactly had been the point of their discussion? They had told Loften little that he did not already know or could not have guessed, nothing had been said that could have helped him to make up his mind. Did that mean he had decided on his course of action even before discussing it with them? But, then, why get them together, why all the argument?

Something that Loften had just said gave him the clue.

'What did you mean by saying 'if we are prepared to be reasonable'?' he asked evenly.

Loften turned to face him. The smile was still there.

'Well — ' he said, and paused. He picked up a dead match from the ash-tray and began to twirl it between finger and thumb. 'Maybe you chaps don't know this, but my share in the business is small. I'm not a rich man — far from it, unfortunately. Things were looking up, however, until you took a hand. I don't know what happens now, but I'm damned certain you've done me a power of no good. I've seen White's solicitor, and he says that so far he has found no trace of a will; if there isn't one the garage may have to be sold. If I had the money to buy it I would — to my mind it's a damn' good proposition. But as things are . . . ' He sighed. 'Well, you've done me out of a living, I shouldn't wonder.'

'How are we supposed to be reasonable?' Wickery persisted.

'If I'm to stick out my neck to save yours I'm not doing it for nothing,' said Loften. 'It wouldn't make sense, would it? Not after you've done your damnedest to ruin me.'

Forthright took a deep breath. 'So that's it,' he said. 'Blackmail, eh? Another White.'

'Not blackmail, Harry.' Loften looked hurt at the accusation, vaguely surprised that such a thought could have entered the other's head. 'Just a little monetary appreciation of what I'm doing for you.'

'Appreciation my foot!' Chitty stood up. 'Why, you dirty — '

'Just a moment, Dave.' Wells turned to Loften. 'How much?'

'Well, the money you pinched from the garage was partly mine, so I imagine I'm entitled to at least half of it. Suppose you hand that over for a start?' He turned to

Wickery. 'If your wife is the sole relative, Bert, she may inherit. In that case you might care to increase my share in the business; it'd be a gesture, don't you think? Or you might care to sell out on somewhat advantageous terms — advantageous to me, of course. As I told you, I'm short on capital. However, that must wait — but I could do with a hundred or two right now.'

They were all on their feet now. They stood close to the table, a mixture of emotions depicted on their faces. Chitty's was the most expressive; anger, fear, frustration — they were all there. And, looking at those four menacing figures, Loften's smile became a little forced. His mouth twitched nervously.

'Rough stuff won't help you,' he said, his eyes fixed on Chitty's large hands now curled into fists. 'Knowing the type of men I was dealing with, I've taken the necessary precautions. My solicitor has a sealed letter containing all the details. If anything happens to me that goes to the police.'

If violence had been in their minds that

stopped them — all, strangely enough, except Forthright. It seemed that his self-control, so patiently exercised until now, had at last been exhausted. Pushing Wells aside, he walked slowly round the table, his grim face contorted with rage. Loften got up quickly, placing the chair between them.

'I warn you, Forthright, you'd better not start anything.' His voice was pitched a little higher, but it was still under control. 'You'll hang if you do, all of you. I'll see to that.'

Wells and Wickery came quickly to his aid. They knew Harry, knew that there wouldn't be much left of Loften once Harry started on him. And although the sight of a well-battered Loften might afford them some satisfaction, it would be very short-lived. Loften, as he had threatened, would see to that.

But Forthright did not move, made no effort to free himself of their detaining hands. He just stood there, his face a mask of hate. To Wells, fearful of what might happen if he went berserk (for Chitty, he knew, would aid him), the moments passed like hours.

Slowly their captive relaxed.

'All right,' he said hoarsely. 'All right, I won't touch him.'

The hate left his eyes; his face was without expression. He walked back to where his beer stood on the table and drank deep. Wiping his mouth with the back of his hand, he said, 'You won't get any money out of us, Loften. We don't know where it is or who has it.'

Loften's face darkened. It may have been due to the dropping of the 'Mister' or to the refusal of the money.

'That could be as unfortunate for you as it is for me,' he said.

Forthright shrugged his shoulders, indicating that he washed his hands of the matter. Wells hastened to explain about the money.

'Too bad,' said Loften. 'Well, if you can't persuade the thief to disburse you'll have to fork out some other way. We could try White's method, for instance.'

He had by now dropped all pretence, he was just a blackmailer seeking to make what he could out of their critical position. 'I need money, and you chaps are going to provide it — or else.'

'You've got a big mouth, you swine,' said Chitty. 'Don't open it much more or one of us is going to close it for you good and proper.' He stretched a brawny arm across the table and slowly clenched his fist. 'See what I mean? We've done one murder and we may as well make it two.'

But Loften was not intimidated; he knew that the moment of violence, if there had been such a moment, was past. Words could not harm him; they were welcome to their words.

He shrugged his shoulders and casually lit another cigarette.

Wells wanted to get the conversation on to less explosive lines. 'Maybe it's fair you should get something for helping us,' he said. 'But we're broke, and that's that. You can't get blood out of a stone.'

'If you *are* helping us,' Forthright added. 'It's my belief you're running with the hare and hunting with the hounds. Why else should the police be raking up the accident to Mrs Gooch?'

'Who says they are?'

'Willie Trape. And you're the only one, outside of us, who could have told them.'

Loften looked surprised. 'They didn't get the idea from me,' he said. 'And I'm not the only person who knows, either. There's Susan.'

'Leave my sister out of this,' Chitty said roughly. 'If she didn't tell them about White she certainly wouldn't let on about Mrs Gooch.'

'Please yourself,' said Loften. 'There's no one else.'

'That's where you're wrong,' said Wickery. 'There *is* someone else.'

At first he had not listened to their talk. He had been thinking of Doris, of what she would do if she were to inherit her uncle's share in the garage. But mention of Mrs Gooch had returned his thoughts to the evening it had all begun, and in a moment of clarity (and there had been few such moments since) he had realized something which had hitherto occurred to none of them.

They looked at him in surprise tinged with suspicion. Had Bert gone nuts? There *couldn't* be anyone else. Only

White — and he was in no position to talk.

'I don't get it,' said Loften, as puzzled as the others. 'Who?'

'We were mugs not to think of it before,' said Wickery, shaking his head. 'Or maybe we had so much on our plates we just couldn't cope with any more. But what was White doing, parked in a car at that time of night?'

'We've been into that before.' Forthright sounded impatient. 'He was with a woman.'

'That's right — he was with a woman.' Wickery's voice came alive. 'But what woman? That's the point, you see. Because, whoever she was, she must have had just as good a view of what happened as White did. *She* knows we killed Mrs Gooch.'

They had not switched on the radio that evening; Forthright had explained to his mother that Loften was coming, that they had important matters to discuss concerning their future at the garage. Only the ticking of the clock on the mantelpiece disturbed the sudden silence that now fell on the room. Their minds, attuned as they were to disaster, seemed unable to cope with this further shock, this spectre that Wickery had conjured out of the past to mock their futile efforts to evade the consequences of their crime. They were as statues, gazing blankly at Wickery. A cigarette drooped from between Chitty's lips, his hand arrested in mid-air on its way to remove it; Wells sat with his hands on his knees, elbows out, his wizened face puckered into still more lines; Forthright's hand rested at the back of his head, which he had been scratching in bewilderment at Wickery's assertion that there had been another witness to the accident. Even Loften seemed disconcerted. His lower jaw had dropped slightly, his eyes were fixed intently on Wickery.

Wells was the first to speak; not an intelligible statement, merely a string of oaths. But it brought the statues to life.

They had dealt with White, and no doubt they would find a way of dealing with Loften; and Susan did not constitute a serious threat. She was Dave's sister;

she would not give them away. But this unknown woman whom Bert had so suddenly resurrected — they could not deal with her. She took no form in their mind's eye, they could not point a finger or utter a name, saying 'it is this woman' or 'that'; and because she was so utterly and completely intangible, the menace of her existence was the greater.

'It might be anyone,' muttered Forth-right. 'Anyone. We could pass her in the street and not know her. It's . . . it's . . . '

For once words failed him.

Chitty said nothing. He looked baffled and bewildered. He could not relieve his feelings in anger, for there was no one on whom to vent it. And anger was Chitty's safety-valve.

'Yes, that's quite a thought,' said Loften. 'I'm surprised none of you got around to it before, seeing you've had over a year to chew on it. It didn't occur to me, of course, because I've only been in the know for a week.' He lit a final cigarette. Wells fancied he expected them to say something, but no one did. After a moment or two Loften stood up, pushing his chair under the table. 'Well, I'll leave you to deal with it; it's your worry, not mine. Only don't forget that this woman is only a witness to Mrs Gooch's death — not to White's. If she exists at all, that is. And White's death is your biggest worry, I imagine.' He paused, then picked up his hat and coat and walked to the door before continuing. 'Don't let it slip your minds that I'm expecting something on account — and that I'm not prepared to wait indefinitely.' Again he paused, and again no one spoke or even looked in his direction. 'Well, good night,' he said, rather more subdued. 'See you in the morning.'

When the door had closed behind him Forthright got up and opened a window. 'We can do with a little fresh air,' he said. 'The room stinks.'

'We always said he was a mean devil,' said Wickery. 'Well, now we know just how mean he can be.'

'We can deal with Loften,' Forthright said. 'It's this woman of yours that's the real menace now. If she's told the police about Mrs Gooch it'll be because she knows White was blackmailing us. She'd have told them before, else. And with a cast-iron motive like that they'll chivvy us around until they get us.'

'Maybe White paid her to keep her mouth shut,' said Wells.

Chitty was more interested in Forthright's first statement. 'How do you reckon we can deal with Loften?' he asked.

'Not the way you think.' Forthright was curt, suddenly remembering how he had allowed his temper to get the better of him during his verbal duel with Loften. That annoyed him. It was one thing to tell a man what he thought of him, to curse him, even to hint at reprisals; but to offer physical violence and then not go through with it was a betrayal of his own manhood. 'String him along for a bit, and in a week or two he damned well dare not go to the police.'

'H'm. I'd feel safer if he was out of the way.'

'That's what you said about White.' Wickery's tone was bitter. 'And look where we are now. Harry's right. If we can keep Loften away from the police long enough we're safe. As far as he's concerned, anyway. But can we? I doubt it.'

He had already discarded his belief that Loften only wanted power.

'So do I,' Wells agreed. 'He's a greedy devil, and he wants that money. If he don't get it I reckon he'll turn nasty.'

Wickery nodded. 'He's no fool; he knows it's now or never. And he probably thinks we're bluffing about not knowing who's got the money.'

'Well, he won't get it by going to the police,' said Forthright.

'No. But you heard what he said about White not having made a will and Doris being his only relative.' Wickery spoke softly, almost apologetically. It was a possibility he did not wish to publicize. 'Well, I don't know much about the law, but I shouldn't think Doris would ever get the money if it was proved we killed him. That might mean Loften would be able to buy the place dirt cheap. I don't know, of course; but he might. And in that case it'd pay him to get us out of the way. Particularly if he thinks we're not going to hand over the money.'

'Yes, there's something in that,' Forthright agreed.

'And even if he doesn't expect to make a bean out of it he's a big enough swine to shop us just for the hell of it,' Wickery continued. 'You can tell that from the way he carried on tonight.'

'What happens if the police arrest just one of us?' asked Wells, following his own train of thought.

'They wouldn't do that. It'll be all or none.'

'But they might,' the little man persisted. 'They might hope he'd split on the others.'

'He'd be a damned fool if he did,' said Forthright. 'That'd be signing his own death-warrant. He'd just have to sit tight and say nothing until we got a lawyer to act for him.'

'About Loften,' said Wickery, impatient at this deviation. 'It seems to me it's up to the chap that took the money to hand it over to him. That'll keep Loften quiet long enough to make it dangerous for him to talk.'

'He could still double-cross us,' Wells said. 'Keep most of it, perhaps, and hand over the rest to the police, saying we was trying to bribe him. That'd be a bit more evidence against us, wouldn't it?'

'It could be,' Forthright said thoughtfully. 'But it could be evidence against him, too.'

'Against Loften? They're not after him, are they?'

'Not yet.' Forthright did not wish to pursue that train of thought; it needed more careful consideration. 'Anyway, how could a chap hand the money over to Loften without giving himself away?'

'He could leave it in the office when no one was around, or shove it through the letter-box at Loften's house,' Wickery suggested. 'There's lots of ways.'

'Let's hope he does, then,' said Wells. 'I'd like to think we hadn't got that devil chasing us. But about this woman, Bert? What the hell can we do about her?'

'Damn all,' Forthright said briefly. 'We haven't a clue.'

'Haven't we? I'm not so sure.' Wickery looked at Wells. 'Molly's been out in White's car, hasn't she?'

Anger blazed instantly in the little man's eyes.

'Damn you, Bert, you've no call to say a thing like that. Molly wasn't one of White's fancy pieces, and you know it. All she did was to accept a lift once or twice.'

Chitty came to his support. 'You leave Molly out of this, Bert Wickcry. She wasn't ever in White's car except as Pop said — and that was only after me and her had quarrelled. A year ago she'd hardly spoken to him.'

'Are you sure?' Forthright asked dubiously. 'I remember Pop saying — '

'I don't care what Pop said; I tell you straight, Molly never went with White until we quarrelled. And that was months after the old woman was killed.'

'You'd say that, of course,' said Wickery. 'You and Pop are bound to stick up for her. But there's no proof — '

'We don't need proof, blast you!' Wells might occasionally speak disparagingly of his daughter, but he would allow no one else to do so. 'Molly isn't that kind of girl, and I won't have you or anyone else saying she is. Maybe she acts a bit silly at times, like all young things. But that don't mean she's bad, like you're trying to make out.'

'I'm not trying to make out anything of the sort. I'm only saying that — '

'Molly was out that night,' Forthright interrupted. 'I remember now — Dave said he'd called to tell her about the job, and she was out. Know where she went, Pop?'

'How the hell *should* I know? And even if I did, I wouldn't remember it now. That was over a year ago.'

'But it was a rather special evening,' Wickery pointed out. 'Me, I can't forget a single damned minute of it. I only wish I could.'

'That's different. That part of it has nothing to do with Molly,' Chitty said angrily. 'Shut up about her, damn you, or I'll knock your block off.'

'You could ask her, Pop,' Forthright persisted, ignoring Chitty's outburst. 'It wouldn't do any harm. And it seems a bit odd to me that Molly should have gone out that evening. She must have known Dave would want to tell her about the job he'd been after.'

That jolted Wells. Even he could appreciate the force of Harry's argument. But he would not allow them to see that his loyalty was shaken.

'Nonsense,' he blustered. 'Damned nonsense! And anyway, how do you expect the girl to remember? It wasn't a special evening for Molly, like it was for us.'

Forthright looked at him thoughtfully.

'It could have been,' he said. 'See what I mean? I think you'd better ask her, Pop.'

# 9

## Design for a Scapegoat

None of the men bothered to be punctual at the garage the next morning; had they had something better to do, or had they not felt that it was at the garage that either their hopes or their fears would be confirmed, they might have stayed away altogether. It would have shown Loften better than any words could do what they thought of him, and after coping for a day on his own he might not be so eager to hand them over to the police. Even the fact that it was pay-day made little or no difference: if Loften was out to soak them he wouldn't be paying any wages — there would be no money for them *that* week.

But the garage drew them, and they came, however reluctantly.

Wickery had had a bad night. The tension between himself and Doris was increasing; if she spoke to him at all it was

242

only on trivial everyday matters, and neither White's murder nor the activities of the police were ever mentioned. Although Wickery was glad to be free of that topic, it frightened him to see how rapidly the rift between them was growing. He had always relied on Doris's moral strength, her calm assurance when faced with the many little difficulties that had beset them in the past. Now, in this major crisis, he needed it more than ever.

Not until dawn was breaking had his tormented brain allowed him to sleep. It had seemed to Wickery then that he had not slept for weeks, and his last conscious act before dozing off had been to push down the little plunger on top of the alarm-clock by his bedside. To hell with Loften! he thought bitterly. I'll have a bit of a lie-in if I can. I'm not getting up early for *him*.

Forthright too had slept little. But the habit of years had awakened him at the usual hour, and he had got up reluctantly. Loften or no Loften, there was his mother's breakfast to prepare.

When he took it up to her she watched

him anxiously as he busied himself with the tray and the bed-table. There were dark circles under his eyes, and his face was drawn and grey.

'You look tired, Harry. You've been working too hard and keeping too many late nights. It's a holiday you're needing, boy.' The many lines on her forehead grew closer together. 'You wouldn't be worrying about this murder, would you?'

'No, Ma. I'm all right.'

'The police haven't been bothering you?'

'No. They're not interested in me. Don't fret yourself so.'

Downstairs again, he wandered aimlessly about the house. But he did not want to be there when the woman came, and presently he put on his coat and went out.

He went by the road, and not by the track through the woods. He had taken a dislike to the track. As he neared the garage Bert Wickery crossed the road from the fields.

'Something's up,' said Wickery. 'There's quite a crowd there.'

They quickened their steps. From the lean-to beside the garage most of the cars had been moved into the yard, and beneath it workmen were busy with pick and shovel. A pile of rubble showed that they had been busy for some time.

Wells saw them and came to meet them. He seemed agitated.

'Where the hell have you been?' he demanded of Forthright. 'I was scared stiff thinking you wouldn't get here in time.'

'In time for what? What's going on here?'

'They're opening up the old drain, the one you dropped the key into.'

'Hell's bells!' said Wickery, aghast. 'Who told them about that?'

'Loften, I suppose. He's there with the Inspector.'

Wickery hurried across to the pile of rubble. Loften saw him and nodded, frowning. But there was no opportunity for private talk; apart from the Inspector there were other policemen about. Wickery stood beside Chitty, and in silence the two watched the pile of rubble grow.

'How deep is it?' Forthright asked Wells. He seemed reluctant to approach nearer to the scene of operations.

'I don't know. It doesn't signify, anyway. They'll go on digging until they find it.' Wells looked up at him, fear writ large on his brown wizened face. 'What'll we do, Harry? This'll sink us.'

'It may not,' Forthright said thoughtfully, trying to calm the other's agitation. They ought to look at ease, no matter what their feelings; one or other of the police might be watching them. 'It may not, Pop. In fact, now I come to think of it I'm not sure we can't make a good thing out of this. Let's go into the garage; I want to talk to you.'

They were standing by a car, apparently working, when Loften came after them. As soon as they saw him they bent over the engine.

But Loften was not deceived. 'You chaps turn up at any old hour of the morning and then stand about gassing,' he said crossly. 'It's time someone did some work in this place.'

'What's going on out there?' asked

Forthright, disregarding this outburst.

'They're digging up the drain. The Inspector wants to have a look at that key you lost.'

'Who told him about the key?'

'I did, of course. He asked me if I had one, and I told him what had happened to it.' Loften lowered his voice as he asked, 'Why the interest? Anything wrong?'

His annoyance seemed to have left him. Forthright wondered if it had been assumed for the benefit of possible listeners outside.

'If they're looking for the key it means they think there was something fishy about my losing it,' he answered. 'I hope they find it. That'll teach 'em not to be so ruddy suspicious.'

'Oh.' Loften was taken aback. 'Well, I'm with you there. The Inspector didn't call me a liar straight out, but he couldn't have looked more disbelieving.'

'Getting worried?' Forthright's tone was deliberately insolent. He wanted to rile Loften. An angry man would be less likely to think carefully before he spoke.

The trick worked. An angry flush spread over the other's pale face.

'You chaps are a damned sight too uppish for my liking; it's time you learned on which side your bread is buttered if you want to keep yourselves all in one piece. I've a good mind — '

He broke off abruptly. Inspector Pitt was at the door of the garage, apparently fiddling with the lock. Presently he walked across to them, followed by another detective. Wickery and Chitty hovered in the entrance.

The Inspector held out his hand, palm uppermost. 'Is this your key, Mr Loften? No — don't touch it, please.'

Loften peered at it. 'I suppose it is. But one Yale looks very much like another, doesn't it?'

'How about you, Mr Forthright? Would you say that is the key you dropped down the drain last week?'

'Goodness knows, Inspector. But if that's where you found it it must be, mustn't it?' Forthright's tone was casual, almost disinterested. 'Not likely to be a whole collection down there, is there?

Why not try it in the lock? That'll settle the matter.'

'I've already tried it,' said the Inspector. 'It settles nothing — except that it doesn't fit.'

'Oh!' Forthright turned to Loften. 'You must have given me the wrong key, Mr Loften.'

He seemed in no way put out. But Loften was.

'I didn't do anything of the sort. It was the right key, and you know it.' He looked at Pitt. 'I don't know what all this is about, Inspector, but I'll swear I gave him my own key to the garage.'

The Inspector nodded.

'You'll have to do better than that,' he said to Forthright. 'If Mr Loften gave you the wrong key you couldn't have used it to get into the garage — as I understand you did.'

'Then you understand wrongly,' the mechanic said cheerfully. 'I didn't need it — one of the other chaps opened the door for me.' He turned to speak to Wells, but the little man had joined the others at the entrance. 'Hey, Pop!' he called. 'Come over here a minute, you're wanted.'

Inspector Pitt frowned. It was his business to summon a witness, not Forthright's. But his annoyance was mild compared to Loften's.

'That's not true!' he shouted. 'You put the key in the lock. Damn it, I was watching, I saw you do it! Nobody opened the door for you, that I'll swear.'

Forthright shook his head. 'No need to get upset, Mr Loften. I dare say it looked that way to you, but — Pop, remember last Friday when I dropped Mr Loften's key down the drain?'

Wells nodded nervously. He wished Wickery or Chitty had been given his rôle. 'What of it?' he asked.

Forthright started to explain, but Pitt stopped him. 'Let's have it from Mr Wells, please.'

Wells did his best to look puzzled.

'I don't know much about it,' he said haltingly. 'Dave and Bert and me was in the workshop at the time. We heard someone bang on the door (we'd closed it to keep out the draught, the wind fair whistles through this place), but we didn't pay any attention because Harry and Mr Loften were working on a car outside and could see to any customers what turned up. Then suddenly I thought maybe it wasn't a customer, but one of them two wanting to get in. So I went and opened the door, and there was Harry. He came in for something they wanted, and then he went out again. It wasn't until afterwards I heard he'd lost the key. I didn't see him drop it.'

'Had Forthright put the key in the lock when you opened the door?' asked the Inspector.

'I don't think so.' Wells sounded cautious. 'He was holding it in his hand like he was just going to do so. He looked quite surprised, me opening the door at that moment.'

'And when you turned the lock you didn't feel any help from outside?'

'No,' said Wells. 'Oh, no.'

'Thank you, Mr Wells,' said Pitt, and looked inquiringly at Loften. Forthright remained silent. Any expression of triumph would be harmful, he thought.

Loften glared at him balefully.

251

'It's not true,' he fumed. 'It's — it's not true, Inspector. I *know* I gave him the right key. What other key *could* I have given him?'

'I don't know, sir.'

The Inspector's voice was cool. Forthright decided it was time for him to turn the screw a little farther.

'I remember you said at the time that you never used your key, Mr Loften. 'I *think* that's the one,' you said when you gave it to me. I dare say that's how you came to make the mistake.'

'Did you say that, Mr Loften?' asked Pitt.

'I . . . I . . . I don't remember. Yes, I probably did. But that's beside the point, Inspector. I tell you I *know* it was the right key. There's absolutely no doubt whatever.'

The Inspector's eyebrows rose a little higher.

'Apparently you weren't very sure at the time, sir. Why are you so certain now?'

But Loften could only repeat, with increasing anger and incoherence, what he had already said. It was obvious that the Inspector was not impressed by his performance, and Forthright began to wonder, somewhat uneasily, whether Loften would be goaded into denouncing them. He had not realized that the man would so deeply resent this attempt to turn the tables on him; for Loften as yet had nothing to fear from the police and should, if he wished to help them, readily have shouldered the blame for what could have been made to appear as a perfectly innocent mistake. He heaved a sigh of relief when the Inspector cut short the argument, gave orders for the excavation to be filled in, and departed with his assistants.

Loften watched them go; then he turned menacingly on the four men. Now for it, thought Forthright, and nodded reassuringly at the others. They could not afford to panic at this juncture.

'So that's it, eh? You substituted a key of your own for the one I gave you, dropped yours down the drain, and kept mine. That's how you got into the garage Tuesday night, is it?'

There was no surprise in his voice, only anger.

'That's it,' Forthright agreed blandly. 'I wonder you didn't get around to that before.'

The two looked at each other steadily. Outside the workmen were busy with their shovels. Forthright hoped Loften would keep his voice down; he had no wish for their discussion to be overheard. 'If you accept the murder I don't see why you're raising such a rumpus over our tricking you into letting us have the key,' he said.

'I'm not,' Loften said unexpectedly. 'As you say, I ought to have guessed what you were up to. What angers me is your deliberate attempt to put me in the wrong with the police.'

'But I didn't.' Forthright's tone was no longer insolent or provocative. Now that his object had been achieved he wanted to calm the man down. Loften was still a menace to them. 'I merely said you gave me the wrong key by mistake. No one could blame you for that, could they? And how else could I explain away the key they found down the drain? You've got to be reasonable, Mr Loften.'

'I've been a damned sight too reasonable, if you ask me,' Loften retorted. 'I didn't ask to be saddled with all this responsibility, and I'm damned if I can see why I should be made a scapegoat for a bunch of tricksters like you four. I don't mean to be, either.'

'The Inspector wouldn't have thought anything of it if you'd agreed with me that you might have been mistaken about the key,' said Forthright. 'Even now I can't see that there's much harm done.'

'A hell of a lot,' Loften said grimly. 'He thinks I'm a liar; that I still have the key.'

Forthright said nothing. He could hardly admit that that had been his intention.

'If you want to stay out of trouble you'd better not try anything like that again,' Loften went on. 'Maybe you think it's too late for me to tell the police the truth, that you're sitting pretty. Well, I wouldn't bank on it if I were you.' His tone changed. 'Now — how about that money? When do I get it?'

'You haven't had it?' Wickery asked.

'You know damn' well I haven't had it.'

Forthright tried to explain how they had hoped that the thief would hand it over anonymously, but Loften refused to listen. 'You get that money and get it quick; I'm not giving you any more rope — except the one that'll hang you,' were his parting words.

They went into the workshop and stood around talking. Events were moving faster than some of them could cope with.

'I thought he was certain to give us away when he was arguing with the Inspector.' Wells had not yet recovered from his fright. It had been touch and go, he knew that. 'What do you think stopped him, Harry?'

'I was wondering the same thing,' Forthright admitted. 'I suppose he still thinks he's on to a good thing and he can't bring himself to let it go. What's more, he knows damned well that, whether we hang or not, he'll have a hell of a lot of explaining to do if the police find out the game he's been playing. He's in it almost as deep as we are now.'

'You needn't have piled it on so thick, though,' said Chitty. He understood action, but he could not appreciate this trifling with words. You don't tease a tiger, you shoot him; and if you don't want to shoot him then leave him alone. That was the way he looked at it. 'No point in getting his goat unnecessarily.'

'But it *was* necessary.' Forthright spoke impatiently. 'You heard what he said — the police think he's lying about the key. If he hadn't been angry he wouldn't have made such a fool of himself, he'd have made the whole thing seem unimportant. That would have foxed the police, they wouldn't have known which of us was telling the truth. Now they think it's us — which means they'll keep a suspicious eye on friend Loften for a bit. That won't do us any harm, will it?'

'There's nothing else against him,' said Wickery.

Forthright picked a spanner from the bench and swung it idly between finger and thumb.

'There could be,' he said.

'What do you mean by that?'

The spanner slipped and fell. The noise as it hit the concrete made them jump.

'I got to thinking about it last night,' Forthright explained. 'Suppose we get Susan to tell the truth — that Loften wasn't with her Tuesday night, but up here — wouldn't that make the police sit up and take notice? I bet it would. He's hard up and he's got an expensive wife — there's your motive, for a start. And now they think there's some funny business about the key! If I were a copper I'd take a damned sight more notice of Loften than I would of us. At least we had an alibi.'

'It sounds all right,' Chitty agreed. 'Only if Susan tells the truth she'll tell the whole truth; she's like that. So the police would know why Loften was here that night.'

'That wouldn't matter so much. We could say Susan was right, that we did plan to rob the garage but called it off later. And Susan would agree that both Bert and I said there was to be no murder. That'd be a point in our favour.'

Wells nodded approvingly. At that moment he would have grabbed at any lifeline that was offered, and Forthright's suggestion seemed to him a stroke of genius.

'Loften had a key and we didn't,' he said. 'And as the garage wasn't broken into the murderer *must* have had a key.'

'It'd be better still if Loften had the money,' said Forthright. 'If the police found that on him he'd be cooked to a turn. He'd never convince them we gave it to him, not even if he admitted blackmailing us.'

Uneasiness crept into their faces at mention of the money. It reminded them that they were by no means united, that there was a traitor among them. 'There's time yet,' said Wells. 'Give the chap a chance. He couldn't do much this morning with all that shemozzle over the key.'

Wickery had taken no part in the discussion, but had listened, at first with indifference and then with disgust, as his companions had so skilfully and callously laid the foundations of their plot to involve Loften. It was a plot based on lies, but lies so twisted and perverted that they could be made to appear as truths; and if they persisted in it, perhaps embroidered it further, it might well succeed. They could establish their innocence to a charge of which they were guilty, and at the same time rid themselves of a man whose continued existence constituted a threat to their lives and liberty.

It was so perfect that it fascinated Wickery. Disaster had followed so closely on disaster that he had begun to believe there was no way out; and it was only when he realized that it involved the conviction and death of a man who, if not innocent of all crime, was certainly innocent of the crime they sought to pin on him, that he rebelled. Much as he hated Loften, and sweet as life seemed to him, he could not stomach that.

'You can't do it,' he said earnestly. 'You just can't do it, Harry. We *know* Loften didn't kill White. He may be the biggest blackguard on earth, but he's not a murderer. You can't plan to get a man hanged for a murder you committed

260

yourself. It's . . . it's . . . '

Words failed him as he looked to the others for support. There was none. Chitty was scowling at him, openly hostile. Wells turned away; he knew Bert was right, but his own scruples were less exacting. Self-preservation, that was the main thing. Kill or be killed, the law of the jungle. It was Loften or themselves.

Forthright's feelings were much the same as Wells'; but he was more honest, he was not afraid to air them.

'Don't be a damned fool, Bert — Loften's not worth it. He'd have handed us over without a pang — delighted in it, in fact — if he hadn't hoped to profit by not doing so. You know that.'

'But it's not the same thing, Harry. We're guilty, he's not. Surely you can see the difference?'

Forthright brushed the objection impatiently aside.

'You won't see the difference so clearly when you're in the dock,' he said scornfully. 'Anyway, it's only an idea at present; maybe it won't work and maybe it will. And there's always the possibility,' he added cunningly, 'that we won't have to use it. Let Loften know what's coming to him if he doesn't play ball and I reckon he'll see it the way we want him to.'

Wickery knew he was being side-tracked, that the sop Harry had thrown him was no more than that. Hating himself, he accepted it.

'That'd be different,' he said haltingly, stifling his conscience.

Chitty was still pondering the problem of his sister.

'If Susan's going to tell the truth she'll tell 'em about Mrs Gooch. We can't put *that* on to Loften.'

'Maybe we could get her to leave it out,' said Wells.

'Loften wouldn't leave it out. He'd plug it for all it was worth.'

'He was in Tanbury that evening, same as us,' Forthright said slowly. 'We all left the pub together, remember? Who's to say it wasn't Loften who killed Mrs Gooch, and not us? There's no proof he didn't.'

He felt elated, amazed at his inventive genius, warmed by the open admiration expressed by Wells and Chitty. Even the incredulous and horrified look that Wickery gave him was somehow stimulating.

'Loften left Tanbury at ten o'clock,' said Wickery, glad of a chance to upset the other's reckoning. 'And Mrs Gooch wasn't on the road until half-past. He'd have been home before then.'

'He didn't go home,' Chitty said. 'At least, I don't think he did. I think he was out with Susan.'

'All the better,' said Forthright. 'She's not likely to remember what time he picked her up — not after all this while. Which means he's got no way of proving he didn't kill Mrs Gooch. And look here, Dave — you've got to talk to Susan. Make her see what a nasty piece of work Loften really is. If it comes to a showdown we want her on our side, not his.'

Wells shook his head. 'Susan wouldn't take sides, she'd just tell the truth. And you forget one thing, Harry. We left Tanbury *after* Loften that night. If you try to make out it was him killed Mrs Gooch then we ought to have seen the body and reported it, didn't we?'

Forthright was annoyed. This was the first serious objection he had encountered since he had embarked on his flight of fancy, and he could see no way round it.

'All right,' he admitted grudgingly. 'If it comes to it we *did* see her. We can say we were scared; we'd no right to be out in a customer's car, and if we'd reported the accident White would have come to hear of it. We might have lost our jobs. And seeing she was dead and there was nothing we could do for her, well, we just scarpered.'

It was, he told himself complacently, a masterly second-best.

'There's something else you've forgotten,' Wickery said. 'What about the woman who was with White in the car?'

The dismay on their faces brought balm to his wounded conscience. Let Harry talk himself out of *that* one, he thought grimly.

But Harry did not even try. 'I'd clean forgotten her,' he admitted. 'Blast the woman!'

Wells and Chitty were silent; they knew what was coming next. As Forthright turned to him Wells braced himself.

'Did you speak to Molly, Pop?'

'Yes. She didn't know a thing about it, like I said.'

'You mean she denies being out with White that evening?'

'Be your age, Harry,' said Wells. The admiration evoked in his narrow mind by Forthright's inventive genius was forgotten now that he was battling for his young. 'How could I ask her what she was doing the night Mrs Gooch was killed? She'd think I was daft, expecting her to remember a thing like that. *And* she'd want to know why.'

'You could have asked her why she didn't stay in that evening to hear if Dave had got his new job,' said Wickery. 'She'd remember that.'

The little man looked at him with pitying scorn. 'You think it'd sound natural to ask a question like that fifteen months after it happened? Don't be daft, Bert.'

'He can't help it,' Dave said sourly.

'Those two have got Molly on the brain.'

Wickery ignored this. 'What *did* you say to her, then?'

'I just asked when was the first time she went in White's car. She couldn't remember for certain, but it was after she and Dave had that bust-up, she said. And that was ages after Mrs Gooch was killed.'

'It gets us nowhere,' Forthright said impatiently. 'If Molly was with White that night she's not going to admit it now. Why should she?'

Wells exploded into a string of oaths.

'For God's sake use your loaf, Harry,' he said. 'Molly's only a kid; if she'd seen us knock down that old woman and then scarper, d'you think I wouldn't have known it the next day? Molly couldn't shut up a thing like that inside her without either Sarah or me knowing something was troubling her.' He spat in disgust. 'Dave's right — you and Bert have got Molly on the brain, seems like.'

Support came to him from an unexpected quarter.

'Maybe you're right,' Wickery agreed.

'Chaps in our position just naturally get suspicious of everyone. But I remember now meeting Molly a few days after the accident. We even talked about Mrs Gooch — Molly did, anyway. Talked quite naturally, too. I don't think she was putting on an act.'

Wells looked at him gratefully. Even Chitty gave a grudging nod of approval.

'Who the hell was it, then?' asked Forthright.

Wickery shrugged. 'Somebody we've never even heard of, I imagine. White wasn't in the habit of bringing his lady friends to the garage.'

'She can't be all that important, anyway,' said Wells. 'If she's been to the police already they'd have hauled us in by now. And if she hasn't — well, I reckon she never will.'

'That's true,' Forthright agreed. 'Only why did the Inspector want that report from Willie Trape?'

'They could have got on to it some other way,' Wells suggested. 'It didn't *have* to be the woman, did it? Someone who saw us on the road, perhaps, or who recognized you and Dave in the Boar's Head.'

The spanner in Forthright's hand fell with a crash.

'Cripes, Pop, you've got it! That's it! That's who he was!'

They looked at him in astonishment. 'What on earth are you babbling about?' asked Wickery.

'Why, that fat man who called in here yesterday morning with the Inspector — the one that kept nosing around until Dave told him to clear off. I *knew* I'd seen him some place before. And that's where it was — the Boar's Head. He was the chap behind the bar!'

★ ★ ★

The kitchen was warm and cosy. The modern cooker was one of the few concessions to easier housekeeping that Dave had made before the drop in income had limited the spending of money to the bare necessities. Susan lavished great care on it; it looked as bright and sparkling now as when it was installed two years before. That was why she never liked Dave to have anything to do with the cooking. He was clumsy in the house and not over-clean; food spilt on the shining enamel would stay there until she herself removed it, and he was careless with the pots and pans.

They lived in the kitchen. It saved fuel in the winter and wear and tear on the already threadbare armchairs in the front room. But Susan was happiest when she had the kitchen to herself, with the curtains drawn and the world shut out; she had been alone so much that now her dreams were almost more real to her than reality. With her brother she felt nervous and uneasy; there was no strong bond of affection between them, and he never put himself out to be pleasant. Even George Loften's proffered friendship had come too late to make any real impression. She liked the occasional stimulus which his society provided, but she still preferred her own.

As she busied herself with the washing-up that Friday evening she kept hoping Dave would go out, even though she knew it meant a visit to the pub. Since the previous afternoon he had ignored her, making no reference either to Loften or to the scene in the garage. Was that because he was angry, or because he was ashamed of his behaviour? The former, no doubt; he had never exhibited shame before, he had always been the confident, domineering male, his youth and strength his only assets.

But Dave made no move. He sat at the table drinking his tea, casting occasional sidelong glances at her when he thought she was not looking. Harry had said to talk to her about Loften, but the prospect of soliciting her help embarrassed him. It was alien to his nature and to the relationship that existed between them.

But it had to be done. He took the plunge boldly.

'Just what is there between you and this fellow Loften?' he asked.

He had meant to speak lightly, but his embarrassment took charge of his voice. It was gruff, abrupt. Susan was on her guard at once.

'Nothing. I told you before, he's just a friend.'

'Can't understand what you see in him,' he grumbled. It was a bad start, but having made it he must go on. 'The fellow's an absolute rotter.'

Anger rose in her. She had no high opinion of George Loften. He was amusing, he ' took her out of herself,' as she put it; but deep inside her she knew that sooner or later he would expect more than friendship. He was putting on an act, gaining her sympathy, selling his personality to her; all part of a plan, no doubt, and not a particularly moral plan at that. But for her brother, a murderer and a thief, to dismiss him so contemptuously . . .

'So you say. I prefer my own opinion.' Despite her anger a lifetime of being on the defensive, of taking his word as law, forbade a more offensive retort.

Desperate, he tried another tack. Much as he hated doing so, he must humble himself, appeal to her sympathy.

'I'm not trying to interfere, Sue, but you ought to know the man he is. You see one side of him, we see another. You think he's being decent over this business of White, that he's said nothing to the police because he's got a kind heart. Kind heart my foot!' Bitterness crept into his voice, and self-pity. 'All he's thinking of is number one. He's on the make, that's all. It isn't you or us he's thinking of — it's himself.'

'How is he on the make?'

'Why, blackmail, of course. Pay up or hang — that's his attitude. He's just another White, that's what he is.'

Susan was frightened. Not for her brother, but because she feared that what he had said might be true. She had guessed that Loften could be merciless, that he was certainly mean. Yet he had been her friend, and with Dave in this awful trouble she was going to need a friend more than ever before. If Loften failed her . . .

She shut her eyes tight to force back the tears. 'Why should he do that?' she asked faintly. 'He knows you haven't any money.'

'He thinks we have. He thinks we've

272

got White's — the money that was stolen.'

'Oh!' She had forgotten the robbery — it had paled into insignificance beside the murder. 'Well, you have, haven't you?'

'No. At least, one of us has.' He embarked on a rambling, unintelligible attempt at explanation which left her completely bewildered. 'And unless Loften gets it he's going to the police, blast him!'

The girl said nothing. Mechanically she dried her hands and began to wipe the dishes. It did not occur to Dave to help her; he had never done so in the past, and now he was seeking words with which to beg the help they needed.

'It isn't only that,' he said. 'It looks as though the police are on to us about Mrs Gooch.' He told her of Willie Trape's report, of the red-faced man from the Boar's Head, of the unknown woman in White's car. 'That's given them a motive, see? You know we didn't plan to kill White, and none of us has any idea how it happened; but it did happen, and with this motive against us the police'll never believe we didn't mean it. And if Loften tells them what you told him — well, that'll be the end. We'll all hang. Not just the one who did it, but all of us.'

This unintentionally dramatic finish to his appeal was wasted on her. It evoked no sympathy because somehow it was too big, too brutal. They didn't hang people one knew, people among whom one lived and worked; that horror was reserved for strangers, people one had never heard of before, people who seemed more fictional than real. But because he obviously expected her to say something she said vaguely, 'I'm sorry.' And then, realizing how ludicrously inadequate that sounded, 'I wish I could help, Dave. You can't expect me to approve of what you've done, but I'd help you if I could.'

That gave him the opening he needed. 'You can,' he said shortly.

'Me?' She was genuinely surprised. Her offer had been mechanical, the sort of thing one said to a person in trouble. That he might take her up on it had never occurred to her. 'How on earth can *I* do anything to help?'

Watching her anxiously, he told her.

And if he did not tell it well, he had the essential facts.

Susan listened — at first in bewilderment, then in disbelief, and finally in horror. She could not credit that four quite ordinary men — men she had known for most of her life, and one of them her brother — could devise and intend to carry out such a devilish plan. And they even expected her to take part in it, to help them hand George Loften over to the hangman in order to save their own miserable skins.

'No!' she cried. 'Oh, no! I won't do it.'

He jumped up and caught her arm.

'You must,' he said fiercely. 'You don't have to tell any lies, only the truth — that Loften wasn't with you Tuesday evening like you said, that he was at the garage. If you want to you can even say *why* he was there — only leave out Mrs Gooch, we don't want any questions about her. And why the hell should you shield Loften instead of us? Does he mean more to you than your own brother, damn it?'

He let her go, and she sat down on the chair he had vacated. She was not crying, she was too stunned for tears. She looked at him across the table, and realized yet once more how little they had in common. That he could even *think* that she might agree to such a diabolical proposal!

'No,' she said again. 'I won't do it, Dave. I don't care what you say about George, at least he isn't a murderer. And I won't help you to prove that he is, to — to hang him.'

He was about to protest, to shout at her, to try to exert his influence over her. Then he remembered Forthright's sop to Wickery.

'You've got it wrong,' he said. 'We wouldn't go as far as that.' Her eyes narrowed, but they did not leave his face. 'All we want is to frighten him so that he won't give us away to the police; and if he thinks you're on our side, that he can't depend on you to back him up — well, he'll think twice about it, anyway.'

She did not believe him. It was too crude, too obvious. 'I'll not do it,' she said again.

Had they been closer, had she had for

him the normal affection of a sister for her brother, he might yet have persuaded her. But because he did not understand her, did not even know *how* to persuade her, he gave up. He resorted to his normal method of argument on the few occasions in the past when she had defied him. He lost his temper.

'A nice sister you are, and no mistake. You'd rather help that swine Loften than you would your own brother,' he stormed, pacing angrily up and down the small kitchen.

She followed him with her eyes. 'No,' she said quietly, 'it isn't that at all. I don't want to help either of you, I don't want to be mixed up in it. I wish to God I'd never gone near Mr Forthright's cottage last week.' Her voice rose. 'Why can't you leave me alone? I didn't ask to be let into your secrets, did I? Why should I be pestered and questioned and frightened the way you're all going on at me? Leave me *alone*, damn you!'

He was startled. Susan had disagreed with him before, but never had she raised her voice to him, never sworn at him. He was so surprised that he sat down on the other chair and lit a cigarette, his anger momentarily forgotten. He felt he ought to say something — but what? He did not know.

Susan got up, walked wearily to the draining-board, and resumed the drying-up. Her outburst had taken most of the vitality out of her, and she felt tired and empty.

Some time later Chitty remembered that he had not yet completed his task. He leaned across and turned down the radio.

'There's something else I want to ask you,' he said diffidently. 'You saw Loften the night Mrs Gooch was run over, didn't you?'

She did not answer, but gazed woodenly at a lurid print of the Bay of Naples that hung on the opposite wall. He repeated the question impatiently.

'I told you, I don't want to talk about it any more. Just leave me alone.'

'But this is different,' he pleaded, angry with himself that he dare not be angry with her. 'Loften was in Tanbury that evening. We had a drink at the George with him, and he left just before us. He went to meet you, didn't he?'

'Yes,' she said wearily, a trifle sullenly. 'What of it?'

'You were at Mrs Quayles', you said. What time did he pick you up?'

'I don't remember.'

Well, that was something, thought Chitty. At least Loften can't prove he was back here before the old woman was killed.

'No idea at all?' he asked.

'Only that it was between a quarter- and half-past ten,' she answered. 'I can't be more exact than that.'

Chitty swore.

'You're certain?' he persisted.

'I saw his wrist-watch while he was driving.' Now that she had started she was glad to talk. The long silence, with Dave glowering at her, had been even more unnerving than his anger. She had wondered what new devilry he was planning. 'It was half-past ten, and we'd been in the car a few minutes.'

'His watch could have been wrong. Did

you look at the time before you left Mrs Quayles?'

'No.' She remembered that she had said all this before, and a flicker of real interest shone in her eyes. 'Anyway, he didn't pick me up at Mrs Quayles', I met him on the main road. But his watch wasn't wrong, I checked it when I came in.'

That seemed decisive, for the kitchen clock, the only one in the house, kept excellent time. 'What made you do that?' he asked curiously.

'It was five past twelve by his watch when he dropped me at the end of the lane. The time seemed to have gone so quickly I thought his watch must be wrong, but it wasn't. Our clock said ten past when I got in, which would allow five minutes for the walk. That would be about right.'

He nodded glumly. Then, as he leaned forward to turn up the radio, she said, 'You wanted to put that on to him also, didn't you? Mrs Gooch's death, I mean. You thought I wouldn't be able to give him an alibi.'

'Rubbish! Nothing of the sort,' he said, annoyed that she should have seen through him so easily. He turned the knob to full volume, and the sickly harmony of a girls' choir filled the room.

'The Inspector had the same idea,' she shouted.

That startled him. He jumped up, and once more the room was quiet. 'How the hell do you know that?' he asked.

'He was here this afternoon, and he asked me almost the same questions as you did.'

'And what did you tell him?'

'What I've told you, of course. So at least it won't be much good your trying to blame the old lady's death on to George Loften, will it?' she said, with a touch of malice.

# 10

## The First Arrest

Wickery wondered why Forthright should look so drawn and haggard that Saturday morning. He hasn't got wife trouble, he reflected bitterly; he can go home of an evening and be free of all this. Ma doesn't look at him the way Doris looks at me sometimes — as though I'm something the cat brought in.

He checked his thoughts abruptly, ashamed of his disloyalty. Doris wasn't to blame. If he'd stood firm on what he knew at the time to be right he wouldn't have landed them both in the cart.

Loften too looked far from well, as though he had slept little. Apart from an abrupt good-morning he ignored the men; there was no reference to the money or to the events of the previous day. 'Maybe he realizes it's not going to be all jam,' Wells said hopefully. 'He looks real worried.'

'There was a light on at his place at four o'clock this morning,' said Forthright. 'I saw it from my bedroom.'

Wickery was about to ask why he was awake himself at that hour when they were startled by the arrival of Chitty and his sister. 'What the hell made him bring *her* along?' he asked anxiously. 'I hope it doesn't mean more trouble.'

It had been Dave's idea. Afraid that they might think he had bungled it, he had insisted that Susan should tell the others what she had told him; and when Susan had objected that there was no need to go to the garage for that, that they could come to her if they wished, he had stressed that it would be easier for her at the garage. With Loften around they would have little opportunity to try to dissuade her from her decision.

'Just tell them you don't want to be mixed up in it either way,' he had said. 'They'll have to leave it at that.'

But he hoped they would not. Since he could not convince her himself, he hoped that the combined persuasion of the other three might do the trick. That had been his main reason for wanting her to go to the garage.

But they listened to her in silence. There were no questions; no one attempted to coerce her. 'Okay, Susan,' said Forthright, when she finished with a stumbling apology. 'It doesn't matter. You do what you think is right.'

Chitty was puzzled, unable to understand this spineless acceptance of her refusal to play ball. Yet he could not argue against it in Susan's presence.

She was about to leave when Loften came out of the office. He looked thoughtfully at the girl and then walked over to greet her. 'I'm glad you're here,' he said. 'I want to talk to you.'

Susan eyed him with trepidation. She had spoken the truth when she had said she did not wish to be involved. It seemed she had convinced Dave and the others of this; did she now have to convince George Loften?

'I won't keep you long,' he said. 'It's just something I think you ought to know.'

Something about her brother, she wondered. If so she did not want to hear it. But because she was tired of argument she went reluctantly into the office with him.

Chitty made to follow, then turned angrily on the others.

'Why the hell didn't you talk to her?' he demanded. 'That's why I brought her along. She was stubborn last night, but I reckoned the four of us together might wear her down. And now that devil's got hold of her there's no knowing what he may not put her up to.'

Wickery thought again what an unpleasant, boorish oaf Chitty was. That a man could talk so of his own sister! What the hell was Pop thinking about, letting a fellow like that marry Molly? Maybe he was attractive to women, and he was a beefy brute who was not averse to throwing his weight about; but what sort of recommendations were those in a prospective husband?

'Susan can't do us any harm,' said Forthright. 'Not if she just tells the truth, as I think she will. I thought about it a lot last night — that's what kept me awake — and I reckon the truth from Susan'll be all in our favour. It'll do more harm to Loften than to us.'

'Maybe that's the way he sees it,' said Wells. 'Maybe that's why he wanted to talk to her.'

'I'm not worrying,' said Forthright. 'It's a pity he's out of the picture as far as Mrs Gooch is concerned, but that doesn't mean *we* must have killed her. It could have been anyone. As long as White's woman keeps her nose out of it we can still say she was dead when we found her.'

They're still at it, thought Wickery, annoyed. First they try to wheedle me into agreeing with them and then they just ignore me. Well, this is one time nobody's going to tell me what to do.

Inspector Pitt arrived. He bade the men a gruff good-morning, inquired after Loften, and went into the office.

'It's a good sign, him asking Susan all them questions about Loften,' said Wells, nodding in the direction of the office. 'Shows we've got him thinking. Must have been the key as done the trick.'

Susan came out with the two men, and Loften and the Inspector went off in the latter's car. The mechanics watched them go and then turned to the girl.

'What did Loften want?' asked Wells.

'Nothing. It was just to tell me that his wife's left him.'

Forthright whistled. 'What, again? Seems like it's becoming a habit with her.'

Chitty sighed. He wouldn't want to marry anyone but Molly, but there was something about Mrs Loften that Molly hadn't got. She did not often come to the garage, but when she did it always made him feel hot under the collar. It could have been her perfume, or the way she dressed, or the bold, appraising way she looked at him. She was a hot one, he thought. It had been Mrs Loften who had intensified his dissatisfaction with Chaim, who had strengthened in him a longing for the big cities where there were many women who dressed and looked as she did.

'I wonder if she's gone for good this time,' he said regretfully.

'He seemed to think so,' said Susan.

'He showed me the note she left.'

'He did? What was in it?'

'Just that she couldn't stand it here any longer, that this — this business of Andrew White (those were her own words) was the last straw. She was through with him for good, she said.'

'When did she go?' asked Wickery.

'He doesn't know. He said she was there yesterday afternoon, but when he got home after having dinner with a friend she'd gone.'

'So that's why he had a sleepless night,' Forthright reflected aloud. An idea occurred to him. 'Did he say you could tell us about it, Sue, or were you supposed to keep it a secret?'

'He asked me to tell you. He said you'd get to hear of it sooner or later.'

'Trying to arouse our sympathy, I suppose,' Chitty said scornfully. 'He's got a hope!'

'That's not true. If you'd seen him when he was telling me about it you'd know. He's terribly upset.'

'But why?' asked Wells, puzzled. 'I thought they fought like cat and dog, hated the sight of each other. You'd think he'd be glad to see the back of her.'

'Pride,' Wickery said briefly.

'Eh?'

'Pride. It makes a chap look a fool when his wife leaves him. Everyone thinks he's a poor sort of bloke — something wrong with him, perhaps. A chap like Loften who's full of his own importance would hate it like hell.'

Chitty eyed his sister speculatively. Was it possible, he wondered, that Loften's liking for Susan might be partly responsible for his wife's departure? It wasn't in the note, from what Susan had said; but then Susan wouldn't have mentioned it anyway. Suppose there was a divorce, would Loften marry Susan? Loften hadn't much to recommend him as a man, but he wasn't a bad prospect as a brother-in-law. If they got out of their present trouble Loften might be useful.

Chitty decided that it might be wise to adopt a more friendly attitude towards his employer. He'd have to toe the line with the others, of course, but if it came to a showdown he could keep in the background. And perhaps in private . . .

'Where's he gone with the Inspector?' Forthright asked the girl.

'To his house, I think. I wasn't really listening.'

Had her thoughts been running on similar lines to his own, wondered her brother.

'We might be able to make some use of that,' said Forthright, when Susan had gone.

'How?' asked Wells.

'I don't know yet.'

Normally the men took it in turns to work on a Saturday afternoon, but when Loften returned he told them curtly that he would need none of them. He would look after the place himself, he said.

Neither he nor they referred to his wife.

'And a fine mess he'll make of it,' said Wells. 'However, it's his worry, not ours.'

'Funny he didn't say anything about the money,' said Forthright. 'Looks like he's going soft. Must have lost his grip along with his missus. I wonder if there's any hope of getting some wages out of him?'

'No harm in trying,' said Wells.

They tried. But if Loften was going soft he wasn't going that soft. He did not refuse to pay them, but said there was no money on the premises — *they* had seen to that — and arrangements would first have to be made for him to draw on the firm's banking account. At present he had no authority to do that.

'And what are we supposed to live on in the meantime?' asked Forthright.

'That's your worry, not mine,' Loften retorted, with some of his old spirit. 'You'll not starve. Not on the money you filched from White.'

'But we told you before only one of us has got that. What about the rest of us?'

'That's your worry too. You'd better try and persuade the thief to disburse — and don't forget my share while you're about it.' He looked directly at Forthright. 'You didn't honestly expect me to fork out, did you?'

'Yes, I did.'

Loften's gaze strayed to the other three. Wickery and Wells said that they too had expected to be paid. Only Chitty was silent.

'How about you, Dave?' asked Loften.

Chitty shifted his weight from one foot to the other. 'I could do with the money, of course,' he said awkwardly. 'But if it's difficult for you I — well, I dare say I can manage without it.'

He kept his head down, not wishing to meet the angry glances of his workmates.

'I'm afraid you'll have to,' Loften said drily, and went into the office, closing the door behind him.

No one spoke. They stripped off their overalls and donned their jackets. Chitty was the first to leave. Without a word to the others, without even looking at them, he hurried out of the garage.

'What the hell's he playing at?' said Forthright, completely bewildered. 'Has he gone soft too?'

Wells shook his head. He was as mystified as Forthright. But Wickery was in no doubt at all.

'Dave's got an eye to the future,' he said bitterly. 'With Mrs Loften out of the way he's hoping Loften'll ask Sue to

292

marry him. That'd suit Dave fine. As for him not needing the money — well, we all know why *that* is.'

'I don't,' said Wells.

The look which Wickery gave him was half pitying, half contemptuous.

'A week's wages don't mean much to Dave,' he said. 'Not with White's money safely tucked away.'

★ ★ ★

Unaware of the reason ascribed to his behaviour by his workmates, Dave Chitty hurried home. He wanted to talk to Susan; to sound her out, as it were. She had insisted that she was not interested in Loften, but that was before she knew that Mrs Loften had left her husband. Her thoughts might already be running in the same direction as his own. If not, he intended to see that they did.

As he climbed the stile into the lane he saw a police-car outside the cottage, and his pace slowed. There were men in the garden, a uniformed constable outside the front gate. Uncertain what to do, he walked slowly on; he knew he had been seen, that any attempt to run would be useless. But his boots felt like lead, and a butterfly fluttered in his stomach.

Inspector Pitt met him at the gate. Susan was there, and behind her Doris Wickery. The frightened look on the girls' faces was, Chitty knew, reflected on his own. There could be only one reason for the presence of so many policemen.

The Inspector held out a metal box. Damp soil adhered to its edges. 'Have you seen this before, Mr Chitty?' he asked, his voice grave.

'No,' said Chitty.

'It has been identified as similar to the cash-box belonging to Andrew White,' said Pitt. 'The box that was stolen from his room on the night he was murdered. It was dug up in your back garden.'

Chitty wanted to protest, to demand what right they had to dig in his garden without his permission, to deny that the box had ever been in his possession. He wanted to blast them with his wrath, to shatter them with some undeniable evidence of his innocence. But the anger would not come, the words remained unspoken. He felt cold and sick and lost, and very, very frightened.

'Oh!' That was the total of his eloquence.

'I must ask you to accompany me to the police station at Tanbury,' said Pitt.

'Why?' asked Chitty. 'Are you arresting me?'

'We have a few questions to ask you,' said the Inspector. 'And I should warn you that you will probably be held in custody on a charge of being in possession of stolen property. Because of that I should also warn you that anything you say now may be taken down and given in evidence later.'

No mention of the murder. Was that a trap, or was it because they weren't quite sure? Well, if they hoped to get a confession out of him they'd got another think coming.

He squared his shoulders. 'All right,' he said.

And then suddenly he was filled with a violent rage that empurpled his face and shook his whole body. The faces in front of him were no longer the faces of the Inspector, of Susan, of Doris Wickery; they were other faces, grinning at him, mocking him. He wanted to smash his fist into them, to tell them . . .

With a tremendous effort he controlled himself.

'All right,' he said again, his voice expressionless. 'You're wrong, of course. I don't know anything about that box — never seen it before, as I said. If you found it in my garden someone else must have put it there. I didn't.'

Inspector Pitt looked at him curiously. Then he shrugged his shoulders.

'We'll go into that later,' he said.

★ ★ ★

'Will Dave keep his mouth shut, like we agreed?' said Wells, nervously licking his thin lips. 'That's what worries me most.'

This time there were only three of them in the Forthrights' front room. Yet the absent figure loomed larger in their thoughts than it had ever done when present.

'If he was right in what Susan heard him say to the Inspector — if he thinks one of us *did* plant that box on him — then he won't feel bound by any agreement,' said Forthright. 'He won't trust us, and he'll do what he thinks is best for himself. But if he killed White and took the money he's got nothing to gain by talking.'

'Of course he killed White!' Wickery spoke impatiently. 'Everything points to it, doesn't it? His broken specs, and then his refusal to tell us where he broke them. And wasn't it Dave who was all for killing White in the first place? Of course he did it. And what I say is, why should we bother to help him now? The police have got the murderer, haven't they? We don't owe him anything, not after the way he double-crossed us over the money. Let him stew in his own juice, that's what I say.'

'You mean you'd let him hang?' asked Wells, aghast. 'What sort of a friend are you?'

'Dave and I have never been friends,' Wickery growled. 'You know that.'

'So what? Wasn't it you who put him up to it in the first place? If you hadn't come out with this bright idea of yours for getting even with White — '

'Cut out the sentiment,' Forthright said gruffly. 'We've got to help Dave whether we like it or not. We gave him an alibi, and if Dave killed White the police will say it was done with our consent.'

'We ought to get him a lawyer,' said Wells.

'So we will. But a lawyer can't get him off. The only way to do that is to give the police a nice red herring.'

'Loften, eh?'

'Yes. They didn't charge Dave with murder, so I reckon they're still interested in Loften. Maybe they think he killed White and that Dave knew about it. Something on those lines, anyway. It could be that they hope to get at Loften through Dave.'

'But why should they suspect Loften when Susan gave him an alibi?'

'They know there's something between them, don't they? And with Mrs Loften clearing off it makes Susan's alibi look a bit fishy. They wouldn't put a lot of weight on it, anyway.'

'But what can we *do?*' asked Wells. 'We can't just go to the police and say we think Loften killed White. They'd tell us to mind our own ruddy business.'

'Not if we feed them some of the truth,' said Forthright. 'Not if we tell them we planned to rob White and then called it off — and then get Susan to tell her side of it. The police couldn't ignore a lead like that.'

They're still trying to shut me out, thought Wickery. They think that when it comes to a showdown I'll give in same as I've done before. Harry's so sure of that that he doesn't even bother now to pretend they're only trying to frighten Loften. If they can hang him they will — and they don't care what I think, they don't even bother to consult me.

But he said nothing. He soothed his anger and resentment with anticipation.

'We've got to be damned careful,' Wells was saying. 'No rushing our fences. It's all got to be tied up good and proper, so that he can't wriggle out of it.'

Forthright nodded absently.

'I wonder why the police searched Dave's place first?' he said. 'Could Loften have put 'em up to it? He was out with the Inspector this morning.'

'Loften wouldn't know which of us had it,' Wells objected. 'And why should he do a thing like that if he hopes to get money out of us?'

'Perhaps he's tired of waiting, thinks we're not going to stump up. Well, if it was him that sold the idea to the police he's put another nail in his coffin. He went back to see Susan after he left the garage Tuesday night — that'll come out when Susan says her piece. The Inspector won't have to do much thinking to realize he could have hidden the money in Dave's garden then.'

Wickery could stand it no longer.

'Haven't you forgotten me?' he asked, his voice trembling. They looked at him, startled, a little ashamed because they *had* forgotten him. 'I said I wasn't going to have you do this, didn't I? Well, I meant it — by God I meant it! You try and pin this on Loften and I'll tell the whole story — Mrs Gooch, White, everything. I let you talk me into running away from Mrs Gooch, but you won't talk me into this. Not in a month of Sundays you won't.'

He stood glaring at them, fists clenched, his body quivering with passion. And Forthright knew that he was beaten. Maybe, when death was a little nearer, when the law had him in its grasp, Bert would weaken. But not now.

'Okay, Bert, have it your own way,' he said quietly. 'I'll think of something else.'

Wickery had worked himself into a mood ripe for battle. This sudden capitulation by the enemy left him at a loss. Victory had been too easy. He had wanted a fight, and now there was no one to fight. Mouth slightly open, he sank into a chair.

'You mean that? It's not another of your blasted tricks?'

'Of course I mean it. Hell, we couldn't pull it off without you, could we?' Forthright said reasonably. But anger and resentment burned deeply in him. It was true they couldn't do it without Bert, but why should the fool choose this of all times to assert himself? Now, when they had Loften where they wanted him!

Wells had taken no part in this flare-up. It had been so sudden, had died so quickly, that he hardly realized it had happened. But as the significance of it gradually dawned on him he began to protest volubly.

'Damn it, Harry, we must go on with it; it's our only chance.' He turned angrily on Wickery. 'You and your perishing scruples — who do you think you are, the Archbishop of Canterbury? You won't feel so damned righteous when you're sitting in the condemned cell, mate. But you're not going to put me there, I'll see to that. Not ruddy likely!'

'Shut up, Pop.' Antagonism, Forthright knew, would only harden Wickery in his attitude. If he'd made up his mind to be a martyr he would welcome it. 'You can't force a chap into doing something he doesn't think is right.'

'But what else can we do?' wailed the little man.

'We can tell the truth,' said Wickery. He

was filled with a sense of well-being, and for the first time since that night fifteen months ago he was almost happy. He had stood out against the others and won; and what made him feel so good was that he knew he was right. 'If we have to, that is. But they've got Dave and — '

There was a loud knock on the front door. The three men looked at each other. 'The police?' suggested Wickery.

'Perhaps. Might be Loften.' Forthright turned as he reached the hall. 'If it's the police, Bert, you keep quiet. Understand?'

Wickery shrugged. 'I'm not looking for trouble. But you keep off Loften, that's all.'

It was the police.

'Glad to find the three of you here,' said Inspector Pitt. 'Saves time.'

He settled himself comfortably in Forthright's armchair. A detective-constable waited by the door. Wells licked his dry lips and wondered if there were other police outside the house.

'What's up now?' asked Forthright. He proffered a cigarette, which the Inspector refused. 'Seems like you chaps can never leave us alone.'

'You can't expect anything else if you get involved in a murder,' Pitt said cheerfully. 'I suppose you know we've arrested your friend Chitty?'

Forthright tried to match his cheerfulness.

'He'll be back. Dave didn't kill White, Inspector.'

'So he tells me.'

He seemed in no hurry to continue, and the men grew restless under his thoughtful gaze. Wells said, trying to keep the conversation on a light plane, 'Are you here on business, Inspector, or is this just a friendly visit?'

'You might call it that.' Pitt drew a notebook from his pocket and thumbed the pages. 'I've been looking into the death of a certain Mrs Gooch, an old lady who was killed by a hit-and-run motorist about fifteen months ago. Remember?'

Although it came as no surprise, it was an unpleasant shock to be actually confronted with the crisis they had been dreading.

'I remember,' said Forthright. 'But why bring that up now? And what's it got to do with us, anyway?'

'I rather fancy you killed her,' the Inspector said calmly.

Forthright hesitated, uncertain whether to be amused or angry. He chose the latter course.

'That's a damned lie!' He dared not look at the others in case their expressions might unnerve him. 'And if the police were satisfied at the time that we had nothing to do with it, why the hell should you start accusing us now?'

'I know. Most regrettable,' said the Inspector. 'I'm afraid the police slipped up badly there; they shouldn't have so readily accepted your statement that you came home on leaving the George at ten o'clock. But you mustn't blame me for their mistakes. Did you recognize the barman from the Boar's Head when he called at the garage on Thursday?'

'No,' said Forthright. 'Why should I? I've never been in the Boar's Head.'

'Well, he recognized you and Chitty. And according to him, the two of you were in his pub until ten-thirty the night Mrs Gooch was killed. Mrs Gooch happened to be his wife's aunt, which fixed the evening in his mind; and apparently the Boar's Head doesn't get many customers drinking whisky the way you two seem to have downed it. Makes a difference, doesn't it?'

They sat looking at him, trying to hide their concern. But they said nothing. It seemed useless to deny the accusation, yet they would not admit it until they had to.

The Inspector raised his eyebrows.

'You don't see the difference, perhaps. Well, you told Constable Trape that you were back at the garage by ten-twenty, so that was lie number one. Lie number two was your statement that you didn't see Mrs Gooch — you *must* have seen either her or her body, for she started to walk home at the same time as you left the Boar's Head. And it's my belief that lie number three was when you said you didn't kill the old lady.'

'You can't produce a witness to that, at any rate,' Forthright said boldly. The

Inspector, he thought, would have been more positive had the woman in White's car come forward.

But Pitt was not to be drawn.

'That's as may be,' he said. 'But if you didn't kill her why deny seeing her?'

'Because we — '

They all looked at him; the Inspector with interest, the others frightened and angry. Forthright hesitated, and was about to continue when Wickery interrupted, his voice unsteady.

'Shouldn't you warn us, Inspector, before making these charges?'

'I'm not making any charges, Mr Wickery, I'm merely stating my beliefs. I told you this is in the nature of a friendly visit.'

'You've got a witness.'

Pitt turned to the detective by the door and nodded. The man left the room, closing the door behind him.

'Well — you were saying, Mr Forthright?'

A nod from Wickery gave Forthright his cue.

'All right, then, we saw her,' he said

defiantly. 'But we didn't kill her, and that's gospel.' He launched into his previously prepared account of how they had seen the old woman lying in the road and, finding she was dead, had placed the body on the grass and cleared off. 'We realized we ought to have reported it; but a job's a job, Inspector, and White wasn't the sort to overlook it if he'd found out we'd been joy-riding in a customer's car.'

Pitt thought this over.

'Not bad,' he admitted. 'Not bad at all. Except that there *was* a witness to the accident, of course.'

Forthright gulped. 'Who?' he asked.

'Why, Andrew White. Wasn't that why you had to kill him — because he was blackmailing you?'

He said it so naturally that Forthright found himself wanting to deny the reason rather than the fact. He spurred his anger into action.

'Have you gone barmy?' he demanded. 'You know damned well we never killed White, that we were playing cards all that evening in this very room.'

'It was stupid of you to pretend to the womenfolk that you'd had your wages cut,' went on the Inspector, ignoring this outburst. 'I wonder they believed you; wages go up these days, not down. It certainly didn't cut any ice with me — particularly after I'd had a look at the books. So why, I asked myself, should three apparently sober-living men (I'm excluding Chitty) have to resort to such a clumsy lie? Blackmail, I said. And when I discovered that your troubles began immediately after the accident, I put two and two together and made four.'

'You may be good at arithmetic,' said Forthright, 'but that doesn't make you a good detective.'

'Then I considered this so-called alibi of yours — the card-party racket.' The Inspector was unperturbed. 'I didn't think much of that either. It proves nothing except that you didn't all leave this house together; Mrs Forthright herself admits that one or two of you could have done so without her being any the wiser. So we arrive at the conclusion that only one or two of you actually committed the murder, but that all were a party to it.'

Wickery shifted uneasily in his chair, and Forthright gave him a warning glance. He wanted no outburst from Bert at that stage. Inwardly he cursed the other's presence. Without Bert this would have been a good time to distract the Inspector's attention from themselves by introducing Loften as a red herring.

'You've got it all worked out, haven't you?' he said.

'Not all. There are still a few gaps, but we'll fill them in in time.' It sounded as though he were trying to complete a crossword puzzle. 'I was rather hoping you fellows might help me there.'

That shocked them.

'Got a nerve, haven't you?' said Wells. 'First you tell us we killed White and then ask us to help you prove it. You think again, mate. We're not that crazy.'

'What was it you expected us to tell you?' Wickery asked curiously.

'What happened to the money, for one thing; the box was empty when we found it. And how you got into the garage

— Loften's key, I suppose, eh? Chitty's spectacles — they fit in somewhere, don't they? The little details, you see, that tie it all up. And I'd certainly like to know what made you decide, after all this time, that you'd had enough of being blackmailed.'

At least one of them thought how much he too would like to know what had happened to the money. *And* Dave's spectacles — it was odd how much fuss they'd made about those spectacles and how little they seemed to matter now. Come to that, even the money was no longer important. There was no need to buy Loften's silence now — they had a better way than that to deal with him. And for themselves there was a bigger issue at stake than a few hundred pounds.

'You're off the beam, Inspector,' said Forthright. 'We had nothing to do with White's death, and we don't know about any blackmail.'

'The cash-box was found in Chitty's garden,' Pitt reminded him. 'How do you suppose it got there?'

'Planted. Dave wouldn't be such a

damned fool as to put it there himself, would he?'

'Planted by whom?'

Forthright looked at Wickery. What he saw on the latter's face deterred him. 'How should we know?' he growled, angry at having to ignore such a golden opportunity. 'That's your business, not ours. What did Dave say?'

'That's my business, not yours,' the Inspector retorted without rancour.

There was a short silence. Wells took a crumpled packet of cigarettes from his pocket. 'I don't get this,' he said, really puzzled. 'Seems an odd way for the police to go about things, don't it, asking chaps to help convict themselves? I shouldn't have thought there was much future in it.'

'Neither should I,' Forthright agreed. 'And if you arrested Dave why didn't you arrest the lot of us, Inspector, if you think we were all in it?'

'Ah!' said Pitt. 'I was coming to that.'

He was so long in coming to it that Forthright began hopefully to wonder whether the police case was so thin that they had had to resort to bluff, and whether, having had their bluff called, they had no answer to it. But eventually Pitt said, speaking slowly and weightily as though every word counted, 'I said this was in the nature of a friendly visit, didn't I? Well, I've got a good case against the four of you — for if one of you killed White you're all equally guilty. In law, anyway. But between ourselves I've an idea that you might not all be — well, morally guilty, shall we say? So I'm giving you the benefit of the doubt.'

They eyed him uneasily. Was this a trick? 'Not quite so cut and dried, eh?' said Forthright.

'You'll see what I'm getting at,' the Inspector continued. 'You all had a strong motive for murder but that's not evidence in itself. It could be that your Tuesday evening card-parties weren't a put-up job, that you three at least had no thought of murder and took no part in it. I'm thinking that Chitty could have made some excuse to leave you that evening, slipped across to the garage, killed White, and returned here without you fellows being any the wiser.' He paused, looking

313

from one to the other. But they had nothing to say; they were too astonished, too doubtful of his motives. 'I'm told he's got a nasty temper, has Chitty; so perhaps he didn't knuckle under as easily as the rest of you, or maybe he just needed the money.' He turned to Forthright. 'There's a query there. Unless you gave him the key that you pinched from Loften, how did Chitty get into the garage?'

Forthright stared at him, shaking his head in bewilderment — not at the question, but at everything the Inspector had so far said.

'Well, we'll leave that for the present. Of course, we can't deny that you would all be accessories after the fact. When White's body was found I presume you either guessed or learnt from Chitty what had happened and decided to give him an alibi. That was stupid of you — stupid and criminal. But I suppose it's only natural to want to stand by a pal.'

'So what?' asked Wickery, although he knew well what was coming.

'A confession from the three of you on those lines and we'd have all the evidence we need against Chitty. Mind you, I'm not bargaining. All I can do is report the matter to the proper authorities, stressing your help to the police. It should make things a lot easier for you. But don't quote me on that.'

They stared at him incredulously. Then, as full realization of the Inspector's words came to Wells, he went red in the face with fury.

'You rotten perisher!' he roared. 'You think we're the kind to shop a pal to save our own ruddy necks? You get out of here quick, before there's another corpse around these parts. Go on, hop it! We all took our . . . Ouch!'

He stopped suddenly, as a savage kick from Forthright landed on his ankle.

'Aren't you rather overdoing it, Inspector?' Forthright said, with an eye on Wickery. 'I reckon you'd find yourself in hot water if we were to report this to your boss.'

The Inspector was unperturbed.

'Don't you worry about that, sir. We have a strong case against your friend Chitty; the only doubt in my mind was whether he killed White with the full knowledge and approval of the rest of you or whether you knew nothing of the murder until after it had happened. I wanted to be clear on that before going ahead.' He stood up. 'You chaps have landed yourselves in quite a mess, but if I feel any sympathy for you — well, that's unofficial. I know what blackmail can do to a man. However, as a police officer I don't let sympathy interfere with duty, and I warn you that I'm out to get White's murderer, blackmail or no blackmail.'

Wickery took little part in the heated discussion that followed the Inspector's unhurried departure, speaking only when appealed to, and then in the vaguest terms. The Inspector's suggestion seemed to him the ideal way out, but Pop, he knew, would never countenance it. If he wanted to discuss it with Harry he would have to wait until they were alone.

He brooded miserably on their predicament, the angry arguments of the other two forming a fitting background to his thoughts. He hated Loften, and he was fast losing the little moral courage left to him, but he still refused to contemplate the sacrifice of an innocent man. And why should he, when this alternative offered? Even if Dave had not actually killed White he was guilty of intent, and obviously the police favoured him as the culprit. The rest of them would have to shoulder their share of guilt and punishment; but at least it would only be a minor share, the Inspector had as good as said so. Pop was the only obstacle; Harry, he guessed, had no scruples either way — all he wanted was to save his own neck. Who died to save it, Loften or Dave, didn't matter a damn to Harry. But Pop, presumably on Molly's account, would rather let the innocent Loften take the blame than the guilty Dave.

Damn him, thought Wickery, scowling across the room at Wells.

Wells did not see the scowl. Taking Wickery's lack of protest as grudging acquiescence, he and Forthright were planning the details of the case that could best be made out against Loften. Wickery let them plan, his anger smouldering, his dislike of them increasing. It surprised him to remember that these two men had once been good friends of his. He wondered how he could ever voluntarily have borne their company, let alone have sought it.

But when Wells departed to try and cement their plan by obtaining Susan's co-operation Wickery dissembled his anger and dislike in a final attempt to win Forthright over to his way of thinking. The other listened to him in silence, nodding or shaking his head occasionally in sympathy or disagreement; but when Wickery had finished he would not commit himself, although he made it plain in which direction his sympathies lay.

'You'll never get Pop to agree to it, you know that,' he said. 'Can't say I blame him, either; Loften's a damned sight better candidate for the rope than Dave. And without Pop's support where are you?'

'He might agree if you were to back me up. What else can he do if the Loften plan is definitely out? It's either Dave or him, and Pop can't be so fond of Dave that he's willing to risk his own neck. Not that that would save Dave's. We'll all be for it unless we can get Pop to toe the line.'

The other frowned.

'It beats me why you can't see it the way we do,' he said. 'If Loften takes the can we get off scot-free, but there's no guarantee what'll happen if we shop Dave.'

'You can cut that right out, Harry. I'm not having any.'

'But why the hell not?' Forthright's anger was rising. He was not a man to suffer interference or opposition easily. 'Suppose we do as the Inspector suggested, say Dave killed White without our knowledge, that we gave him an alibi because we were a lot of sympathetic fools? What about Susan? Is *she* going to agree to that? You know damned well she won't. Susan'll tell the truth — and then where are we?'

Wickery was silent. He had forgotten Susan. Yes, Susan could wreck it, he realized that.

'Maybe we'd better tell the whole truth

and be done with it,' he said slowly. 'I can't stand much more of this.'

'Come off it!' Forthright was alarmed. 'We're not beat yet. Here! Have a drink.'

Wickery shook his head.

'I'm going home,' he said. 'I want to think this out.'

'Well, thinking won't hurt,' the other conceded. 'But no funny business with the police, mate, if you want to stay in one piece.'

# 11

## Pieces of Paper

Dave Chitty's arrest caused an even greater stir in the village than the murder of Andrew White had done. He was not particularly popular — there were many who considered him capable of having committed the crime for which (in public opinion) he had been arrested. But White had been an outsider and Chitty was one of themselves, and Chaim folk were clannish.

Doris Wickery did not belong to the village any more than her uncle had done. She liked Susan Chitty, but not Susan's brother; and she knew or guessed more than the village of the events leading up to her uncle's death. She could not share their sympathy, only their horror; and she had in addition her own private fear.

She saw her husband for only a few moments after Dave's arrest, for as soon as she told him of it he hurried from the house. For the rest of the afternoon she waited, her fear growing with every hour that passed.

It was late when he eventually returned, looking tired and frightened; but he vouchsafed no information, and she was too fearful to ask. She fetched his supper from the oven and watched his pretence of eating.

Presently he pushed the half-empty plate away from him and stood up, searching the mantelshelf for his pipe.

'The Inspector was round at Harry's place this afternoon,' he said. 'He thinks we killed your uncle.'

The tears started from her eyes, although she was unaware that she was crying until she tasted the saltness on her tongue. Now it's coming, she thought. Perhaps Dave had confessed, perhaps at any moment they will come for Bert. And suddenly she wished not to know the truth — not to have to think for him, advise him, as she would have to do once he had unburdened himself.

'No,' she said. 'Oh, no!'

He misunderstood her protest. He thought it showed concern for himself and began to speak hurriedly, sparing her nothing — Mrs Gooch, White, Loften, their quarrels among themselves, the Inspector's visit that afternoon. It was a relief to tell her, to know that he now had a confidante on whose counsel he could rely. He had bottled it up too long, he should have shared this burden with Doris, as he had shared others, from the beginning. Doris always knew what was best to be done.

'I wanted to tell you before,' he concluded, staring into the fire. 'It was the others wouldn't let me. But now it's done and — well, what do we do next?'

Doris did not answer. It was the 'we' that seemed to her the final straw. He was making her a partner in his guilt, pushing his responsibilities on to her, asking her to decide something he should have decided long ago. She wanted to protest, to deny the partnership; but she could not.

Her silence mystified him. 'You take it pretty coolly, I must say,' he remarked, hurt that she should withhold her sympathy. 'One would think — '

Then he saw the tears on her cheeks, the strained look on her white face, the way her hands gripped the sides of the high-backed chair. He moved towards her quickly, kneeling beside her and putting a large, calloused hand on hers.

It was his touch that broke the last shred of her reserve. The hand was the hand of her husband — and of a murderer, perhaps. Screaming, she leaned forward, beating at him with her clenched fists. Through her tears she could see the horrified look on his face as he bent away from her, gazing at her mutely. Screams gave way to speech, and she started to revile him, using words she had never uttered before, calling him foul names — until the stinging slap of his hand on her cheek stopped her.

She leaned back in her chair exhausted, the hysteria passing as suddenly as it had begun. Bert stood looking down at her, his twitching hands hanging loosely by his sides. But before either of them could speak there was an imperative knock on the cottage door, and he hurried from the room.

It was the woman from next door.

'I heard Doris screaming,' she said, trying to peer round him into the hall. 'I didn't know you was home. Is she all right?'

'Yes, thanks.' It seemed inadequate, and he added, 'She was a bit hysterical. It's been a trying time.'

'One takes more notice of a scream these days,' she said. 'Murder — it makes one think, doesn't it? You sure Doris is all right? Nothing I can do for her?'

'Nothing, thank you.'

She went away reluctantly.

Doris had stopped crying, but she had not moved from her chair. 'That was the Drake woman,' he said. 'She heard you screaming. Thought I was beating you up, I expect.'

'I'm sorry.' Her voice was weak but controlled. 'I just couldn't help it.'

'I guess you didn't mean all those things you said,' he answered, relieved at the apology. 'It must have been the shock.'

She shook her head. She could not tell

him that there had been no mental shock, that she had already guessed much of what he had told her. It had been a physical reaction, a sudden, uncontrollable aversion to his touch. She wondered why she had not felt it before — he was no different today from what he had been yesterday. But then yesterday she was only guessing; today she knew.

When he tried to put an arm round her she got up quickly and stood by the fireplace. His eyes followed her, hurt and puzzled.

'What do you think we should do?' he asked.

She winced at the 'we.' 'Tell the police,' she answered harshly.

'You mean — as the Inspector suggested?'

'Of course not. I mean the truth — about Mrs Gooch, and Uncle Andrew, and anything else there is to tell them,' she said, watching him carefully. 'Trying to put the blame on Dave or Mr Loften is just shirking the issue — and it probably wouldn't work; the police must know a great deal more than the little the

Inspector told you. You just tell the truth and leave them to fix the blame. If you don't — well, what sort of a future will there be for us, Bert? What you've done would always be between us.' Her voice lost its harshness, became vibrant with emotion. Her purpose was no longer to hurt him, but to make him see it her way. 'I know I couldn't stand it, and I don't think you could either. In time we'd come to hate each other.'

'But I can't do that, Doris!' Only a little while before he had contemplated taking that very step, but it disturbed him that she should suggest it. 'There's the others to consider.'

'Why? They're guilty, aren't they?' she said scornfully, hurt that he should rate his friends' welfare more important than herself. 'One of you killed Uncle Andrew, and if you're not prepared to help the police then you're all as bad as the murderer. Dave's in prison already, and that's where the rest of you belong.'

'You mean you want us to hang?' She started to cry, but he persisted. 'Is that it, Doris? Is that what you want?'

'No,' she wailed. 'Of course it isn't. But I'd rather you were dead than go on living as we are. I can't stand it, Bert, I just can't.' And when he did not answer she added, hysteria returning, 'What's more, I won't. I'll give you until tomorrow, Bert, and if you haven't been to the police by then I'll go myself. Maybe I'll kill myself afterwards, but I'll go. I swear I will.'

She ran out of the room and up the stairs. He made no attempt to follow her. Hours later, when he went to bed, she was lying on her back staring at the ceiling. She did not look at him, but moved away as he climbed into the big double bed.

Long into the night they lay awake. Sometimes when he shifted his position Doris tensed her body in an agony of apprehension, shrinking still farther away from him. But he made no attempt to touch her.

As dawn was breaking he went downstairs to make tea. He brought it up to the bedroom, and they both drank avidly. Doris's eyes were sore with crying and lack of sleep, and her head ached abominably. If only I could sleep, she thought, and never wake up. Her mind trying to grapple with the problem that confronted her, she stared unseeing at her husband's back as he sat on the edge of the bed in his dressing-gown, gazing out of the windows at the world coming to life in the faint morning light. She felt some pity for him, but mainly anger that he should so wantonly have wrecked their marriage. Where there was only one person in your life, she reflected sadly, everything was lost if he failed you.

The sun was dispersing the morning mist and chasing the shadows out of the corners of the room as Wickery began to dress. Doris watched him covertly. His movements were sluggish, he looked tired and much older. I've failed him too, I suppose, she thought. He expected help from me and I've let him down. But I can't help him — not the way he wants, I can't.

Miserably her mind turned from her husband to the murder itself. How they must have hated Uncle, she thought. Yet they had not planned to kill him — or so

Bert had said. If only she could believe that! There was Susan, of course — she could ask Susan. But then Susan had overheard only a small part of what was said. And that was a week before the murder — they could easily have changed their plans after that. And if they had changed them to include murder, would Bert have admitted it to her? Yet how could four such men, no matter what the provocation, come to plan so terrible a revenge? Harry Forthright, perhaps — there was something elemental about him. But the others . . .

She remembered it was Dave who, according to Bert, had committed the actual murder. In imagination she saw him climb the stairs to the flat, a spanner gripped firmly in his hand. She saw him bend over the sleeping figure of her uncle, the weapon poised to strike . . . the swift, decisive blow . . .

Doris shuddered. Dave was an ugly customer, a bully. But would he really . . .

'Why are you so sure it was Dave?' she asked, breaking the long silence. Curiosity had temporarily replaced horror.

Wickery explained eagerly, grateful for the interest in her voice. But when he had done she did not seem impressed.

'Was he drunk?'

'Not drunk. He'd had one or two, but he seemed sober enough to me. Why? Don't you think he did it?'

'I suppose so,' she said doubtfully. And then, after an interval, voicing the final stage in her train of thought, 'What did you do with yours?'

'My what?'

'Your piece of paper. The one you said had NO written on it.'

'I tore it up. Why?'

She did not answer. Presently he said bitterly, 'You wanted to see it, I suppose, to make quite sure I didn't kill your uncle.'

Doris flushed. That had certainly been one reason for her question. But there was another.

'I was thinking you might just have crumpled it up and thrown it on the ground — it wouldn't have any significance to anyone but the four of you. And if the others did the same — well, if we could find their pieces of paper we'd know who killed Uncle Andrew.'

He stared at her, eyes wide.

'By God, Doris, that's an idea! And I know where each of us stood; more or less, anyway. They'd probably take some finding, but it's worth trying.'

His enthusiasm damped hers.

'It's four days now. They may have blown away, or perhaps the others tore them up too.'

'Yes, of course. But I could ask them — not Dave, of course, but Pop and Harry. If we concentrate — '

'Don't be a fool, Bert.' Doris's voice was sharp. 'You don't imagine they'd tell you the truth, do you?'

Half-way into his jacket, he turned in surprise.

'Why not? If we can prove that Dave killed White there won't be any more argument, we can do as the Inspector suggested.'

'And suppose it wasn't Dave? Suppose it was Mr Forthright? He'd take good care you didn't set eyes on *his* piece of paper. No, Bert, you leave this to me.'

His eyes narrowed. 'You? What about me?'

'You must show me where you each stood, of course, but I'd better do the searching. It may take a long time, and they'd miss you at the garage.'

'It's Sunday,' he reminded her, his voice hard. 'The garage will be closed. We'll both look.'

Doris hesitated. To indulge in a little detective work on her own was one thing, to do it in company with her husband was another. She knew that he had misunderstood her interest, assuming it to spring from a desire to help him. Well, there was that too. But her chief purpose was to get at the truth; and if the truth involved Bert more deeply than he had given her to suppose he would certainly do his best to hide it from her.

'All right,' she said reluctantly. 'And while we're at it we'll see if we can find the pieces you tore up. You might need them later.'

Wickery was not deceived. His freshly shaven face reddened, but he made no comment.

There was no one about when they reached the garage. Behind it, except on the tracks, the undergrowth was heavy from the rain. Although this made their search the more difficult it reduced the likelihood of the pieces of paper having been scattered by the wind.

Hurt and angered by Doris's suspicion of him, Wickery insisted that they look first in the spot where he had waited that Tuesday night; and because he knew exactly where to look it did not take them long. Many of the pieces were missing, but they found enough; and as she looked at the creased and dirty jigsaw of paper in the palm of her hand Doris felt slightly ashamed.

The pencilled NO was unmistakable.

'Satisfied?' asked her husband.

Doris nodded.

'Good. Better put them back where we found them, then.'

She knew he was probably right, but now that she had them she could not bear to be parted from them. She took an envelope from her pocket.

'I'd rather keep them, Bert, if you don't

mind. I don't suppose the police will take much notice of them, but at least they're safer with me.'

It was nearly midday when they found the piece of paper dropped by Dave Chitty. It was not torn, as Bert's had been, not even crumpled. It might have been placed there carefully, on purpose — or it might have fluttered there gently and slowly, dropped by a nervous hand. It had been slightly stained by the weather, but the pencilled YES was not obliterated.

'So I was right,' Wickery exulted. 'It was Dave.'

Doris stared at it thoughtfully. 'I suppose it's the right piece of paper,' she said.

'Of course it is. There's no mistaking Harry's writing.'

'No. But doesn't it seem odd that Dave should have dropped it like that, without crumpling it up first?'

'Oh, I don't know. It probably gave him quite a jolt when he read it, and he just let it slip out of his fingers.' He stopped. 'No, that's unlikely, too. Dave wouldn't be scared, he was all blood and thunder before the job.'

Doris shook her head.

'Thunder, perhaps, but not blood. Dave talked big, but I always thought he was a bit of a coward. Yes, I believe you're right, Bert — he *was* scared.'

'He didn't strike me that way,' Wickery said doubtfully. 'And if he was scared why did he kill White? That was his idea, not ours.'

'I don't know. Perhaps Uncle Andrew woke up and Dave got frightened and — ' She shuddered. 'Let's look for the other pieces.'

'But why? Isn't that enough?'

'It should be,' she admitted. 'But somehow — well, I'd just like to see the others. To make sure.'

The path which led from the garage to the Forthright cottage was not concealed from the road. 'Anyone can see us,' Wickery objected nervously, as they began their search. 'They'll wonder what we're up to.'

Doris took no heed. Even the further suggestion that Harry himself might be watching did not deter her. 'We can say we're having another look for the glass from Dave's spectacles,' she said.

But they found no more pieces of paper, neither there nor on the track taken by Wells.

'What next?' asked Wickery, as they stood together at the back of the garage. Now that he had this new evidence, and with Doris to help him, he felt a different man. His voice was almost cheerful.

But the morning's search had not altered Doris's outlook as it had his. 'Go to the police and tell them everything,' she said firmly. 'It's the only thing to do.'

'But good heavens, Doris, why? Now that we know Dave is guilty there's no need to tell them the whole truth; we can do as the Inspector suggested. Why ask for trouble?'

'It's not a question of need, it's what's right that matters,' she snapped, weary of his arguments, tired physically and mentally. 'And do you think the Chittys will keep silent when you give evidence against Dave? Of course they won't. You do as I say, Bert, and tell the police the truth. Otherwise — well, I will.'

Her reference to the Chittys almost convinced him, but he was not yet ready to admit defeat. 'I must speak to the others first,' he hedged. 'It wouldn't be right not to let them know.'

'You're a fool if you do — they'll only try to dissuade you. But remember, Bert, I'm serious about going to the police. Dead serious. So it's up to you.'

She walked away without waiting for his answer. He watched her until she left the road and disappeared behind the hedge that bordered the field. Had she looked back, had she given the least sign that she wanted his company, he might have followed her. But she did not, and he turned and walked slowly along the path to the cottage.

Wells was there with Forthright. 'This place is becoming a sort of club,' the latter said when Wickery entered. 'What's up with you, Bert?'

Wickery told him. Not the whole of it, for he feared the older man's wrath if he were to learn that Doris had been made a confidante. He said he had found the piece of paper that Chitty had dropped, so that now there could no longer be any doubt of his guilt. 'We can go ahead with a clear conscience, Harry,' he said, not looking at Wells. 'Do what the Inspector suggested, I mean. It's either that or the truth.'

'It's my neck I'm worried about, not my conscience,' growled Forthright. 'Let's see this bit of paper.'

That shook him.

'I gave it to Doris,' he said; and added hastily, 'It's all right, she doesn't know what it's about. I just asked her to look after it.'

'You keep Doris out of this; there's enough ruddy women mucking up the works without her. As for knuckling under to the police — not me, mate. Not as long as there's another way out.'

'But what other way is there?'

'Loften,' Wells said succinctly.

So we're back on that lark, are we? Wickery thought. 'You won't get around Susan, you fools,' he said.

'No,' Forthright admitted. 'Pop's tried that. But she'll have to admit that Loften was up at the garage that night, and that's all we need. Anything else she says we can discredit by stressing that Loften was her lover, that she's trying to shield him. Dave'll back us up — he'll probably invent a few savoury morsels for the jury if we put it to him.'

Wells nodded agreement, licking his lips. But Wickery was filled with disgust.

'What a filthy thing to do!' he said angrily. 'You've sunk pretty low, Harry, if you can do that to a decent girl like Susan.'

Forthright flushed.

'I don't like it any more than you do,' he said, 'But I can't afford to be squeamish. I've got Ma to think of. How will she make out if they shove me in gaol?'

'I don't know and I don't care. And you can drop any idea of getting Loften and Susan involved in this, because I won't have it. Dave killed White, and if anyone swings for it it's going to be him. I'll see to that.'

'How?'

'By telling the truth, that's how. And if I don't Doris will, so you might as well get used to the idea.'

It was not until after he had spoken that he realized what he had done. Even then he did not greatly care — they'd have to know sooner or later.

Forthright stepped closer to him, his bullet head thrust forward.

'So Doris knows, does she? You were lying when you said you hadn't told her?'

Wickery did not flinch.

'Yes, I was lying. But there's been a damned sight too much lying in the past, and from now on I'm telling the truth.' He did not wish to antagonize them unnecessarily, and in a quieter tone he added, 'I'm sorry, Harry — but I know I'm right. And in any case there's no alternative now. Doris really meant it when she said she'd go to the police, and it's better if it comes from us.'

Neither of the other two spoke, neither of them moved. For a moment Wickery hesitated, uncertain.

'Like that, is it?' he said eventually. 'Well, I'm off.'

Forthright moved swiftly, barring his way.

'No, you don't,' he said, his teeth bared, close together. 'First thing you've got to do is go home and knock some sense into Doris's head.'

'You leave Doris out of this.'

'Leave her out, eh? And who the hell brought her into it in the first place, I'd like to know? You do what I say, mate. Go back home and tan the hide off her, the ruddy, interfering little bitch. And if you won't then I'll damned well do it for you.'

Wickery hit him — a glancing blow on the cheek. His rage blinded him to the fact that he was no match for the older man, despite his advantage in height. But luck was with him. Forthright hit him in the eye with a straight left, but as he followed this up with a swinging right Wells, frightened, caught at his jacket and threw him off balance. Wickery ducked, and Forthright, unable to stop himself, tripped over a chair and fell heavily.

Wickery watched him for a moment, rubbing his eye. The fallen man had hit his head against the wall and was temporarily stunned; but as he opened his eyes, shook his head vigorously, and, swearing profanely, began struggling to his feet Wickery decided it was time to leave. Pushing aside the protesting Wells, he ran out of the room and out of the cottage.

'You're a fine help, you are,' said Forthright, rubbing the back of his head. 'Why the hell did you have to interfere?'

'I didn't want a fight. We ought to be able to settle it without that.'

'Bert'll settle it all right, blast him!'

'Do you think we ought to go after him, Harry?'

'What's the use? Short of murder, there's no way of stopping him now.'

Wells winced. He didn't like the way Harry said that.

'We can't just wait for the police to arrest us,' he protested. 'We must do something.'

'Such as what? There's nothing we can do, unless — ' Forthright paused. 'You clear off home, Pop; I want to think. And keep your mouth shut if the cops pick you up — tell 'em you're saying nothing till you've seen a lawyer. I'll find a way to beat 'em yet, Bert or no Bert.'

# 12

## Death in the Forest

Inspector Pitt rattled a pencil thoughtfully between his teeth as he looked long and searchingly at his visitor. Then he took the pencil from his mouth, laid it carefully and exactly along the centre of the big blotter, and leaned forward across the desk.

'Why didn't you tell me all this on Wednesday morning, Mr Wickery?' he asked sternly.

'It would have gone pretty bad with us if I had, wouldn't it?' Wickery felt good, better than he had felt for what seemed like almost a lifetime. It had been so easy; no interruptions, no awkward questions. He had been allowed to tell his story in his own way and at his own pace. And although he knew that the questions must come he felt confident that he could deal with them now that he was sticking to the truth. Unless they got on to the subject of Mrs Gooch. He hadn't mentioned her.

'And what makes you think it won't go bad with you now?'

'Well, it's different, isn't it? We know now that it was Dave killed White. And then there's his sister — *she* can tell you we never planned it that way, that we only meant to get back the money White owed us.'

'How did White come to owe you this money?'

But Wickery was not as yet prepared to answer that. Later, perhaps, when he had seen a lawyer, and if the latter considered it necessary.

'How about the others?' asked Pitt. 'Are they willing to confirm your statement?'

Wickery shook his head.

'I don't know,' he said. 'I tried to persuade them to see it my way' — here the Inspector's glance rested on the other's swollen right eye and he nodded understandingly — 'but they're a bit suspicious. They think maybe you'll go back on the offer you made yesterday.'

'I made no offer,' Pitt said sharply. 'Don't you try to pull that one.'

Wickery hastily assured him that he didn't intend to pull anything. All he meant was that the others thought the police might not be quite so willing to accept the fact that they were innocent of murder once they had confessed to a plan to break into the garage.

'Depends on the evidence,' Pitt said gruffly. 'For instance, why all the elaborate precautions for secrecy among yourselves?'

'I don't know. It seemed a good idea at the time. We weren't too sure of each other, I suppose.'

'Sounds daft to me,' was the Inspector's blunt verdict. 'How about Chitty's spectacles? Where did he break those?'

'Not on his way home, anyway,' said Wickery. 'They were broken before we got back to the cottage.' He explained how Chitty had fallen, and how on the next day they had been unable to find a trace of broken glass on the path. 'He never would say how it happened. We thought it must have been in White's room, which was why he flew off the handle when we mentioned it to him.'

Inspector Pitt frowned. 'Not there,' he said, and stood up. 'Well, let's get along to the garage. I'll have another car pick your wife up and meet us there.'

'Am I under arrest?'

'You're being held in custody — for the present.'

The news of her husband's confession came as a shock to Doris, despite the fact that she had prompted it. She had not really believed that he would go to the police, was not even certain that she could force herself to carry out her threat to do so if he refused. But she felt no regret at spurring him to this action. The months of uncertainty and fear had been as harassing for her as they had been for him, and she was glad that they were over.

Bert was at the garage when she got there, and she smiled at him, trying to convey her approval of what he had done — wondering, too, when she had last given him a kind look or a kind word. The Inspector was there, and a number of other policemen, and Loften arrived shortly after to open the garage for them. There was no sign of Wells or Forthright.

At Pitt's request she gave him the pieces of paper they had picked up in the forest. He showed little interest in the fragments that Bert had claimed to be his, but the uncreased YES that they knew had been drawn by Dave Chitty obviously puzzled him. Doris wondered whether he had the same doubts about it as she had had. If only he would give her the chance she would expound her own theory.

But the Inspector put the paper away, and they went out of the garage for Wickery to show them where the four of them had stood that Tuesday night. Loften tried to follow, curious as to what was going on, but was turned back by a constable. He was not in sight when they were brought back to the garage to await the Inspector's pleasure.

There was little they had to say to each other that was not private, and the presence of a constable forbade privacy. Doris wondered if this was the last time she and Bert would be together, and the awful thought kept nagging at her that her passion for the truth might cost her husband his life. With that in her mind it was dreadful to have to sit together and say nothing, and she was glad when the arrival of Pop Wells created a small diversion. Despite her knowledge of what he had done she smiled at him. He nodded curtly in reply, and the look he gave Bert showed that he was in no friendly mood.

It seemed hours before the Inspector returned. As he sat on the edge of the desk firing questions at Wells — questions which the latter stubbornly refused to answer — he had something in his hand which he kept tossing into the air and catching, something that glistened in the weak sunlight. The continuous movement got on Doris's already strained nerves, so that eventually she could not refrain from interrupting him.

'What *is* that you're playing with, Inspector?'

He looked down at it, still for a moment in the palm of his hand. 'That? Just a piece of glass, Mrs Wickery.'

The glass began to dance again as he turned once more to Wells. Doris made no comment, but for her husband the word 'glass' had a special significance.

'Do you mean — is it a piece of Dave's specs, the ones he broke?' he asked.

'It could be, Mr Wickery. I'm only a policeman, however, and I fancy we'll need an optician to tell us that.'

His tone was of bored and suffering politeness, but it did not deceive Doris. He's on to something, she thought, and he doesn't want us to know it.

'Where did you find it, Inspector?' Wickery persisted.

This time the voice was not so polite. 'Suppose I ask the questions and you confine yourself to the answers?' snapped Pitt. 'We'll get along better that way.'

But they did not get along better. There was nothing more to be got from the Wickerys, and Wells remained obstinately mute. When two detectives returned to say that Forthright was not at the cottage Pitt looked almost relieved at the need for action.

'Probably gone to earth in the forest,'

he said. 'Well, let's try and winkle him out.'

★  ★  ★

Forthright knew it would not be long before they came for him, but at least he had a small margin of time. Even if Bert did not go to Tanbury, but telephoned the police from the village call-box, they could not act at once. Half an hour, perhaps — not more. Well, it would do.

He ate a hurried meal, took food up to his mother, and, after telling her that he had to go out, that he might not be back until late but that she was not to worry, he ran down the road to a neighbour. To him he explained that he had to go away, that he might not be back that night, and would the neighbour's wife be kind enough to keep an eye on Ma?

Then he made for the forest. He did not go far. He found a vantage-point from which he could watch the road and the garage, and sat down to unravel the tangle that was his mind.

The forest held a fascination for

351

Forthright that he recognized but could not explain, and he knew it as he knew his own garden. Since boyhood he had roamed its tracks, penetrated into every dense clump of tree and bush, climbed every ridge, and explored every gully. Now, he thought, this knowledge was to do him good service. The police would not find him in the forest — there were hiding-places that only he knew of and where even in winter a man could lie hid for days.

But in his case it would serve no purpose to lie hid. Unless he acted quickly Pop and Dave might think he had deserted them, they might even follow Bert's example and confess for want of an alternative. He had to act at once or not at all; but the devil of it was, he couldn't make up his mind *how* to act. The inventive genius on which he had prided himself seemed to have deserted him, and the close pressure of time and the need to keep a sharp look-out were no aids to clear thinking.

Who would the police believe, he wondered, if the rest of them denied

Bert's confession and offered Loften in exchange? Bert had Susan to support him, but Susan threatened no danger if they were prepared to admit that there *had* been a plan to rob the garage and that they had then discarded it. Besides, they intended to discredit Susan, to implicate her with Loften.

Forthright frowned, recalling the disgust on Bert Wickery's face when he had spoken of this earlier. It was a dirty trick, he knew that, and he wouldn't play it unless he had to. But he wasn't going to let respect for a girl's reputation stand between him and freedom, perhaps between him and life.

The main danger lay in those pieces of paper that Bert and Doris had picked up — no use trying to disclaim them, some expert was bound to prove that the handwriting was his. And in face of that damning evidence was it possible to persuade the police that Bert had confessed to a crime he had never committed?

Gloomily he came to the conclusion that it was not, that Bert had stymied him. And now they could not even take the way out suggested by the Inspector.

A police car stopped outside the garage. He could see Pitt and Wickery, and presently there were more cars and more policemen. And Doris. Then a car stopped outside his own cottage, and he watched anxiously as two men got out and went round to the front. I hope they don't put the wind up Ma, he thought.

Suppose he and the others toed the line and confessed, would the police believe that there had been no intention to murder, that White's death was an accident they could not account for? There was a clear case against Dave, and it could be made still clearer by stressing how from the beginning Dave had been all in favour of murder. Would that satisfy them, or would they want more?

The men came out of the cottage and went back to the garage, and presently some dozen or so policemen left the building and, spreading out as they went, moved in a long line into the forest. For a moment Forthright waited, trying to gauge the extent of the ground they were likely to cover; then he turned and disappeared.

He did not panic. Picking his way carefully, he went eastward, towards that part of the forest that lay north of the garage. It was thicker there; and the police would surely expect him to go west, anticipating a break for freedom.

Excitement grew in him, and a strong determination not to submit tamely to capture. Let them have a run for their money; and then, when it was dark, he would go down to Loften's house and have it out with him. If Loften could be threatened or cajoled into a reasonable attitude all might yet be well; suitably cut, his evidence could be made to appear overwhelmingly in their favour. And if Loften refused . . .

They nearly got him then. Just in time he heard them coming, and knew that he had underestimated the Inspector. There were more police, men he had not seen from his vantage-point; and they were coming from the east.

Even then he did not panic. He turned sharply, doubling back on his tracks and then striking off to the north-west. The trees and shrubs were thick here, the undergrowth sparse; he had concealment without hindrance. Stepping lightly for a man of his build, he set a pace that the slow-moving police were unlikely to match.

Something white, speckled with what looked like blood, attracted his attention. It had been caught on the branches of a thorn-bush, and mechanically he picked it off, examining it as he went. The spots were not blood, but part of the material-design; and he was about to throw it away when something — a memory from the past, a tiny incident he had thought forgotten — clicked in his brain. He stopped suddenly, the men behind him dismissed from his mind as though they had ceased to exist. Once more he examined the small fragment of material, incredulous of the crazy idea that was forming in his brain. Then, exultant and purposeful, he went slowly forward, his sharp eyes following the trail that had unwittingly been blazed for him.

'Why search the forest?' asked Loften, as the last man disappeared from view. 'Forthright wouldn't know you wanted to see him, would he? He's probably just gone for a walk.'

The Inspector said he had his reasons, and Loften had to accept that unsatisfactory reply; but as Pitt turned to speak to a colleague he went into the office, hoping for further information from the Wickerys. He had put his first question when he became aware that the Inspector had followed him and was regarding him in displeasure.

'I must ask you to wait outside, Mr Loften,' Pitt said curtly.

Loften shrugged his shoulders and left. Pitt turned to Doris.

'I'm sending you home now, Mrs Wickery. There's a car ready to take you.'

'What about my husband?' she asked, a quiver in her voice.

Pitt shook his head. 'Not at present, ma'am. He's needed here.'

'Are you going to arrest him?'

But the Inspector was not to be drawn. 'You'll be kept informed of what happens, Mrs Wickery,' he said patiently. 'Now, if you're ready . . .'

Doris departed, tearful and red of eye. It would be the first time she and Bert had been separated for a night, she thought unhappily, as she got into the waiting car. The fact that the separation was largely due to her insistence on Bert's confession did not make it easier.

Pitt turned to the two men.

'When the car returns I'm sending you into Tanbury. You will be taken to the police station and charged with conspiring to commit a felony. You have already made a statement admitting that, Mr Wickery, and you will be asked to sign it; whether you do so or not is up to you. If you want to see your solicitor first that can be arranged.' He looked at Wells. 'I presume you still wish to say nothing?'

'That's right.'

'Well, we can't make you talk. You'll both be held in custody over-night and will come up before a magistrate in the morning.'

They went out into the yard to await the return of the car. But already news of the police activity had spread through the village, and on the opposite side of the road a small crowd had collected. A few passing cars had drawn up by the kerb, their occupants anxious to miss nothing of what might happen.

Pitt eyed them with distaste. 'We'll wait in the garage,' he said, turning — and then stopped. From behind the back of the garage came Forthright, a policeman on either side of him. He was smiling, a grim smile that made Wickery wonder.

When he saw Pitt he stepped towards him eagerly, but the police held him back. A detective hurried forward.

'So you got him, eh?' commented the Inspector. 'Nice work.'

'Well — not exactly, sir,' answered the men. 'When we found him he was coming this way. Gave himself up, you might say. He says he wants to talk to you.'

'The desire is mutual. Bring him into the garage.'

The big doors closed behind them, shutting out the waiting crowd. It was dark inside, and Loften switched on the lights. Then he went to stand near Wells and Wickery, anxious to hear but not anxious to be observed.

'Well, Mr Forthright, I understand you have something to say to me,' said Pitt. 'We'd better go into the office.'

'No,' said Forthright. 'What I have to say is best said right here with everyone present.'

'Just as you like. But I must warn you — '

'You've got the wrong idea, mate,' the other interrupted him. 'It's an accusation I'm making, not a confession. I'm telling you who killed Andrew White.'

If the Inspector was surprised Wells was not. He had guessed Harry would fix it, that Harry hadn't done a bunk just because he'd got the wind up. He glanced at Wickery and Loften; both looked angry and somewhat apprehensive. Bert knows what's afoot, he thought, but not Loften. Loften had a bit of a shock coming, unless he was much mistaken.

'And who might that be?' asked the Inspector.

Forthright turned slowly, intentionally dramatic. It was his big moment, and he meant to make the most of it.

'Him,' he said, pointing. 'Loften.'

Face white, fists clenched, Loften started forward. 'You damned liar!' he shouted. 'What the hell . . . ?'

Pitt stopped him. 'If you don't mind, sir, we'll hear what he has to say. You'll have your chance later.'

'But I do mind, Inspector. The fellow's lying, I tell you.'

Support came to him from an unexpected source. 'Mr Loften's right, Inspector,' said Wickery. 'Forthright's been cooking this up for days; he — '

'Shut up, you!' Forthright's tone was vicious. 'You've opened your big mouth once too often already. Open it again and I'll ruddy well close it for good.'

The Inspector lost his temper.

'That'll do,' he almost shouted. 'Any more of this and I'll clap the lot of you in gaol.' He turned to Loften and Wickery. 'I'm going to hear what this man has to say. Neither of you has to stay here and listen, but if you do you'll damned well listen in silence. Is that understood?'

They nodded, eyeing each other suspiciously. Neither had expected to find the other in the same camp.

'Now,' Pitt said to Forthright.

'Well, I don't know what cock-and-bull story Wickery has told you, Inspector; maybe there's some truth in it, but not much, I'll be bound.' Forthright spoke slowly, savouring his triumph to the full, delighting in the helplessness of his enemies. 'The fact of the matter is, the four of us chaps had got in bad with Mr White. He'd been doing the dirty on us for months, and one evening, after we'd had a few drinks, we got talking about how we might get back some of the money that we'd been done out of. We never meant any harm to White, only to make him give us the money he owed us. But Chitty's sister heard us talking, and her and Loften being the way they are' — here there was a violent outburst from Loften, instantly suppressed by Pitt — 'it was only natural she should tell him about it. And that gave Loften the idea, I suppose. He could kill White and let us take the can back.'

'How?' asked Pitt.

'Easy. He had a key to the garage, didn't he?' Here Forthright realized he was on tricky ground, and he went on hastily, 'He told us himself he was there that night. That was when he started his blackmailing lark, saying he'd keep his mouth shut about us if we made it worth his while. Ask Susan Chitty — *she'll* tell you he was there. He spun her some yarn about going up to the garage to try and stop us, and then got her to give him an alibi so as you fellows wouldn't suspect him of the murder.'

'Why *should* we suspect him?' asked Pitt. 'What motive do you suggest he had for killing White?'

'He had a motive all right. White had been playing around with his missus.'

It was too much for Loften.

'You damned scoundrel!' he shouted. 'I'll not stand any more of this. You and your so-called friends murdered White. If you think you can put it on to me — '

He made to rush at his tormentor, but two policemen caught and held him. Pitt walked over to the struggling group.

'I warned you, Mr Loften,' he said sternly; and to the constables he added, 'Take him into the office and keep him quiet.'

Wells watched Loften's removal with satisfaction. He was full of admiration for Forthright's performance. Loften could deny Harry's accusations until he was blue in the face, but he couldn't *prove* any of them to be false. Not even that last crack about his wife — for White was dead, and Mrs Loften had cleared out. Even if the police found her, and she denied it, they were unlikely to have much confidence in her denial after that note she had left for her husband.

I suppose he'll cut loose and spill the beans, thought Wells. Well, he can't do us much harm now, not after Bert's little effort. It'll damage him more than it will us — if the police believe him.

Wickery was angry; angry with Forthright for denying the truth and angry with the Inspector for listening to him. But he did not wish to suffer Loften's fate, he wanted to know what other lies Harry had managed to concoct. So he said nothing.

'Anything else?' Pitt asked Forthright.

'Yes, the cash-box. Loften went back to Dave's place after he left here — Susan'll tell you that. I expect he forced the lock, kept the money, and buried the box where you found it. I knew Dave wouldn't have put it there — it had to be someone else; and none of us was round that way.'

'Very plausible,' said Pitt, not taking his eyes off the other. 'But you say he had a key. I understood he gave it to you?'

'He gave us the wrong key, I told you that before,' lied Forthright. 'Maybe he meant to or maybe it was a mistake, but that's what happened.'

'He gave you the right key,' Wickery burst out, unable to restrain himself longer. 'You put it in the garage door Tuesday night so as one of us could get in. That's just another of your damned lies.'

This time Forthright remained calm. He even smiled.

'Lies, eh? I'll show you whether I'm

lying.' He turned to Pitt. 'Get Loften out of there, Inspector, and I'll give you all the proof you want that he's a murderer.'

The Inspector nodded, went to the office door, and opened it. 'Bring him out,' he said sharply.

Wickery felt dazed. The Inspector couldn't possibly have been taken in by Forthright's bluff — not after he had heard Wickery's own confession and had seen the slip of paper that had led to Dave's killing White. Why didn't he stop this nonsense and arrest the three of them as he had arrested Dave?

Between two constables Loften stood glaring at Forthright and the Inspector. 'Haven't you arrested him yet?' he said. 'If it's evidence you want, ask me. I can give you evidence enough to hang the four of them twice over.'

'A pity you didn't do so earlier, then,' said Pitt, his voice cool. 'Where's this proof of yours, Mr Forthright?'

'In the forest, Inspector. I'll show you. But I want Loften to come with us. *And* those two doubting Thomases over there. Let them see for themselves.'

Wells wondered why he should thus be linked with Bert Wickery. He had never been a doubting Thomas — Harry had always had his full support in his scheme to incriminate Loften. But as he went through the yard and into the forest, with Wickery beside him and policemen behind and in front, doubt began to assail his conscience. He had never really believed that the plot could prove completely successful, that Loften would ultimately hang for their crime. He did not believe it now. And yet with Harry so confident and the Inspector apparently hood-winked . . .

Was it possible, he wondered, watching Forthright striding ahead with the Inspector at his side, that Harry had become so obsessed by his scheming that he had actually come to believe it was the truth?

He glanced back at Loften. Loften was lagging behind; the police had hold of his arms and were almost dragging him along. He looked terrified, afraid of the unknown towards which Forthright was leading them. Wells thought he could understand his fear. To be accused of a crime of which he was innocent, to hear a damning, almost irrefutable case cunningly built up against him — and then this gruesome approach through the forest to — to what?

Wells shuddered. For the first time since the fight in the cottage he spoke to Wickery.

'I'm scared, Bert,' he admitted. 'Scared stiff. What's Harry up to?'

Wickery glanced at him contemptuously.

'You ought to know,' he said. 'You helped him, didn't you?'

Forthright had stopped, was pointing out something on the ground to the Inspector. The two men knelt and, with the assistance of a constable, began to remove a layer of dead leaves and bracken. Wells and Wickery, impelled by a dreadful curiosity and unrestrained by the police, stole forward to crane their heads over the kneeling men.

The soil under the leaves was loose, had obviously been recently disturbed. Already the men had removed a small pile of it, were digging deeper with their hands around something partly uncovered, something that —

Wells stiffened, clutching at Wickery for support.

'No!' he said, his voice hoarse. 'Oh, no, not that!'

It was a human foot. A small, slim foot, the toenails still adorned with traces of scarlet varnish. A woman's foot.

Wickery said nothing. His stomach heaved. Teeth clenched, he tried hard not to be sick as he watched the gradual uncovering of the body — a body clothed in white, a white that was spotted with scarlet dots.

Inspector Pitt stood up, beckoned with an imperative finger. Behind him Wickery heard oaths, a scuffle. He turned to see three policemen pushing forward a grey-faced, struggling figure.

And then Loften screamed — a single, piercing scream. And after that — nothing.

'He's fainted,' said a voice. 'Passed out cold.'

The Inspector looked away and down at the now almost uncovered body. She lay on her side, her red hair dulled with the soil that filled it, her face hidden. Then he bent down and gently lifted the inert head, turning it so that the lifeless eyes stared up at them accusingly.

'Who is it?' he asked quietly. 'His wife?'

'Yes,' said Forthright, his voice no longer exultant. 'His wife.'

# 13

## The Pieces Are Fitted Together

'Well, you were right, Mr Forthright,' said Inspector Pitt. 'I don't know how you stumbled on it, but you were dead right. Loften has confessed to both murders — no fight in him at all.'

Once more the four of them sat, together with the Inspector, in the front room of Forthright's cottage. For the last time too as far as I'm concerned, Wickery said to himself; I'll never enter this damned room again if I can help it. Nor am I likely to be invited, he thought, glancing at and then away from the stern face of Harry Forthright. There's been too much bad blood between us this past week for us ever to be on friendly terms again.

He looked at the others. Both Wells and Chitty showed the strain they had undergone. I suppose I do too, he thought; but it's funny, you'd think we'd all be busting with delight instead of looking like a lot of wet Sundays. Perhaps that's because it's too soon; we haven't yet had time to appreciate how lucky we are. It all happened so quickly; yesterday we thought ourselves murderers, and now we're free. Or nearly free.

Only Inspector Pitt seemed quite at ease. Wickery experienced a strong surge of gratitude towards the gaunt, solemn-faced policeman. He knew he ought to feel the same way about Harry, for it had been Harry who had found Mrs Loften, Harry who had clinched the case against her husband. But he could not. And you can't compel your own emotions, he told himself.

'Thank you for not objecting to our being granted bail this morning, Inspector,' he said. 'It meant a lot to me.'

It meant a lot to Doris also, he knew. Had that one night he had spent in gaol marked her as he felt it had marked him? He looked at Chitty. Dave had spent two nights in gaol, and with no expectation of release in the morning. That must have been a grim experience.

Pitt grunted.

'You're not out of the wood yet, you know. You still have to face your trial. Don't start thinking it's all finished and forgotten, Mr Wickery, because it isn't.'

'I know,' said Wickery. 'I'm not counting any chickens, Inspector.'

They fell silent, each of the four conspirators wondering what lay ahead. Presently the Inspector said, 'I asked you men to meet me here because I need your help. I've got Loften's confession, but it leaves a few gaps — gaps I fancy he couldn't fill because he didn't know the answers.'

'And you think we do?'

'I hope you do, anyway.'

'What do we get out of it?' asked Chitty. He did not share Wickery's liking for the Inspector.

'Nothing,' Pitt said curtly. 'As I said before, it won't do your case any harm if the police can assure the court that you gave them all the assistance you could. But nothing apart from that.'

You didn't say it to Dave, thought

Forthright. You said it to the rest of us when you were trying to get our support against Dave. I wonder what he'd say if he knew about that!

'What can we lose?' he said. 'Only how about making a bargain, Inspector, and swopping your information for ours?'

'Good idea,' said Wells. 'Even now I can't figure out how Loften managed it.'

Pitt looked inquiringly at the other two, who nodded their assent.

'Good. Well, as Mr Forthright guessed, when Loften heard from Miss Chitty that you were planning to break into the garage he saw his chance; after you had stolen the money he merely had to walk in and kill White, and when the robbery was later traced to you (through a hint from him, if necessary) it was unlikely that your denial of the murder would cut much ice. He says now that he didn't intend to implicate you unless the police took too great an interest in himself; and of course he had no idea that you chaps would believe that it was one of *you* who killed White. That was a piece of jam he hadn't counted on.

'On Tuesday night he went up to the garage and waited for you to arrive. He saw the key put in the lock, and wondered why none of you went in; and he wondered still more when about half an hour later you removed the key and cleared off.'

'Wait a minute,' said Wells, astonished, his eyes darting from Chitty to the Inspector. 'Are you saying that *none* of us entered the garage that night?'

'That's right.'

'But — '

'We'll deal with that later, if you don't mind. But you can take my word for it that that's how it was.'

They looked at the red-faced Chitty, who nodded sheepishly. But Pitt gave him no time to explain.

'For a while I often waited, thinking you might return,' he continued. 'When you didn't he decided he could safely go ahead. Miss Chitty's evidence would ensure that you were still involved; and now, in addition to killing White at your expense, so to speak, he could also take the money. And that's what he did

— burying the empty cash-box in Mr Chitty's garden when he went back there to report to his sister.'

'But how did he get into the garage?' asked Wickery. 'He *did* give Forthright the right key — no doubt about that.'

'Miss Chitty heard you say that you hoped to get hold of a key. That meant *his* key, he thought — it wouldn't be White's — and so he had another cut in readiness. Your little ruse didn't deceive him — he welcomed it, in fact. Having handed his key over to you he was, so far as anyone knew, without one. And that, he thought, should remove him from all suspicion.' The Inspector smiled. 'Now you can see why he was so angry when you accused him of having given you the wrong key. It cut that particular piece of firm ground from under his feet.'

'He didn't know we'd planned to leave the cash-box under the scrap-heap, of course,' said Forthright. 'If he'd taken the money out and then put it there we'd have been properly flummoxed.'

'Why did he try to blackmail us into

handing over the money when he knew we hadn't got it?' asked Wells. 'That was a bit daft, wasn't it?'

'I don't think so. He reasoned that that was what you'd expect him to do, so he did it. But there was more to it than just playing a part. He was greedy. Since you couldn't hand over White's money he reckoned on adopting much the same tactics as White had done — docking your wages.'

'What a swine,' growled Chitty. 'Trying to put the screw on us for a murder he'd done himself!' His indignation was not assumed; he saw no parallel in his having been a party to the plot to frame a supposedly innocent Loften. 'What's funny about that, Inspector?' he demanded, as Pitt smiled.

'That wasn't the only occasion on which you were hoaxed, Mr Chitty,' said Pitt. 'You see, you didn't kill Mrs Gooch either.'

Forthright remembered in time that they had never admitted responsibility for the old woman's death — not even Bert. He shot a warning look at the others, who were gazing in bewilderment at the Inspector.

'No,' he said casually. 'That was just one of your crazy notions.'

Pitt smiled.

'All right, Mr Forthright, we'll leave it at that. But it happens to be my crazy notion that you *thought* you killed Mrs Gooch — which was why you paid up when White went in for blackmail. But, as I said, you didn't kill her. Loften did.'

'But — ' began Wells — and stopped. He wanted to explain that Loften *couldn't* have killed Mrs Gooch; hadn't they seen the dead body, felt the car pass over it? Yet to explain would be to admit their guilt.

'Tricky, isn't it?' said Pitt. 'You don't believe me, but you can't argue without putting yourselves in the cart. Well, I'll make it easy for you. Loften left the George at ten that night, but he hadn't gone far when the car went dead on him. He had a choked jet, and it took him some time to clear it (I gather he's not much of a mechanic); and by the time he got going again he can't have been more than a few minutes ahead of you.

'He was late for his appointment by now, and he drove faster than he should have done. It was raining hard, and the road is narrow and full of bends; he says he never saw the old lady until he was almost on top of her, and then it was too late. He got out of the car to find her dead; and as there seemed to be no one about he took a chance and drove on.' The Inspector's eyes narrowed. 'Too many of these hit-and-run drivers, don't you think?'

'Did Loften tell you all this?' asked Wickery, ignoring the question.

'He did. It was the old lady's dead body that *you* ran over. It doesn't excuse your failure to report the accident, but that's what happened.'

None of them spoke. They waited, hoping he would continue without prompting, still reluctant to admit their fault.

'I hope that makes you think,' said Pitt, a trifle smugly. 'If you'd acted correctly and got in touch with the police maybe you wouldn't have had to pay all that good money to White merely for running over a dead body. Of course, you weren't his only victims; he was blackmailing Loften as well. That was why Loften killed him.'

'Good Lord!' said Wells.

'We have to do a bit of guessing here,' Pitt went on, 'but I imagine White saw the first accident and, after Loften had cleared off, was just going to investigate when you four turned up. But the fact remains, he blackmailed the lot of you.'

'Loften never said anything about it to us,' muttered Wells.

'Why should he? Did you tell him? And that was what White banked on, that the victims of blackmail seldom *do* tell.'

'But wait a minute,' said Chitty. 'Susan told me that Loften picked her up that night before ten-thirty. She said she saw the time by his wrist-watch as he was driving; and it's no good saying his watch was wrong, because she checked it with our clock in the kitchen when she got back. He *couldn't* have killed Mrs Gooch, no matter what he said.'

'Yes, she told me that too. It puzzled

me a lot. But apparently Loften put back the hands of his watch before he met her, hoping she would be able to give him an alibi if he should be suspected. Later in the evening he put it right again, so that she wouldn't notice any discrepancy when she got home.'

'She might have looked at a clock *before* she met him,' said Wickery.

'Yes, of course. He realized that, but hoped she would take his watch as being correct — as she would have done, no doubt, when she found that it tallied with her clock at home. In any case, it was the only chance that offered.'

'He was lucky,' said Wells. 'Damned lucky.'

'In that, yes. Not that it's done him much good.' Pitt turned to Forthright. 'I suppose you had no idea of all this when you accused him of murdering White?'

'No,' said Forthright. He flushed slightly. 'I thought it was one of us.' Haltingly, with occasional shamefaced apologies, he described how he and Wells had built up the case against Loften. 'Even when I found Mrs Loften's body I never connected it with White's death; I just thought he'd done her in during one of the rows they were always having. Only seeing as how he was guilty of that, I thought — well — '

'You thought he might as well shoulder responsibility for the other, eh?' said Pitt. 'How did you come to find the body?'

'There was a bit of stuff caught on a bush — it reminded me of a sort of housecoat thing I'd seen her wearing once when I called at the house. It wasn't what you'd expect her to wear outdoors — and she never went into the forest anyway, she hated the country. And seeing as she'd disappeared — and that Loften was worried, which he never was when she left him before — well, it all struck me as being a bit fishy.'

'Did it take you long to find her?'

'No. A man carrying a heavy burden like that leaves quite a trail if you know how to look for it. And he hadn't buried her deep, only a shallow grave with dead bracken and stuff piled on top. You couldn't miss it.'

'He was in a hurry,' said Pitt. 'He

meant to go back and finish the job later; he didn't expect anyone to be wandering around that part of the forest in winter.'

'Was I right about why he killed her?' asked Forthright.

'No, quite wrong. At least, you were right in thinking she and White were having an affair. But that wasn't why Loften killed her; he'd known of it for a long time and couldn't have cared less.'

'Then why *did* he kill her?' asked Wickery.

'She was with White the night Mrs Gooch was killed,' said Pitt. 'That's why.'

'Good Lord! So that's who it was!'

'Yes, Mr Wickery, that's who it was. And the tragedy of it is that even from her husband's point of view her death was quite unnecessary. She didn't know it was her husband who killed Mrs Gooch, didn't know you four were involved, didn't know you and he were being blackmailed by White. She was sitting in his car on the far side of the hedge and never saw a thing. She stayed in the car while he got out to investigate.'

'Didn't White tell her?'

'Only that there'd been an accident, and to keep her mouth shut. It might cause a scandal, he said, if their association became public knowledge. After you'd gone they cleared off as fast as they could.'

'Where did you learn all this?' asked Wells.

'From Loften. She told him. It seems you fellows put the wind up him Thursday night when you mentioned that White must have had a woman with him. It had never occurred to him before; but knowing the way it was between her and White, he guessed it must have been his wife. He taxed her with it, not knowing she was completely ignorant of what had happened that night; he even accused her of being a party to the blackmail; and only after he'd given himself away completely did he realize his mistake. All he could do then was to kill her; she was too anxious to be rid of him, he says, for him to expect her to keep her mouth shut.'

'She'd kept it shut for over a year,' said Chitty.

384

'Only because she didn't know. And if he'd thought it over calmly before accusing her he might have realized that. But then, few men in his position *do* think calmly. That's why they get caught.'

Where Wickery felt grateful to the Inspector, Wells was full of admiration for Harry Forthright. It was Harry, not the police, who had given them their freedom; without Harry's assistance the police would never even have suspected Loften. He said, rather patronizingly, 'Bit of luck for you, wasn't it, finding White's cash-box in the first place you looked? I bet you're not often as lucky as that.'

'Strangely enough we are,' Pitt answered equably. 'But the police don't rely entirely on luck, Mr Wells, although we're always glad to have it with us. In this case we just chose the most likely spot.'

'Why was my garden more likely than the others?' asked Chitty. 'You knew we were all in it together.'

'Exactly. And if a man has something incriminating to conceal he doesn't choose his own garden or that of a friend

— not with a perfectly good forest handy, where its discovery can do harm to no one. On the other hand, he might, provided he was that sort of chap, leave it where it could incriminate an enemy. That was why I picked on your garden.'

'But Dave wasn't our enemy,' Wells protested.

'He was Loften's enemy,' Pitt answered quietly. 'You all were. But Mr Chitty's garden came handiest for him that night.'

It took a moment or two for the implication of this statement to sink in.

'You mean you actually suspected Loften?' asked Wells, incredulous.

'Of course. Mind you, it didn't come suddenly — it sort of grew on me,' Pitt said modestly. 'First there was that argument over the key. Guilty or innocent, he wouldn't deliberately have given you the wrong key — you would have discovered it the moment you tried it in the lock. So why all that fuss, I asked myself, if he was innocent? On the other hand, if he'd been planning to murder White himself why give you the key when he'd need it himself? It didn't make sense either way.

'Then there was the motive. The motive that fitted you also fitted him, for he was in Tanbury the night Mrs Gooch was killed, and left only a little while before you. Miss Chitty told me that Loften met her before ten-thirty; but she added that, although he mentioned the time as they were driving out of the village, she also saw from his wrist-watch that it was correct. That, I thought, was *most* significant.'

'I don't see why,' said Forthright.

'You don't? Ever noticed on which wrist Loften wears his watch?'

'On the right,' said Wells and Chitty together.

'Yes. So I noticed. But if Miss Chitty was able to read the time by it as Loften was driving he must have been wearing it on his *left* wrist. And a man doesn't alter a habit like that without a very good reason.'

'I seem to remember that it was on his right wrist when we met him at the George,' said Wells.

'I'm sure it was. He changed it over so that Miss Chitty could confirm his version of the time they met.'

'What about that note his wife left for him?' asked Forthright. 'Susan Chitty saw it, and she's positive it wasn't a forgery.'

'Of course it wasn't,' Pitt agreed. 'And it was the note that really confirmed his guilt in my mind. When he showed it to me I went up to his house to have a look round, and I couldn't find any similar paper anywhere. So I had the ink analysed — and learned that the note must have been written at least several months ago. It was, you see, written on the last occasion she left him.'

'But that's impossible,' said Forthright. 'She referred to White's murder in it.'

'No, she didn't. Her actual words were 'I've been planning for months to leave you, and this business of Andrew White is the last straw.' She wasn't referring to the murder when she wrote that, but to Loften's discovery of her affair with White.'

'Could you have nailed him for his wife's death if he hadn't lost his nerve?'

asked Forthright. 'There wasn't anything to *prove* he did it, was there?'

'I should say there was plenty. For one thing, he told us he last saw her on Friday afternoon — whereas medical evidence shows she was dead at least twelve hours before that.'

'He must have killed her Thursday night, then, after he'd heard us talking about the woman in White's car,' said Wickery. 'Why didn't he tell us the next morning that she'd gone? Why wait until Saturday?'

'He couldn't find the note,' Pitt explained. 'He needed that to confirm his tale that she'd left him. He spent all Thursday night and most of Friday night looking for it. He says that was why he didn't have time to go back and make a better job of concealing the body. Personally, I don't believe that; I think he was just plain scared. He wasn't busy Saturday night.'

Pop Wells was still reluctant to acknowledge any debt to the Inspector for his deliverance. He didn't go much for policemen, he told his wife later. Willie

Trape was all right, of course, he was one of themselves; but those detective chaps from Tanbury — well, it seemed like they were always right even when they were wrong.

'If you were so sure it was Loften done it why didn't you let up on us?' he asked now, hoping to score a point.

'I couldn't see the wood for the trees, Mr Wells,' said Pitt. 'You fellows kept getting in the way; I didn't know whether you were on your own or in partnership with Loften. Saturday evening I even tried to provoke you into talking, but it didn't work; and it wasn't until Mr Wickery decided to come clean that I was able to pick up the pieces and put most of them together. Even then I couldn't get confirmation. Mr Forthright decided to disappear, and you and Mr Chitty wouldn't talk.'

'You can't blame us,' said Wells. 'We looked all set for the high jump. Of course, if we'd known none of us went into the garage Tuesday night — ' He broke off and turned to Chitty. 'You never told us what happened, Dave. Bert says he found the piece of paper with *YES* on it where you were standing. Why didn't you go in and get the money?'

Chitty grinned sheepishly; but before he could answer Pitt said, 'Mind if I try my hand at that one, Mr Chitty? Mr Wells here seems to think that the police get results purely by chance. I'd like to show him he's wrong, that we do occasionally apply our brains to the job.'

'Go right ahead, Inspector.'

'I felt rather pleased with myself when I'd worked it out,' Pitt said boyishly. 'You dropped your glasses, didn't you, before reading what was on the paper?'

'That's right.'

'And when you picked them up they were broken, eh? You couldn't see to read?'

'I dropped the piece of paper as well,' said Chitty. 'It slipped out of my hand as I made a grab at the glasses.'

'Yes, of course. That's why it wasn't torn or crumpled.' Pitt turned to the others. 'You see? It's as simple as that, Mr Wells.'

Wells ignored him. 'What did you do then, Dave?' he asked.

'Nothing,' said Chitty; and then, considering that this was perhaps too brief an explanation, 'What *could* I do?'

'You could have come and told one of us what had happened,' said Forthright.

'And been accused of spying? Not ruddy likely! Besides, it was three to one against my piece of paper having *YES* on it. If White told us next morning that he'd been robbed I'd no need to worry; if not — well, at least you couldn't say it was me that had let you down, could you?'

'But why didn't you tell us later, when we more or less accused you of having killed White?' asked Wickery. 'And why pretend you broke your specs on the track?'

'Well, you'd *see* they were broken when we got back here, and I didn't want any questions asked,' said Chitty. 'I *was* going to explain later; but the way you went for me, saying I must have broken them in White's room and that I ought to be shot — it put my back up properly. To hell with them, I thought — let 'em worry. It can't do me any harm.'

He looked rather ashamed at this last

revelation, but Wells nodded sympathetically. 'It was a mess-up all round, if you ask me,' he said.

'We're well out of it,' said Forthright. 'What do you think will happen to us, Inspector? Will it mean going to prison?'

'That's not for me to say, Mr Forthright. I'm a policeman, not a judge.'

They came back to reality with a bump. Curiosity had for a short while drowned their mistrust of each other and their fears for the future, but now these were with them again. Silence fell on them; they looked furtively at each other and doubtfully at the Inspector.

Wickery stubbed out his cigarette and stood up.

'If you don't want me any more, Inspector, I'll be getting home,' he said. 'And thanks a lot.'

'No more for now, anyway,' said Pitt.

'I'll be making tracks too, then,' said Wells, glad of the lead Wickery had given him. 'Coming, Dave?'

Inspector Pitt stood at the cottage door with Forthright and watched them go; Wells and Chitty walking together,

Wickery a little apart. He felt a twinge of pity. They had probably been decent enough fellows, he thought, before Fate and White and Loften had in turn played their tricks on them. Would they go back to being decent fellows, or would the immediate past and future be too much for them?

The three men left the road and turned into the field, and now only their bobbing heads were visible above the hedges. Forthright turned to the Inspector.

'What do you think we'll get?' he asked. 'You must have *some* idea.'

Pitt eyed him thoughtfully. You're the strong man behind that bunch, he thought; I'd bet a pound to a penny you put them up to it. Maybe without your lead they'd have behaved like law-abiding citizens — have reported the accident and never have known what it's like to suffer the despair and degradation of blackmail. I ought to have included you with Fate and White and Loften.

'Justice,' he said aloud, his voice stern. 'Justice, Mr Forthright, that's what you'll get. And I hope you feel you deserve it.'